PRAISE FOR *ENEMIES AMONG US*

Bob Hamer's debut novel delivers realism only an undercover FBI agent can bring. *Enemies Among Us* will grab you from word one and stay with you long after you've read the last evocative page. Mitch Rapp has a new friend in the world of fictional heroes, FBI Special Agent Matt Hogan . . .

—Vince Flynn, *New York Times* #1 best-selling author of *Pursuit of Honor*

Knowing Hamer "walked the talk" as an FBI undercover agent gives this well-crafted thriller a terrific plausibility, a genuine edge that rings like a struck bell. Hamer hits the nail on the head.

—Kevin Sorbo, producer/director and star of *Hercules: The Legendary Journeys* and Gene Roddenberry's *Andromeda*.

Bob Hamer's real-life experiences as an undercover FBI agent lend an insider's touch to this all-too-realistic tale of terrorism in our time. It's a story of dedicated people who battle bureaucrats and terrorists to keep America safe.

—Charlie Daniels, in his four-decade music career, has six platinum albums, performed for U.S. troops all over the world, and has been honored by two American presidents

Bob Hamer's book, *Enemies Among Us,* doesn't read like a work of fiction—it reads like real life. Only it's a life among dark criminal subcultures that most of us will, thankfully, never know. That's because every scene is born of Bob's personal experience as an undercover FBI agent—and while much of what he did in more than two decades on the job is still classified, many of those incredible experiences find an outlet in Bob's fiction. If you ever wondered about the threats this country faces that never make the evening news—this book will make you thank God ... es in harm's way on the home front so ... l. Don't miss it.

—Chuck Holton, CBN military ... 4 *More Elite Soldier* and the *Task For* ... s

Bob Hamer spent twenty-six years in the FBI—many undercover. He brings a realism to his writing few authors can. He's been there and takes his reader on the same wild ride he traveled while an undercover G-man. His fiction is as real as it gets. In fact, I wonder if this really did happen.

—Karri Turner, actress from the CBS series *JAG* and recipient of the 2009 USO "Heart of a Patriot" Award

The best novels tell riveting stories while extolling truth and goodness. *Enemies Among Us* delivers fully on both counts.

—Bill Myers, best-selling author of *Angel of Wrath* and *The Voice*

Enemies Among Us, what a book! I was drawn in right from the start. It was filled with action and drama. Bob Hamer's Matt Hogan is my kind of hero, a real man. I can't wait to read his next book.

—Blanca Soto, Miss Mexico, www.blancasoto.net

While deployed to Afghanistan, I read *Enemies Among Us*. Bob Hamer gives us an edge-of-your-seat thriller that tells an incredible story of terrorism in our country today. He makes it seem all too real. Thanks for the ride.

—Ryan Smith, U.S. Army

With chilling savvy, Bob Hamer throws light on the darkness. *Enemies Among Us* shatters quixotic notions about life on the streets of Beverly Hills. I'd take Matt Hogan as a neighbor any day.

—Keri Tombazian, radio personality, host of *Night Grooves*, 94.7 the Wave

Where have all the American heroes gone? You'll find one of the best and bravest between the covers of *Enemies Among Us*. Slip on your best Walter Mitty outfit and become Matt Hogan, fearless FBI agent—a tough, no-nonsense hero who rides a motorcycle like a Hell's Angel and yet merits the love of a good woman and hapless children, like a storybook champion. Hamer writes this tome with all the grit and authenticity of the former Marine veteran and FBI award winner he is, and because he's lived it, you'll find yourself living it too; he's just that good. What are you waiting for? Open the book and get on with it. There are bad guys to beat and a mystery to be solved! America is counting on you.

—Bill Corsair, combat veteran, talk show pioneer, and New York actor

Enemies Among Us is a rip-roaring roller-coaster ride of a read that launches undercover agent Matt Hogan as a rising star in the fictional world of 007s. With unbridled conviction and sheer dogged determination, this maverick undercover FBI agent confronts evil and embraces his own personal demons while facing the daunting task of infiltrating a terrorist cell within the United States. Hamer has so skillfully crafted a character with heart, brains, courage, and faith—and presented him to us in an intoxicating joyride of twisted corridors, evil plots, and surprising self-discovery—we will eagerly be chomping at the bit and craving for more adventures in sequels to come.

—Chele Stanton, actress and gospel recording artist

Riveting and realistic, Hamer's *Enemies Among Us* puts you right in the action! The story has momentum from the beginning and builds an intriguing plot that keeps your heart pounding until the very end. I could not put the book down! It was fast-paced, explosive, and definitely packs a punch. Hamer exposes the dark underworld of terrorism as it relates so closely to real world events of today.

Leslie N. Smith, CPT (Ret.), U.S. Army, Wounded Warrior

Bob Hamer, a real-life FBI undercover veteran, is a deft narrator with a clear eye and strong heart. He brings pitch-perfect detail to a story that is as gripping as it is unsettling. In post-9/11 Los Angeles, there are *Enemies Among Us*, plotting our destruction from within. They hate us for our freedom, our values, our faith. Hunting them takes courage, personal sacrifice, and skill—but Hamer reveals that, when you go undercover, sometimes it's just better to be lucky than good. This is a thrilling, timely reminder of who we are fighting . . . and why.

—Brian Alan Ross, New Media Counsel, entrepreneur and family man

As a Hollywood stuntman I enjoy action and drama in the projects that I read. *Enemies Among Us* provides a portrayal of the intensity and discipline it takes to fight the shadow war in the streets of America. As a stuntman it takes discipline and patience to be successful. After reading Bob's first book *The Last Undercover*, a non-fiction chronicle of his life in the FBI and now reading about a new fictional character here, Matt Hogan, I realize it takes discipline and patience to be a successful undercover. Thanks, Bob, for another great read.

—Buddy Sosthand, Hollywood stuntman, 2007 Taurus Award Winner at The World Taurus Stunt Awards in the Best Fight Category for *Pirates of the Caribbean 2: Dead Man's Chest*

Enemies Among Us is a suspenseful thriller that engages your mind while giving you great insight into the FBI undercover world. Bob Hamer, a true hero, brings realization to the frightening world of terrorism, all too often missed by many, as to just how close to home it can hit at any moment.

—Laura Orrico, actress, www.lauraorrico.com

Fun to read. Suspenseful and intriguing. Gives amazing first-hand insight into FBI procedures. Action filled yet tender, shows what is being done to fight the war on terror behind the scenes.

—Geneva Somers, actress

Enemies Among Us is a thrilling ride and I enjoyed every moment! If we only had more men like Matt Hogan—a man every woman wants and every man aspires to be!

—Morgan Brittany, actress

Bob Hamer has captured the realities of the enemy we face today in a very credible and exciting book that shows the reader how terrorists are operating in our midst. As one who knows, Bob shows the terrorist network and tactics in a fast moving, fascinating thriller. Thanks Bob for telling people what the enemy is up to.

—LtGen William G. Boykin USA (Ret), former commander of U.S. Army Special Forces

Bob is a great reminder that there's heroes among us as well!

—Alfonzo Rachel, PJ TV

ENEMIES AMONG US

ENEMIES AMONG US

A THRILLER

VETERAN UNDERCOVER FBI AGENT

BOB HAMER

FIDELIS
BOOKS
NASHVILLE, TENNESSEE

Printed in the United States of America

978-0-8054-4978-5

Fidelis Books, an imprint of B&H Publishing Group
Nashville, Tennessee

Dewey Decimal Classification: F
Subject Heading: SPIES—FICTION \ ADVENTURE FICTION \ TERRORISM—FICTION

Publisher's Note: The characters and events in this book are fictional, and any resemblance to actual persons or events is coincidental.

1 2 3 4 5 6 7 8 9 10 • 14 13 12 11 10

"It is not the critic who counts: not the man who points out how the strong man stumbles or where the doer of deeds could have done better. The credit belongs to the man who is actually in the arena, whose face is marred by dust and sweat and blood, who strives valiantly, who errs and comes up short again and again, because there is no effort without error or shortcoming, but who knows the great enthusiasms, the great devotions, who spends himself for a worthy cause; who, at the best, knows, in the end, the triumph of high achievement, and who, at the worst, if he fails, at least he fails while daring greatly, so that his place shall never be with those cold and timid souls who knew neither victory nor defeat."

—Theodore Roosevelt, "Citizenship in a Republic," Speech at the Sorbonne in Paris, April 23, 1910

Chapter One

The entire week was postcard perfect. Unseasonably warm weather continued to bathe the greater Los Angeles area in summerlike conditions. Even though it was the middle of October, it felt like July. Santa Ana winds, blowing in from the desert, pushed the smog toward the ocean, clearing impurities from the sky. Residents and tourists alike paraded up and down the crowded Beverly Hills streets, ducking in and out of boutiques catering to America's wealthiest. But the sedated buzz of excitement on this chamber of commerce-type evening was interrupted by the roar of a Harley weaving its way through the traffic on Rodeo Drive.

He looked like an urban street warrior—greasy hair, tattered long-sleeve T-shirt, a swastika tattooed on the left side of his neck, and the German SS tattooed on the right. Although he wasn't "flying colors"—wearing a leather jacket designating an outlaw motorcycle gang affiliation—no one would question Matt Hogan's credentials. His menacing appearance caught the attention of everyone on the street, and drivers gave him as much leeway as they could provide.

Hogan's destination on this night was the Mediterranean Enchantment, a favorite restaurant for Beverly Hills' high and mighty. The food was overpriced and not much better than something you could pick up at a local strip mall falafel joint, but "The Enchantment," as it was called by Hollywood aristocracy, had ambiance. What that really meant was rooftop diners with their hookah water pipes and two belly dancers performing hourly to the beat of something from the Baghdad Top 40. As with any Saturday night, the restaurant was crowded with the well dressed and the well favored.

Hogan cruised past The Enchantment's olive green canopy entrance and watched a parking valet take the keys to a car priced higher than Hogan's net worth. He glared at the older Middle Eastern couple exiting the Rolls Royce Phantom. They in turn stared at this unwashed intruder to their elite community. Hogan wouldn't be welcomed at the front door, but that was just fine with him. He couldn't stand the food or the music. Besides, tonight's business was better suited for the back. He raced down the street, took a hard right at the corner and another hard right onto a paved alley leading to the delivery entrance of the restaurant. He parked his bike in the shadows, further concealing his intentions but not his anger. His persona may have been fiction, but his hatred was real.

He marched toward his destination with the determination of a Nazi storm trooper. A reinforced wrought-iron door led directly to a small office located off the kitchen of The Enchantment. Using his steel-toed Doc Martens, Hogan snapped the latch with one powerful front kick.

"What, you don't knock?" asked a wide-eyed Karim Ali Abboud sitting alone at his desk, almost choking on his food.

"Not for you," said Hogan. Then with sarcasm dripping from every word, he added, "Nice security lock. Might want to buy American next time. Costs a little more but keeps you safer."

In contrast to the near spotless dining room and kitchen, the office was filthy and smelled of day-old garbage, the result of a trash bin just outside an opened window. A mildewed mop stood in one corner, flanked by dead roaches and rat droppings. Against the wall was a small cluttered desk, three cases of inexpensive wine, and stacks of lunch menus.

The fifty-six-year-old Iraqi was a major financial supporter of radical Islamic causes. Thin-framed, his reedlike arms were adorned with a Rolex watch and a gold bracelet. His "designer everything" clothing was in sharp contrast to the intimidating Hogan—white sinew in his mid-thirties.

"What's the holdup now, and why isn't this happening?" demanded Hogan.

"It is. He should be here soon," whimpered Karim in strongly accented English.

"That's what you said on the phone an hour ago and three hours before that." Hogan spit a large chunk of tobacco on the floor, another health-code violation, but even if he cared, Karim was too fearful to protest.

"Please, give it some more time. You Americans are so impatient. Have an appetizer."

Karim pointed to a plate of dolma and flat bread. Hogan grunted an expletive, picked up a handful of the delicacies, and flung them across the small office. Rice, ground lamb, and grape leaves all but covered the tiny room.

A startled Karim rose from his chair, attempting to make his way toward the door to the kitchen.

With a powerful left hand, Hogan grabbed the Iraqi's bony shoulder and threw him back into his chair.

"Sit down!"

Karim obeyed. "Please, my friend, soon, very soon your product will arrive."

Both remained silent for a few moments as a tentative calm prevailed. Hogan glowered at a weak Karim, who immediately fixed his gaze on the floor. *Machiavelli was right*, thought Hogan, *it is better to be feared than loved.* And Hogan loved being the alpha male.

When that thought passed, Hogan continued to press. "This isn't the way I do business. If your man can't produce, then I'm outta here."

Karim, seeing profit slipping out the back door, pleaded, "You got the sample. My product is good."

"Anybody can produce a high-grade taste. It's quantity my people want."

Hogan's people did demand more. The sample of heroin, imported from Afghanistan, graded out at over 90-percent pure. Street level "smack" was 2–3 percent. Karim's sample was pure poison, instant death, but a small sample was insufficient for Hogan's purposes. To prove he was a capable supplier, Karim was going to have to produce the kilo Hogan ordered.

"Your people will get quantity and quality."

"Yeah, but how much longer do I have to wait?"

"You'll never find better product."

"Yeah, well you'll never find greener money or a safer outlet."

Karim tried to screw up his courage and attempted to respond with conviction. "So you say."

Hogan liked the feistiness his newfound terrorist friend displayed and accepted the challenge. "Hey, you don't trust me? Then all I have to do is hop on the hog and blow this camel-jockey slop house."

Karim backed down immediately. "Give him a little longer."

"Get him on his cell phone and find out where he's at. I've got people to answer to, and they don't like waitin'."

Just as Karim picked up the receiver and punched in the numbers, his associate, Mustafa al-Hamza, walked in from the kitchen carrying a brown leather briefcase.

Mustafa was shorter than Hogan and less developed, but the thirty-four-year-old Saudi was in shape. Although not a citizen, it was apparent he had been seduced by American culture.

Karim gave Mustafa a puzzled look. "How did you get in?"

"Get in what?" said Mustafa with only a slight accent.

"The kitchen . . . my office . . . this restaurant. I thought you'd come through the alley."

"I came in through the front door."

"The front door? Don't you think that is a little obvious?"

"It's better than sneaking around dark alleys. The more obvious you are, the less obvious you appear. Tonight is business as usual."

"Not sure how many of your customers carry briefcases to dinner on a Saturday night," interjected Hogan, sizing up Mustafa.

"Mustafa, this is our buyer. He got the sample the other night and liked our product. Tonight he brings us my favorite color . . . green."

Mustafa locked his attention on Hogan, and the momentary silence was deafening.

Watch his eyes, thought Hogan. A man doesn't kill with his eyes, but they are a window to intentions. They signal courage, contempt, or fear. But Hogan had to guard his eyes as well. Death was only one mistake away.

"Come on," demanded Hogan.

Mustafa, still being cautious, asked, "What's your hurry?"

"What's my hurry? This was supposed to go down this afternoon, Abdul. Pop it or I'm leaving."

"Who you callin' Abdul?"

Hogan's impatience grew as he glared at Mustafa. "Just open the briefcase. Karim, put a fire under this guy, or I'm outta here."

Mustafa held his ground. "Somebody better teach this piece of trailer trash a little bit about Middle Eastern culture."

"Hey, open it or I'm gone."

Hogan started for the door.

Karim intervened. "Gentlemen, stop it! Mustafa, open it up. We're here to do business, so quit playing your games."

Mustafa slowly aligned the numbers on the briefcase's two combination latch locks. Staring at Hogan with contempt, he released the zinc-plated latches and with all deliberateness opened the briefcase. Turning it, he allowed Hogan to survey its contents.

It was what Hogan had been awaiting since Karim first produced the sample three days ago—a kilogram of heroin wrapped in white plastic and duct tape. When broken into street-level dosages, this package, no larger than a hardback novel, would bring more than three million dollars. Hogan's cost was a mere $200,000.

Karim beamed. "It's fresh off the plane, my friend, just like I promised."

Hogan reached into the back pocket of his worn jeans and with the speed of a seasoned street fighter flashed the eight-inch blade of a spring-loaded knife. His skilled maneuvering startled even the stoic Mustafa, who instinctively grasped at his belt. Hogan noted the move and realized the Saudi was armed.

"Relax, Abdul. If I wanted to kill you, I would have dropped you before you opened the briefcase."

Mustafa just glared.

Hogan pulled a small Marquis Reagent heroin test kit, not much larger than a cigarette lighter, from his pocket.

"What's that?" demanded Mustafa.

"It's a test kit."

"A test kit? What are you, some kinda cop?"

Hogan didn't miss a beat. "Yeah right, and you're Osama Bin Laden. What? You think this is TV and I pull out a beaker and cook it over an open flame? Get real. I don't shoot this crap. You wanna stick it in *your* arm?"

He looked at both Karim and Mustafa. They said nothing. The meek Iraqi restaurant owner stared at the floor. Mustafa, however, maintained eye contact, never wavering.

Hogan then cut a tiny hole through the duct tape and using the tip of the knife blade took a sample of the packaged product. Hogan examined what appeared to be fine textured sand. He moved the knife blade close to his nose and smelled the sample. Then he placed the substance into the clear plastic test kit and sealed it. He methodically broke the three glass vials within the kit and shook the mixture. Holding the kit up to the light, Hogan noted the speed and intensity with which the heroin sample changed color. "Looks good, gentlemen."

Mustafa tensed. "Let's see the money."

"It's at the bike. Let's move our business out there."

Karim stepped in. "No way, my friend. You bring your package here. Our package goes nowhere until we see American currency."

Hogan casually shrugged his shoulders. "If that's your play, I'll be back."

Chapter Two

Hogan stepped out the back door and headed into the alley toward his motorcycle. The bike was parked about fifteen yards from the restaurant, obscured in darkness. As Hogan walked away from the restaurant, he could feel the stares of Karim and Mustafa watching his every move from the rear window.

Hogan appeared to be talking to himself. "It's a 'go,' gentlemen. Karim is in the back office with his supplier. I saw the product and tested it. It is pure dynamite. It's in a brown leather briefcase. The supplier's armed. Be safe. Oh, and you can thank me later for loosening up the back door."

With that, an arrest team of FBI agents, all wearing raid jackets and ballistic vests, armed with MP-5s, Sigs, and Glocks, began to slowly converge on the back door.

From a safe distance in the darkness, Matt Hogan stood by his bike, taking it all in. The agents moved with precision, carefully sliding down the sidewalls of the adjacent buildings to avoid early detection. Matt watched Karim and Mustafa at the window. They were oblivious to what was about to happen.

As the agents moved in, a Mexican busboy, whose immigration status was less than perfect, stepped outside the restaurant and lit up a cigarette. He froze momentarily when he saw the agents then shouted, "La Migra!" and ran down the alley in an effort to avoid capture.

The agents let him run. It wasn't the first time they had been mistaken for immigration officials, and it wouldn't be the last.

The fleeing busboy alerted Mustafa to the activity just outside the window. Craning his neck to see down the side of the building, Mustafa spied the approaching agents. "It's a rip!" shouted Mustafa.

The small office exploded with confusion. Mustafa slammed the briefcase shut as both men raced out of the room through the kitchen and into the main dining area.

The agents gave chase, easily entering through the broken security door.

Chaos erupted in the dining room. Mustafa knocked down an elderly lady hustling toward the restroom and pushed a busboy into a table of diners.

Two agents entering through the front door grabbed Karim, who struggled, but only briefly, before being thrown to the floor and cuffed, his face ground into the dark plush carpeting.

Patrons began streaming out of the restaurant.

Mustafa spotted more agents rushing through the front entrance and from the kitchen. He changed course, heading toward the stairs to the roof. He took the steps three at a time as agents gave chase.

Startled rooftop smokers, clustered around hookah water pipes, watched as Mustafa ran past the tables.

In a futile gesture a pursuing agent screamed, "Halt! FBI!"

Mustafa had no intention of stopping for anyone, especially the FBI. He turned with his weapon drawn in the direction of the lead agent, who ducked behind the open doorway. Mustafa pulled the trigger, but the hammer landed on an empty chamber. Not having the combat sense to pull back the slide and chamber another round, he threw the impotent weapon toward the pursuing agents, momentarily halting their forward progress. In an instant the rules of engagement changed. Now Mustafa was unarmed. The *L.A. Times* would love to headline Sunday's paper *FBI Kills Unarmed Arab.*

Mustafa then flung the briefcase in the same direction. The brief interlude gave him enough time to jump from The Enchantment's roof to a neighboring boutique and slide down a drainpipe to the ground.

He ran out into the street, south on Rodeo where his black Infinity Q45 was parked.

Chapter Three

Matt saw Mustafa race through the kitchen as agents gave chase. Rather than join in the foot pursuit, he mounted the Harley and drove through the alley and out onto Rodeo. From this vantage point he spotted Mustafa enter the Infinity.

Tires squealed as Mustafa sped off. Matt pursued on his motorcycle, and the roar of the bike deafened the screams of frightened tourists.

Mustafa went north on Rodeo and ran a red light, forcing a dark blue Lexus to run up onto the sidewalk, barely missing several pedestrians. He then turned left on Brighton and right on Camden Drive, blasting through another red light at Santa Monica Boulevard.

A Jaguar clipped the rear of Mustafa's Infinity as it sped through the intersection, and the smell of burning rubber filled the air.

Matt was focused in the pursuit but keenly aware of his Beverly Hills surroundings. They passed 810 Linden Drive, *the home of mobster Bugsy Siegel, killed in 1947 when a shotgun blast through the front window ended his life.*

Matt had been in high-speed chases before, and this one had that same surreal feeling. Even though the car and the motorcycle were traveling at speeds in excess of sixty miles per hour on residential streets, perception reduced to slow motion.

Matt remained relaxed and confident during the chase. He was actually enjoying this latest thrill ride. *Ride it like you stole it!*

Mustafa took a right on Sunset, then a quick left on Roxbury past the former homes of Jimmy Stewart, Lucille Ball, and Peter Falk. *Was this a pursuit or a celebrity bus tour?*

Mustafa, unfamiliar with the side streets, was driving with no other goal than to evade the pursuing motorcycle. He continued speeding, circling back toward Sunset Boulevard, but lost control in front of the legendary Beverly Hills Hotel.

Mustafa's Infinity smashed into a street lamp, snapping it off at the base. A chili-red Mini Cooper, now more closely resembling a crushed soda can, received the brunt of the blow from the light pole.

Matt was following close behind—too close. When Mustafa hit the light pole, Matt had no choice but to lay down his bike to avoid crashing into the car. The motorcycle skidded forward into Mustafa's vehicle. Matt managed a tuck and roll as he hit the ground and was prone on the pavement as the bike plowed into the Infinity. Both the motorcycle and the car burst into flames.

Jumping to his feet, Matt limped toward the inferno. Leaking gasoline flowed toward the Mini Cooper, and a small flame followed the stream.

Matt helped the driver of the crushed Cooper as they both stumbled to safety. Once the driver was out of harm's way, Matt turned his attention to Mustafa and the Infinity.

The driver-side window was up, the doors locked, and Mustafa lay dazed in the front seat. Matt tried to open the door, but the heat from the fire transferred to the metal car frame and singed Matt's hand. He ripped off his shirt, wrapped it around his hand and made another futile effort at opening the locked door.

Looking around, he spotted a large rock from a curb-side flower bed. Matt hobbled over to the curb, grabbed the rock, and returned to the burning vehicle. Using the rock, he smashed the driver-side window of the Infinity. Glass splay throughout the interior of the car as he reached in and unlocked the door. Unsnapping the seat belt, he then pulled a bloody Mustafa from the burning vehicle and dragged him safely from the flames.

Mustafa was alive but barely. With partially opened and uncomprehending eyes, he looked up at a smiling Matt Hogan on his knees straddling him.

In a slow, methodical cadence reserved for foreign tourists on Hollywood Boulevard, Matt said, "How do you like America?" Before Mustafa could answer, he lapsed into unconsciousness. Matt flipped him over and pinned his arms behind his back as Supervisor Dwayne Washington ran up on the scene. Washington was new to Los Angeles and had only met Matt earlier in the week when both began work on a newly formed terrorism squad. Washington had a commanding presence compelling respect; a few inches taller and he could be Michael Jordan's twin brother.

"You got cuffs?" asked Matt.

Washington towered over Hogan and his captive. He handed a pair of handcuffs to Matt, who quickly shackled the injured Saudi heroin trafficker.

A quick pat down of Mustafa produced a cell phone that Matt tossed to Dwayne.

"Might be interesting to see who our friend's been calling."

Matt slowly stood up and took a quick inventory of his own injuries. His clothes were ripped, parts shredded, but no bones seemed broken. The lacerations and abrasions appeared minor, and a trip to the emergency room was unnecessary . . . this time.

Washington pretended to be disgusted by Matt but could barely contain a smile. "Good job." He paused then said, "I think. What part of the briefing didn't you understand? Undercovers do not—I repeat, do not—make arrests, let alone engage in high-speed chases through residential streets."

Matt's adrenaline was flowing beyond legal limits, and he grinned. "It's all in how you write the paper. These guys'll plead. They're bought and paid for."

L.A.'s newest supervisor, fresh from headquarters, shook his head and laughed. "I'm more concerned with the civil lawsuits arising from the victims you left in the wake of this joyride."

Chapter Four

A crowd began to gather at the crash site. Paramedic units and patrol officers from the Beverly Hills PD joined the FBI agents as firefighters quickly extinguished the flaming wreckage.

The driver of the Mini Cooper avoided any major injuries but was taken to the hospital in a precautionary move.

A second paramedic unit treated Mustafa, applying a cervical collar, immobilizing him on a long board, and loading him into the ambulance where they began an IV. The prognosis was not good. Two agents crowded into the back of the ambulance and accompanied the Saudi narcotics trafficker to the hospital.

In the back of the crowd, Rashid Khan, in his late thirties, wearing a worn gray sweatshirt with a distinctive green paint stain on his right sleeve, walked toward some heavy shrubbery. At five feet seven inches, the Afghan national was hidden by the mature oleander. He flipped open his cell phone and made a call.

In a heavy accent he said, "Wadi, it was a trap. The FBI arrested Karim at the restaurant. Mustafa tried to escape in his car and crashed on Sunset. The FBI just took him to the hospital in an ambulance. I am sure we lost the kilo."

Wadi Mohammed al-Habishi responded, "Karim does not know we were behind this. Mustafa must never talk. We will be more careful in the future. And Rashid, it is Saturday; destroy the SIM card."

The Afghan replaced the portable memory chip in his cell phone, tossing the old one in the sewer.

Several miles from this evening's action, Ismad, who had been in the city less than a month, was driving southbound on the crowded 405 Freeway. As he inched his way through the Mulholland Pass, he thought about his hatred of Los Angeles, "the entertainment capital of the world," and all that it stood for—moral decadence, pornography, and the celebration of drugs and alcohol.

At the top of the hill, he spied the huge Skirball Cultural Center, a stunning symbol of Jewish life, culture, and to him, *infestation.* The brilliant white walls stood in contrast to the brown hills above the 405. The forty-million-dollar edifice was an icon of what he hated most about the United States. He sneered and swore as he passed it, "May Allah destroy the infidels and the fools who are their allies!"

Ismad pounded the steering wheel. "How dare you deify your democracy over Allah. Crusaders and Zionists!" He spit the words out the open window.

When traffic picked up momentarily, a black Hummer with shiny chrome dubs and huge tires cut in front of him. He pounded the brakes to avoid crashing.

"Death to the Infidels!"

The words of his imam echoed in his mind. He told Ismad before he left for the United States, "You are part of a noble cause, a personal jihad as well as a corporate movement, a movement that seeks not simply to reduce Israeli influence in the Middle East but to eliminate it! As long as infidels inhabit that which belongs to Allah, it is an abomination."

"L.A. is an abomination," Ismad muttered.

Ismad would punish the West during this trip and help bring about its destruction. The war would not be won in a single day or with a single battle. It was a multifaceted attack, from within and without. But if the cause was anything, it was patient. The first attack on the World Trade Center occurred in 1993, the second on September 11, 2001. The ultimate goal was clear. Iranian President Mahmoud Ahmadinejad said it so succinctly: "The U.S., Britain, and Israel will eventually disappear from the world like the pharaohs. It's a divine promise." Ismad was proud to be part of the effort to fulfill Allah's promise and eliminate the Jews and their allies.

Chapter Five

It was well past midnight. As Matt drove home in his Bureau car, he could feel his muscles begin to stiffen. He was in great shape and exercised daily, but no workout could prepare him for the spill he had taken this evening.

He smiled as he thought about dumping the bike—at least, it wasn't his. The motorcycle was seized from a methamphetamine dealer last spring. The federal forfeiture statutes allowed for the seizure of any item used to "facilitate" a narcotics transaction. In April it was a Harley. Tonight the Mediterranean Enchantment became the FBI's latest prize in the forfeiture sweepstakes.

Matt pulled up to the security gate and pressed the remote, opening the main entrance to the suburban Thousand Oaks condominium complex. The fact he and Caitlin could only afford a nine-hundred-square-foot condo grated on his sense of justice. A few years ago when Los Angeles real estate prices made the dream of a larger home just that, a dream, Matt and Caitlin purchased the condo with a creative finance package. Now with a downturn in the housing market, they were upside down on their mortgage, but at least they were upside down in Southern California. Matt still remembered Indiana's cold, dark winters and humid, bug-infested summers. The weather and the casework made L.A. ideal for an aggressive agent with an adrenaline addiction.

He was home—his sanctuary—the one place he felt insulated from the evils of the world. As she did every night Matt worked late, Caitlin left the light on over the stove. He made his way to the kitchen and grabbed a Coke from the refrigerator. Returning to the living room, he gingerly sat in the wooden rocker she bought him when he turned thirty. The rocker had the FBI logo on the front and the words "Special Agent Matthew M. Hogan" laser-engraved on the back.

He rocked, reflecting not only on the evening but on life. He tempted fate again and survived. Was he really this good, or did destiny play a part? The rush he experienced with each undercover assignment seemed to make the risks worthwhile, but it was also the penance he needed to pay. He owed Scott. To some extent the guilt had subsided over the years, but the memories lingered of a lost brother and the warriors who heeded the call and returned to the Corps. The passion Matt brought to the job was more an obsession. Like those he arrested who flipped and became informants, he too was working off a beef, trying to balance an obligation still owed. Matt chose Caitlin, and now he had to pay his debt to the real heroes, those who didn't survive and left grieving wives and children. He needed to make sense of all the blood and terror and the pain and waste.

After he finished his soda, he slowly and stiffly rose from the rocker and headed toward the bedroom where Caitlin slept. He didn't want to wake her, but he needed a shower in the worst way. He last shaved and showered four days ago. Since that day, he had been taking what he jokingly referred to as "French showers." No water, no soap, just watered-down cheap aftershave sprayed on his clothes. Caitlin found little humor in his hygiene practices.

Tonight's cleanup efforts might really be painful because it took a 99-percent solution of alcohol to remove the temporary tattoos he applied to his neck, hands, and fingers. A make-up artist Matt met several years ago showed him the secrets of the movie studio tattoo. He became skillful at applying the Tinsley transfers. Spray the area with a 70-percent solution of alcohol, apply the transfer, dust with baby powder, spray a thin layer of Green Marble SeLr to seal the theatrical makeup and *voilà,* you can look Beverly Hills chic or biker filthy. Tonight was biker filthy.

The left side of Matt's face and neck were badly scraped. Several layers of his skin remained on portions of the Beverly Hills pavement, but there was no way Caitlin would allow the swastika to remain. He would just have to bite the bullet and begin the removal process of rubbing the neck clean. Besides, what's a 99-percent solution of alcohol on an open wound to a former Marine and a macho undercover FBI agent?

He quietly walked into the room and spied a sleeping Caitlin. She looked beautiful in the moonlight-allowed passage through the open plantation shutters. They had been married for nine years, and he continued to be amazed at why she found anything in him worth loving.

He showered slowly, allowing the hot water to pelt his aching back. The heat felt good. He was able to remove all the tattoos, although the removal process was accompanied by spurts of severe alcohol-induced pain. After shaving and washing his hair, he was a new man.

As he walked out of the shower, Caitlin was waiting. The scrapes and the darkening bruises were not easy to miss even in the shadows of the bedroom.

"You okay?" she asked.

"I'll be okay. Nothing a little tender loving care can't repair."

Caitlin laughed. "I'm not that easy, Cowboy. Do I even dare ask how it went?"

"Not bad. Good guys two. Bad guys nothing. Of course, 7-Eleven is down a couple of night managers, but what the heck."

Matt loved to get a rise out of Caitlin, and anything hinting at prejudice produced the intended result.

"Someday your mouth is gonna get you into trouble."

"It's my lying mouth that keeps me out of trouble." Then he winked. "Don't you forget, baby, I'm better at lovin' than I am at lyin', and I'm a great liar."

"You're a bad country song." Caitlin reached over to touch the abrasion on his left cheek. "What did you do?"

Matt responded with pride, "I wrecked the bike."

Caitlin had been through this before. Married to an FBI agent can be stressful enough, but married to an agent who thinks he's Serpico means stress beyond a mere mortal wife's imagination.

"Oh, no! Were you in policy? Please, tell me you were in policy. We're still paying off the Mercedes you wrecked three years ago when OPR said you were, how did they say it, 'outside the parameters of normal work standards.'"

OPR, the Office of Professional Responsibility, was the FBI's answer to internal affairs. Some agents went an entire career without having to deal with the headquarters-based unit. Matt was on their speed dial. He interacted with them on more than one occasion. Several times he won, but on the Mercedes issue, he lost.

"Yeah, it was something like that. I'm not worried this time. This new supervisor seems okay, a street agent's kind of boss, unlike most of the 'blue-flamers' more interested in covering their collective backsides. I think I may like this one."

Caitlin knew Matt's history with supervisors. "Yeah, until he wises up and trades you for some rookie out of Quantico."

"Hey, we got two tonight, and we'll seize a restaurant. That'll cover the cost of the bike and then some. Who knows, maybe I'll get a cash incentive award?"

Caitlin feigned shock. "That bump on the head may have caused you to hallucinate, Cowboy. An incentive award? The only incentive they ever give you comes in the form of a paycheck every two weeks. I'm not holding my breath for an incentive award. Just try not to get fired."

Matt and Caitlin both laughed. He threw his arms around her and they kissed. When Caitlin gave him an extra squeeze, he winced and backed away. Almost simultaneously, they said, "I love you."

Caitlin added. "I just don't know what I'm going to do with you."

"Neither does the Bureau. Let's go to bed."

Chapter Six

Wadi Mohammed al-Habishi leafed through a telephone directory and found the number he wanted. He called from a graffiti-marked pay phone outside an all-night Sunset Boulevard coffee shop. Only two customers were inside. Wadi was checking area hospitals. Fearing the hospitals might have caller ID, he chose the pay phone over his cell phone. He was unsuccessful with the first two calls. The third call was more promising.

"Mount Sinai Medical Center," answered the operator.

"Admissions," said Wadi.

He was quickly connected.

"Admissions, may I help you?"

"Yes, I received a call that my brother was in an accident and was taken to the hospital earlier this evening. Could you tell me if he was admitted?"

"Sir, what is your brother's name?"

"It is Mustafa al-Hamza."

The admissions counselor checked through her computer records. "Sir, I'm not seeing anything under al-Hamza. Let me try Hamza. Do you know approximately what time the accident occurred?"

"It was before midnight . . ."

Before he could finish his sentence, she interrupted, "Sir, I see it. Yes, he was admitted. There is a notation on his file. Let me pull that up." She paused a few seconds, then came back to the phone. "Sir, are you aware your brother is in FBI custody? He is here, but he's not allowed visitors. The notation says all inquiries should be referred to the FBI. Sir, if I could have your name and number, I will have someone from the FBI contact you."

Wadi had the information he needed. He had confirmed the location of Mustafa so he abruptly hung up the phone. He stepped away from the pay phone and walked out to the middle of the coffee-shop parking lot. No one was in the area to hear his call, but he wanted to take the extra precaution. He opened his cell phone and punched in a familiar number.

"Dr. U, I found him. He's at Mount Sinai. Do we have anyone there?"

Dr. Ubadiah Adel al-Banna, a well-respected physician in Los Angeles, sat up in bed. He was alone in the room but was whispering on the cell phone he kept for just such limited communications. "That is very good. We have several there willing to serve Allah and our cause. How ironic that what the Americans call a terrorist was taken to a Jewish hospital for treatment. I will handle the rest."

Wadi replaced the SIM card in his cell phone and headed for his car.

Chapter Seven

Caitlin finished her shower and was getting ready for church. Matt was a light sleeper, and she assumed the noise from the shower would have awakened him.

Wrapped in only a towel, she walked to the bed and leaned over to give him a kiss. The water from her recently washed hair dropped onto his face. He flinched but not much. She kissed him on the cheek and he smiled.

"So you *are* awake. I knew you couldn't sleep through the whine of that noisy shower. Get up and get ready for church."

Matt moaned. "Come on, baby, I'm really hurting. This may be the big one we've been looking for to get that tax-free medical retirement."

Caitlin wasn't buying any of his complaints. "Get that big o' lazy body out of bed and get ready for church."

"Honey, I kept the world safe for democracy last night. God will forgive me if I don't make it this Sunday."

Caitlin pulled back the covers. "God may forgive you, but I'm not sure I will. You promised you'd go with me this week."

With a hint of irritation in his voice, Matt said, "Caitlin, come on. It was a late night. I'm hurting. I don't want to sit through some long sermon. I'll owe you one."

"God protected you again last night. You owe him, not me."

"Please, don't start on me now. I'll go next week, I promise. Besides, I've got a ton of paperwork from last night. I need to get to the office."

Matt slowly lifted his bruised and battered body from the bed. He grabbed Caitlin's towel as she walked away, quickly twisted it, and snapped her now bare bottom, a skill he'd perfected in junior high.

Caitlin would have thought the antic a lot funnier had Matt agreed to go to church. He occasionally accompanied her but more out of obligation than desire. His faith was shattered on Christmas Day 2005, and he had struggled with God ever since. Any excuse was a good excuse, and last night's adventure provided all the reason he needed to back off Sunday services.

HER HUSBAND HELD HIS hand over the mouthpiece and hollered from the living room. "Elissa, it's for you."

"I'll take it in the bedroom."

Elissa picked up the phone, "Hello."

The caller waited for the distinctive sound of the extension phone being hung up before he spoke. "Elissa al-Omari?"

"Yes," she responded.

"I believe you spoke to a friend of mine last week about your parents in Saudi Arabia. You understand?"

"Yes, I understand."

"Good. Tomorrow, at precisely 3:30 p.m., a man will enter your bank. He will be wearing a gray hooded sweatshirt. He will come to your teller window and hand you a note. You will give him everything you have except the bait money. Do you understand?"

She hesitated and then stuttered with her response. "Yes, yes, I understand."

"You will not activate any alarms or any cameras until he is about to exit the building."

"Yes, those were my instructions."

"If you do exactly as you have been instructed, there will be no problems. If you fail to follow these instructions, if you tell anyone, if we are not successful tomorrow, your parents will die," said the voice.

"I understand. Please do not hurt them."

"No one will be hurt if we are successful. *Allah Issalmak*."

The caller hung up without waiting for a response.

Mount Sinai Medical Center in West Los Angeles is consistently rated one of the finest hospitals in the nation, the first choice of those living on the coveted Westside. However, unlike County General, it does not have a jail ward.

Mustafa was in the custody of the FBI but was being housed in a single-bed ICU hospital room for the foreseeable future. As a result of the accident, he suffered serious internal injuries requiring four hours of surgery. Then Sunday morning, while still in the recovery room, Mustafa began to bleed internally and was rushed back to surgery. After another hour under the knife, the hemorrhaging subsided and his condition stabilized.

Dr. Daniel Combs performed the surgery. A former Navy surgeon with a combat tour under his belt, Dr. Combs said Mustafa's internal injuries rivaled what he saw from Iraqi IEDs. He gave Mustafa less than a 20-percent chance of survival and said he would need to remain in the ICU for several days at a minimum. If and when

Mustafa showed progress, he could be moved to the federal prison hospital ward at Terminal Island in San Pedro. He had tubes going in and coming out of every body orifice, and machines monitoring every bodily function. In what seemed like a futile gesture, Mustafa's right wrist was handcuffed to the bed, but he was going nowhere, at least not under his own power.

There were more exciting jobs in the Bureau than babysitting a bedridden criminal, especially on the ten-to-six shift, the dreaded "night watch," but even in the FBI, rookies paid their dues. Both agents who were "knighted" for this plum assignment were on probation.

One agent sat outside the door. The second sat inside the room with Mustafa. The agents alternated the seating arrangements every few hours. The name and time of everyone who entered the room was noted; and throughout the night, doctors, nurses, and medical technicians paraded in and out. The traffic became commonplace. The agents had no medical training and could only assume the medical personnel knew what they were doing. The agents were there to prevent Mustafa from escaping. They were successful in that assignment. They failed, however, in protecting him.

At midnight the night-shift nurses prepared to assume the care of those in the ICU ward. The nurses were alerted to the status of the patient and the reasons for armed guards both in and outside the room. Law enforcement personnel inside the ICU were nothing novel, so the nurses went about their business as necessary.

Hasana Akram, a critical-care nurse from the recovery room, entered ICU. She was about to end her shift and, as was her custom, took one last pass through the ICU. She slowly walked through the rooms of those patients recovering from surgery performed during her shift.

She smiled at the agent sitting outside the room, signed the visitor's sheet, and walked into Mustafa's room. The second agent looked up from the Vince Flynn novel he was reading. She smiled at him and walked over to the patient. She checked one of the IV units, something several other nurses had done throughout the night. She pulled out a hypodermic needle from a pocket of her white nurse's smock, then, calmly, professionally, and in full view of the agent, injected Ultalente into the IV line. The synthetic insulin would immediately enter Mustafa's system but take hours for the desired effect.

Hasana pulled the medical chart from the edge of the bed, made an innocuous notation, and walked out of the room as the agent returned to his novel.

Chapter Eight

Monday morning meant the beginning of a new day and a new workweek. Matt reached over and silenced the 5:00 a.m. alarm. Except on days when he had an undercover assignment or was scheduled to work nights, Matt's routine was predictable.

The morning ritual at home consisted merely of shaving and brushing his teeth. He put on his workout gear and, with a change of clothes in hand, headed toward the Federal Building in Westwood. The condo was exactly forty-six miles from the office. If he were out the door by 5:15 or 5:20, he could put the "Bu car" on cruise control, set it for seventy-five, and drive unobstructed to work, well before most commuters were on the road.

The FBI garage had a weight room and shower facilities, allowing Matt to get in a five-mile run every morning, pump a little iron, and be at his desk before many agents arrived at the office.

Once or twice a week, in the afternoon or early evening, he would stop at the Gallo Boxing Gym in the Valley. Matt would jump into the ring with his amateur Golden Glove skills and go a few rounds with someone training for an upcoming professional fight. Legally Matt couldn't be a sparring partner because he was not licensed by the state of California, but since he received no compensation for getting his head beaten in by those with world-class skills, the point was moot. To Caitlin's dismay, on more than one occasion, he arrived home with a bruised face and a bloodied nose.

This morning Matt was still stiff from Saturday night's crash but not as bad as he would have guessed. Following the run, he showered quickly and hustled up to the office to continue the paperwork he started on Sunday.

Saturday night's buy-bust meant Matt needed to complete the FD-302 of the actual heroin purchase and arrest of Karim and Mustafa, download the device he wore recording the entire transaction that evening, book that recording into evidence and complete the FD-504 chain of custody for the recording, fill out the "overhear" sheet, complete the duplication request form, complete the FD-504 for the heroin, prepare the letter to the DEA lab for drug analysis and a separate letter for the FBI lab for fingerprint analysis, and arrange to have the drug evidence and packaging shipped to the respective labs.

Sometimes the paperwork was almost overwhelming, especially in a fast-moving case, when each stage of the investigation had Bureau-imposed deadlines that had to be met.

Another agent would be handling the filing of the arrest affidavit and complaint Matt wrote on Sunday. That same agent would make Karim's initial magistrate appearance scheduled for the afternoon in federal court.

Thanks to his Evel Knievel driving prowess, Matt also had a detailed accident report to complete. The last agent on the squad to have an accident would be assigned the accident investigation, but Matt would do most of the paperwork, more out of courtesy than obligation. Technically, an "impartial" agent should do the accident investigation, but since Matt was responsible for the problem, he would prepare the paperwork for the other agent's signature. It was one of those unwritten rules street agents observed and supervisors blindly approved. The accident report might take a little creative writing, so Matt welcomed the opportunity to limit his potential liability.

Matt was at his desk in the squad bay working at the computer when Dwayne approached.

"That was a throwaway you seized Saturday night," said Dwayne.

"Doesn't surprise me. Gangbangers have been using prepaid SIM cards for years. You have to figure terrorist drug dealers are locked into the wireless generation as well."

"We checked the call history."

"Anything interesting?"

Just as Dwayne started to answer, his cell phone rang. "Dwayne Washington. . . . Yeah, right away."

Dwayne hung up and looked at Matt. "Boss, needs to see us now."

There was no sense in postponing the inevitable. "Mr. Toad's Wild Ride gonna cost me days on the bricks?" asked Matt.

Matt could not afford a lengthy suspension. He and Caitlin might be able to sustain a few days without pay, but they were almost in a paycheck-to-paycheck status as it was.

Dwayne was not encouraging. "That's up to him and how you write the paper. But I'm not sure Tom Clancy could fictionalize Saturday night's escapade in such a way to save you from a government-imposed vacation."

They walked down the hall toward the office of the Assistant Director in Charge—even the title sounded ominous.

"The Queen Mother may be joining us," said Dwayne.

Matt looked at Dwayne, as if to make sure he really heard what he thought he had, then he laughed.

Within the first hours after Pamela Clinton, Dwayne's immediate boss, reported to Los Angeles as the Assistant Special Agent in Charge of the terrorism squads, she was dubbed the Queen Mother. She had an aura of English royalty, walking erect, almost with her nose in the air, but she was merely in a figurehead position. She suffered from delusions of adequacy. As far as the street agents were concerned, the gates were down, the lights were flashing, but there was no train on the tracks. After a two-year probationary period in her first-office assignment in Kansas City, she raised her hand and was assigned some obscure supervisory position at HQ no one else wanted. She'd been an administrator ever since, parlaying her "by the book" resolve from one administrative post to another. Her reputation was that of an obstructionist who was more interested in penetrating a perceived FBI glass ceiling than solving crime. She knew the "Bureau paper" and could cite chapter and verse of the regulations but had little, if any, clue what was happening on the street. The fact Dwayne picked up the nickname so quickly meant he was well aware of what was being said in the bullpen. *Impressive!*

It had been thirty-six hours since the fiery crash on Sunset. Mustafa al-Hamza remained on life support and still had not regained consciousness. A new set of agents performed the security duties, but Mustafa was going nowhere.

The steady whine of one of the monitors was irritating, and the perpetual beep of another machine made it almost impossible for the young agent to concentrate on the novel he was reading.

All of that changed in an instant. Without warning, the heart monitor alarm sounded. Simultaneously, warning bells rang at the nurses' station. The young agent sprang to his feet as Mustafa began to convulse, his body jumping uncontrollably. The agent opened the door and hollered for help, but his cry was unnecessary. An announcement on the overhead paging system was already alerting the staff to the emergency.

Medical personnel poured into the room. The convulsing stopped and so did the heart. Mustafa flatlined.

A third-year resident grabbed the defibrillator paddles from the crash cart and a well-choreographed medical emergency ritual began. The nurse rubbed the clear defib gel on the outstretched devices. As the doctor placed both paddles on the terrorist's chest, he yelled, "Clear," and the medical personnel retreated in unison. Mustafa's lifeless prone body violently jumped as the electrical charge attempted to jump-start the heart. The doctor repeated the process several times before he stopped the futile efforts. Without much fanfare, he said, "I'm calling it, time of death 9:36 a.m."

The injection Hasana Akram administered almost ten hours earlier had the desired effect. Mustafa was dead, and the cause of death would read "accidental, due to automobile collision." Mustafa's story, had he been willing to tell it, died with him.

THREE MEN WERE MEETING in a small, one-bedroom furnished apartment on Havenhurst Drive just south of Sunset Boulevard. The West Hollywood apartment, sparsely furnished in Salvation Army chic, was dark and uninviting. Most of the furniture was as old as the three Middle Eastern males sitting around the dining room table.

Boxes of clothes and canned food items were scattered through the apartment. A modern computer and three telephones sat atop the unfinished dining room table marred by cigarette burns. Arab-language telephone directories from cities throughout the United States were stacked in one corner of the kitchen.

The one exception to the sparse furnishings was the TV and sound system. Against the far wall was a fifty-inch high-definition, flat-screen TV with surround sound. The unit retailed for more than $6,000. A stack of recently released Blu-ray discs in English and Arabic sat beneath the system.

The TV was tuned to Al-Jazeera, the standard viewing of many Arabs in the United States.

The three men were assessing the damage from Saturday night.

Wadi Mohammed al-Habishi was enrolled at UCLA in Westwood, just a mile from the Federal Building. Rashid Kahn, who witnessed the aftermath of the Saturday night pursuit, was in the U.S. on a student visa but quit attending classes three years ago. Babur Ali illegally crossed into the United States through Sasabe, Sonora, Mexico, a small town sixty-five miles southwest of Tucson, last year. Each was hoping to one day find an American woman to marry in order to gain U.S. citizenship, a valued prize for any terrorist.

Wadi looked younger than twenty-nine, but maybe the frequent facials and $150 Beverly Hills haircuts betrayed his true age. Even though he was the youngest of the three, he was the leader of the Los Angeles-based support cell. He answered to a superior, a superior the other two had never met nor whose name they knew. Wadi was getting his masters in business administration at UCLA, and although successfully managing a terrorist support cell is not something that completes a résumé, he was brilliantly supporting the cause.

From the small West Hollywood apartment, the men solicited financial contributions, food, and clothing from Middle Eastern businessmen living in the United States. They spent hours every week on the phones, seeking donations and arranging for the distribution of those items to other terrorist cells operating throughout the world. It was an assignment the three took very seriously.

Mustafa al-Hamza's mission on Saturday night was to sell high-grade heroin to a motorcycle gang member Karim Ali Abboud brought to him. A completed sale would have resulted in a sizable financial profit for the cause.

On more than one occasion, Wadi and Mustafa had been successful at planning and consummating just such a transaction. Saturday night's mission failed, and Wadi made the decision how best to handle that failure.

"I stand by my decision," said Wadi.

"We are not questioning what you had to do," said Rashid, the smaller of the two associates and the oldest of the three.

Wadi explained, "Mustafa served our cause well thanks to his connections on the street. But he was weak. I have always feared that should he be caught, he would talk. I do not believe he could survive the American prisons. His usefulness was over. With his capture, it was necessary to terminate the only link between Saturday night's transaction and the cause."

"Everyone is expendable when the cause is just," said Rashid with conviction. "We are the righteous warriors seeking to overthrow the infidels who mock Allah's words."

Wadi laughed. "Spoken like a sound bite on CNN."

Babur also laughed, but Rashid could only manage an awkward smile.

Chapter Nine

The Assistant Director in Charge, or ADIC in FBI parlance, was the top agent in Los Angeles. He reported to the Director in Washington. Most field offices had a Special Agent in Charge or SAC, but L.A. was so large it commanded an ADIC and four SACs. The ADIC's office was impressive. The outer office featured a deep green leather couch and matching leather chairs. Turn-of-the-century lithographs of Los Angeles adorned the wood-paneled walls.

Kathryn Wilson sat at her desk near the door to Jason Barnes's office. She was the gatekeeper to the Assistant Director in Charge and had been with the Bureau longer than anyone in L.A. She knew where the bodies were buried and was the last person you wanted to anger. Her matronly appearance belied her authority. Many a visitor mistook the glasses hanging from a chain around her neck as a sign of pre-Alzheimer forgetfulness; Kathryn forgot nothing.

Matt and Dwayne approached.

"He's on the STU-phone with the Director. Have a seat."

The use of the "secure telephone unit" meant the call with the Director was encrypted, something not occurring with most communications between L.A. and headquarters.

Must be important. Hope it's not about me. It was just a motorcycle!

Kathryn added, "Pamela Clinton will be joining you."

The words were not music to Matt's ears.

"I am getting brick time," bemoaned Matt.

Kathryn loved to see agents squirm. She peered over the top of the computer monitor. "Understand they took the training wheels off the other night, and you lost your balance."

Matt could only manage a slight smile. "Something like that."

Knowing the real purpose of the meeting, Kathryn turned up the heat. "Clinton's looking for another notch on her belt."

"If that means she moves on to headquarters and out of this division, I'll be the sacrificial lamb."

Dwayne intervened as he heard footsteps, whispering, "You need all the help you can get right now. Making the ASAC mad isn't the smart move."

Pamela Clinton was an Assistant Special Agent in Charge, but due to the transfer of the SAC, she was now the Acting Special Agent in Charge of the Terrorism Division. Agents loved to gossip; after all, crime was solved by gathering intelligence, so why not refine the technique whenever possible. The latest rumor spreading through the bullpen had Clinton moving into the SAC slot. She was moving up, not out. If it were up to the street agents, she'd be voted off the island, but no one thought that a possibility.

The Queen Mother made her entrance, but her royal subjects failed to bow. They barely acknowledged her presence.

Even before the obligatory pleasantries could be exchanged, Kathryn said, "You can go in. He's off the phone."

Matt stood, grabbed the handle, and opened the door to the ADIC's office. Clinton entered first. As she walked past, she whispered in Matt's ear, "Don't think that *semper fi* crap is going to save your butt this time."

Matt held his tongue and squeezed the door handle until his knuckles turned white, wishing it were the Queen Mother's neck. Dwayne followed mouthing the words, "Stay calm."

Matt looked at Kathryn as he closed the door. She gave him a wink and an impish smile. "By the way, is that a black eye, or is your mascara running?"

Matt failed to respond with a snappy comeback but read the wink to mean he might get out of this meeting with a full paycheck.

Jason Barnes rose and welcomed all to his office. Barnes, a former Marine, knew how to command. He proved himself at Granada when as a first lieutenant he earned the Bronze Star directing his platoon at Pearls Airport. During a helicopter insertion, members of Echo Company were immediately greeted with small arms fire from the People's Revolutionary Army. For several hours in the heat of combat, Barnes guided his men until the enemy threat was neutralized.

"I just got off the phone with the Director. He sends his congratulations for a job well done Saturday night."

Dwayne replied for both of them. "That's very much appreciated."

Clinton had a different agenda. "That's no excuse for an out-of-policy joyride through Beverly Hills."

Matt exploded. "Joyride! That joyride resulted in two towels in custody, and we get a restaurant!"

"There's no call for language like that, and maybe, just maybe the seized restaurant will partially offset the property damage you inflicted on the city of Beverly Hills," barked Clinton.

Barnes intervened. "Both of you relax."

Dwayne took this as an opportunity to divert the controversy. "Matt seized a cell phone from al-Hamza. His call history had three calls to a clinic in Santa Monica, two on Friday and one on Saturday morning."

Barnes was interested. "That may tie into the Director's call. NSA has intercepted overseas chatter that your arrest was linked to a charitable group in L.A."

"Any idea which group?" asked Dwayne.

"Not based on the overhears. Will this Mustafa al-Hamza talk?" said Barnes.

"He's still in ICU. I've got agents on the room." Almost as if on cue, Dwayne's cell phone rang. He looked at the caller ID. "Let me take this; it's the agent at the hospital. Dwayne Washington." He listened for a few moments then responded, "Okay, thanks."

Dwayne glanced up at the ADIC. "Mustafa's not talking. He's dead."

Pamela Clinton's look said, *It's your fault because you were out of policy.* Matt knew her eyes were fixed on him, but he refused to acknowledge her piercing glare.

Barnes wasn't interested in fighting the last evil. There was little sense dwelling on the death or attempting to affix blame. He quickly aborted any discussion by asking, "What do we know about this clinic?"

"It's World Angel Ministry," replied Dwayne.

"We can send some agents over this morning. See if we can marry up a connection," said the ASAC.

She was the only one in the room who thought it was a good idea.

Using diplomacy in front of subordinates, Barnes said, "Pamela, that may be appropriate down the road, but I'm not sure it's the right course of action now."

Dwayne asked, "What are you thinking, boss?"

Jason Barnes thought for a few seconds, looking out the window toward the Santa Monica Mountains. Each knew not to interrupt his thinking. He then looked at Matt, "You ready to play humanitarian?"

"That'll be a stretch," said Dwayne.

Matt knew he had little choice, especially in light of Saturday night. "What do you have in mind?"

"You're a Bureau-certified paramedic."

Matt was cautious in his response. "So are a half-dozen other guys in this office."

Barnes was quick with a reply. "Good, then we can spare you. You've also got the undercover chops I'm looking for. How about using both those skills in a clinic setting? I'm sure a charity is always looking for volunteers."

Clinton could not let the issue die. "I'm not certain this is appropriate under the circumstances. We still have Saturday night to answer for."

If Matt wanted to escape the destroyed motorcycle incident without a suspension, he needed to act decisively. "I already have the proper backstopping. It shouldn't be a problem. I know I can pull it off."

Jason Barnes, a man of action, wanted to implement his idea as soon as practical. "Then it's settled. Get started with the approval process. I'll push it through headquarters. Dwayne, you report directly to Pamela. I want daily updates because I'll need to brief the Director."

The three got up and started to leave.

Dwayne turned to Matt. "Meet me in my office. The ASAC and I need to go over some administrative items before we get started on this project. I'll be there in a few minutes."

Matt thought he had dodged a bullet, but Jason Barnes wasn't that easy. Before Matt could exit the door, the ADIC said, "I haven't forgotten about the motorcycle. Pull this one off and maybe I will."

Matt turned to the ADIC and saw an uncharacteristic smile. *Semper fi.*

DWAYNE'S OFFICE HAD AN air of professionalism. Diplomas from Georgetown, a bachelor's degree in political science and a master's degree in international relations, hung on the west wall. On the east wall were plaques surrounding his autographed photo with the Director. The plaques documented his stays in Pittsburgh, Detroit, and headquarters, as well as a plaque from the CIA thanking Dwayne for his service over a two-year period. Despite what the press stated after 9/11, Matt knew for years FBI agents had been detailed to CIA Headquarters in Langley, Virginia, at their Counterterrorist Center, just as CIA employees were detailed to the FBI's Counterterrorism Division and to the various task forces throughout the country. Dwayne was one of the selected few for the coveted assignment at Langley.

Dwayne's office was on the north side of the Federal Building. He had a beautiful view of the mountains and the Los Angeles National Cemetery where more than 85,000 veterans, including fourteen Medal of Honor recipients, were buried.

Matt stood at the window and looked out. Directly below he could hear car horns blasting and the sounds of protestors chanting an indistinguishable rage against the war. Daily protests at the Westwood Federal Building were the norm. The rants did little but tie up traffic; after all, the war continues under both administrations. Anger fueled Matt's thoughts. *Those marble headstones aren't some glorification of war. They're monuments to the sacrifice of men who gave you the right to spew your daily discontent. Why not think about paying back sometime?*

Matt could see a protestor run into the street waving a sign in front of motorists. *Somewhere a village is missing an idiot. Maybe he'll be roadkill before the light changes.* No such luck. The light changed, but civility prevailed, and the drivers let him race back to the curb.

Dwayne walked in. "We have a very short window on this."

"Why? The ADIC's on board."

"He is. The Queen Mother isn't."

"She overrides the ADIC?"

"No, but she fears undercover operations. Too many things can go wrong, and she's unwilling to risk her career on, as she describes it, your 'cowboy antics.' She is going to keep both of us on a short leash. The first time it seems to be going south, she will do everything in her power to pull the plug."

Matt had seen administrators like this before, and it was one reason for his deep-seated animosity toward headquarters—always quick to take the credit, quicker to place the blame.

"A proactive terrorism squad scares her. You scare her. She was weaned on Bureau-approved intelligence-gathering protocols. Anything outside the counterintel manual can only railroad her ascension to highest levels of management."

Matt shook his head in disgust. "God forbid we stifle her career. I would never want the security of this nation to interfere with her personal ambitions."

"I'll handle her. I need you on the street."

"I'm ready to start today."

"Let's do our homework first. Do an Internet search on World Angel and check indices. Then, if you're ready, we can start as soon as we get the approvals in place."

"I figure we just cold-call 'em. I'll walk in and volunteer. Seems pretty simple—if they bite, we're in. If they don't, the Queen Mother can go overt," suggested Matt.

"I'll set up a fixed surveillance post on the building. We can at least start tracking who's coming and going for the next couple of days. Might give you somewhat of an edge before you go in."

Matt knew certain protocol had to be followed before any undercover operation was initiated. Waiting for the approval process can be frustrating. He was eager to get started. Besides thwarting terrorism, he had the added incentive of proving Pamela Clinton wrong.

Chapter Ten

A decal on the window of the Santa Monica branch of the Wells Fargo Bank announced the bank was insured by the Federal Deposit Insurance Corporation (FDIC), meaning the FBI had jurisdiction to investigate robberies occurring there.

The decal meant nothing to Rashid as he walked into the branch at precisely 3:30 p.m. The bank resembled many in the area. Most seemed interchangeable. With the recent mergers, takeovers, bailouts, and buyouts, the branches lost their individuality. Today's bank might be tomorrow's savings and loan. There was little incentive to make the branches distinctive.

The high ceilings and well-lit lobby area made for a customer-friendly atmosphere designed to encourage a personal banking touch so many banks lacked. Unlike banks in high-crime areas, the tellers were not separated from the customer by thick bulletproof glass requiring a louder than normal voice to communicate with the employee. Most of the customers were regulars, and the tellers knew them by name.

Besides helping Wadi and Babur with the telephone solicitations, Rashid was Wadi's point man in a series of successful, almost risk-free bank robberies garnering additional funds for the cause.

Three customers stood in line waiting for the next available teller.

Two of the tellers were male—one black, one Asian. The female teller, Middle Eastern, was short with dark, smooth skin. Elissa al-Omari was a graduate student at UCLA and worked part-time at the bank. Her jet-black hair and dark brown eyes made her a favorite of many of the Middle Eastern elderly men who frequented the branch. The men often waited in line, allowing others to pass, until Elissa's window opened. Her personality was well suited for interacting with the public.

Rashid stood patiently in line. It was chilly outside so wearing a tattered gray sweatshirt with the hood pulled up did not seem out of place. The back of the right sleeve of the sweatshirt had a recent large green paint stain covering about six inches between the elbow and the shoulder. The blue jeans were old but clean, and his nondescript tennis shoes were hardly alarming. Even if he did not fit the regular customer profile, the branch had not been robbed in three years, so there was no reason for the staff to be on alert.

Rashid's nerves were steady, his demeanor calm, as he waited his turn. Glancing over at Elissa, he made eye contact with her.

The customers ahead of the robber moved forward and were serviced by the available tellers.

A young mother in her early twenties with a child in a stroller was at Elissa's window longer than normal, cashing several checks. The seven-month-old infant began to fuss, forcing the mother to push the stroller back and forth. Attempts to placate the child failed as he screamed, drawing attention to Elissa's window. As the customer in front of Rashid moved to the open window of the Asian male teller, Elissa completed the young mother's transaction. The movement of the stroller toward the door seemed to comfort the child, silencing the explosive cries.

Rashid walked to the available window. He kept his left hand inside the sweatshirt pocket and with his right handed her a note and brown paper bag. Elissa looked at the note and reached into the cash drawer, quickly putting money in the paper sack. She then emptied the bottom drawer of neatly stacked bundles of currency.

Rashid took the bag, turned, and briskly walked toward the door. He kept his head down and the hood pulled high over his head. Just as he approached the door, Elissa activated the silent alarm notifying the police and FBI. Surveillance cameras, trained on the exit doors, were automatically activated. The photos, however, were of no use. They merely showed the top of the hood as Rashid exited the bank. He quickly disappeared onto the crowded sidewalk and down the street.

The tiny Chinese restaurant seated twenty people. The majority of its business, and that wasn't much, was take-out. Wadi suspected the family used the restaurant as a tax shelter to hide the illegal money flowing through the back door.

Whatever money the restaurant earned went only for minimal maintenance, enough to keep the health inspectors at bay. The drab walls and dim lighting were far from inviting.

As the sun was setting, Wadi entered the near-empty restaurant. There was no clamoring for seats, and reservations were never required. Three people, all Asian, were seated at the round table in the middle of the "dining room." They stared at the young Saudi terrorist as he walked in and took a seat in the booth closest to the kitchen. Wadi was not particularly fond of Chinese food, and apparently neither were residents of the neighborhood. But this was the only place Sammy Chu would do business. Sammy's brother owned the restaurant, and it provided a safe meeting location.

Wadi had been here numerous times and ordered the usual—a bowl of white rice, one egg roll, and a Pepsi.

Just as his brother, Jimmy, threw the order on the table, Sammy walked in.

"Ah, Wadi, my Middle Eastern friend, so good to see you."

Wadi returned the greeting and feigned sincerity as much as Sammy did.

Sammy laughed and said, "I see you are having today's special, white rice, my favorite."

Sammy was short, rotund, and nearing fifty. He was a criminal entrepreneur in every sense of the word. Whatever you needed, he could get and at the right price.

Recently he had been specializing in counterfeit cigarettes, but if you wanted jeans, watches, designer shirts, just ask. As Sammy always said, "If you don't see what you want, give me a sample, we'll make it." His costs were minimal because Chinese slave labor came at an inexpensive price.

Everything Sammy sold came from China, and everything Wadi bought was fake. Sammy knew it and so did Wadi. Italian designer jeans selling for two hundred dollars in the finest Beverly Hills boutiques cost Wadi less than eight dollars, and the price included a "genuine certificate of authenticity," also counterfeit; famous-maker Swiss watches going for five thousand dollars in elite jewelry stores, a mere three hundred dollars. The faceplate may say one thing, but Sammy and Wadi knew it was made in China. The product du jour was cigarettes.

For the past several years Sammy had been using his Chinese connections to manufacture, package, and import "American made" cigarettes complete with state tax stamps and warning labels.

In California, cigarettes sold for five or six dollars a pack. Wadi could purchase an entire carton for the same price. He parlayed several successful heroin deals into enough capital to finance a second purchase of an entire shipping container of counterfeit cigarettes.

A quarter of a million-dollar investment stood to earn the cause nearly a half million-dollar profit, with minimal law enforcement risk.

"Your container arrives on Wednesday. We will arrange for delivery to your storage location on Thursday. I'll need the cash that day," said Sammy.

"We are ready. I have rented three storage lockers at a facility in Hollywood. The place is easily accessible for your semi and hidden from the view of inquiring minds."

"Oh, you read the *Enquirer*, too. You have become Americanized since coming here."

Sammy was a naturalized citizen but enjoyed helping young immigrants get started in a life of crime. He appreciated the free-enterprise opportunities America offered, even if every one of his opportunities violated some federal or state statute. Sammy had no idea he was funding terrorist activities and would probably object to Wadi's use of the profits, but as long as he received his compensation, Sammy wouldn't object too loudly.

Sammy leaned over the table and with a pair of chopsticks grabbed a bite of rice. "I will be there on Thursday. We will break the container seal together. I want to prove to you we have not tampered with your product since its arrival in the United States. We are honorable men. You will do well to continue a business relationship."

Wadi had no plans of severing business ties, at least not in the foreseeable future. He finished his meal and promised to see Sammy on Thursday.

Chapter Eleven

Matt was again in the office early, well before the other agents. He completed an FBI computer records search, known as "indices," a term surviving the advent of computers. "Indices" were a throwback to a time when all the key names in a report were listed on index cards and kept in massive file cabinets. The computer check revealed two references to World Angel Ministry, but neither was helpful. A check of the Internet provided numerous references to the organization and gave Matt the appropriate background on the group, but no news article contained a smoking gun. There was no hint of a link to terrorism.

He was still finishing paperwork on the "accident" and wanted to get that behind him so he could devote full time to the undercover operation he hoped to begin later in the day.

Somehow the Hollywood moguls who produced blockbuster cop flicks never quite captured the burdensome paperwork requirements. Matt enjoyed the *Lethal Weapon* series with Mel Gibson and Danny Glover but couldn't imagine the administrative ramifications of just one of their adventures. The reports from each of Matt's shootings were thicker than the substantive criminal reports of the cases he was investigating at the time of each incident.

He was making headway on the accident investigation pounding away on the computer keyboard. He organized the photos, the witness interviews, the legal addendum, and the three estimates for each vehicle damaged. Now he merely had to complete the investigative summary, the cover sheet, and the table of contents. Upon completion, Matt would give the report to Steve Barnett, the agent actually assigned the investigation, for Steve's signature, another ghostwritten report completed.

Matt was engrossed in his writing when Dwayne stepped out of his office and walked up behind Matt. "What are you trying to do, impress your new supervisor by being the first agent in the bullpen two mornings this week?"

Matt jumped. "I thought I was the only one here."

"Didn't mean to scare you. You bucking for a job in management?"

Matt returned to the keyboard as he continued talking to Dwayne.

"Hardly, just trying to finish up the accident report so I can get back to the real work of the Bureau. I think you'll be pleased with Steve's creative writing style. As a matter of fact, Special Agent Barnett found the pursuit to be completely in policy."

Dwayne revealed a slight grin. "I heard great things about Barnett's investigative skills, and I had no doubt you'd be in policy."

Dwayne gently smacked Matt in the back of his head with a folded report from headquarters. "Let's get serious. I spoke with legal and just got off the phone with headquarters. It's a go with the UC op. You ready?"

Matt tried to hide the disdain he was feeling when he heard "legal and headquarters" in the same sentence. "Yeah, I think so. There was a recent article in the *Times* about the organization so I'll play up that angle. It seems pretty cut and dry. I'm well backstopped with my cover. I thought I'd take a run at them after lunch."

"Sounds good to me. If they bite, you better stay out of the office until the operation is over."

Matt gave Dwayne an ear-to-ear smile. "That's all the incentive I need."

"The Amigo," a small taco stand a block from the ocean near the Santa Monica Pier, was always crowded with those from the beach scene seeking a quick Mexican food fix. The red and green wooden building needed a fresh coat of paint, but that did nothing to discourage customers.

Wadi was sitting at one of the picnic tables on the patio, eating an overstuffed burrito, when Ismad arrived.

"*Allahu Akbar,*" said Wadi.

"*Allahu,*" responded Ismad.

They gave each other a traditional hug, and Wadi welcomed his newest soldier to the United States. Ismad noticed salsa on Wadi's shirt and handed him a napkin. Wadi laughed off the etiquette gaff and wiped the tomato mess from the front of his Neiman-Marcus sweatshirt.

"I am here to assist you in your mission," said Wadi. "There are only two in the United States who know of your plans, me and the doctor. Others are here to support you indirectly but will never meet you or know your name."

"Did Mustafa know of my mission?" asked Ismad.

"Mustafa is no longer a problem."

"I am aware of that. Mustafa's name had been given to me by others overseas. He knew I was in this country but did not know the nature of my mission, unless you told him."

Wadi straightened at the less-than-subtle accusation. "I have told no one of your mission."

"Were you behind his involvement in the heroin transaction Saturday night?" asked Ismad.

"That is not for you to know."

"It was sloppy to have someone so weak involved in anything that dangerous, so close to my mission."

"Maybe you do not understand how the organization works. I answer to only one person, and that person is not you. The cause must raise money in many ways; otherwise, you, and others like you, will never succeed."

"I am aware of how the organization works. I have been given a very singular task, and it is most important I am successful. The window of success is indeed narrow. I ask for little, just limited support and a chance to accomplish the goal."

"That you will have."

"I will not succeed if I am discovered because of foolishness like Saturday night."

"There will be no more mistakes," said Wadi. "We can provide all of your needs—money, documentation, transportation, housing, food, and, of course, those items needed for that day."

"I will need nothing but those special items for the day of my mission. My cover is adequate to sustain my daily needs, as you should know."

"We have a strong organization in Los Angeles supporting the cause, and we are available to you," said Wadi. "We have done well in our fund-raising attempts and have contributed much to the overall effort."

"My only concern is fulfilling my assigned duty," said Ismad.

"I have many other concerns but understand the importance of your assignment. We should meet periodically in preparation for that day."

As Wadi was finishing his burrito, Ismad departed without saying another word.

Chapter Twelve

World Angel Ministry was located on Wilshire Boulevard in Santa Monica just a few blocks from the ocean. At lunchtime the staffers could walk to the bluffs overlooking the ocean and eat at the picnic tables. The view was absolutely beautiful if you didn't mind rubbing elbows with the homeless, who staked claim to many of the tables.

The structure housing the offices of the ministry was a two-story beige stucco building with a Spanish red tile roof. Sections of Santa Monica were heavily damaged during the Northridge earthquake in 1994. Almost every tile from the roof of the World Angel building smashed to the sidewalk, and much of the stucco was destroyed. Even though the building was built in 1928, the exterior renovations following the earthquake made it look much newer.

Matt parked on the street. After feeding the parking meter with quarters, he approached the World Angel building. A homeless man, dressed in rags and sitting near the entrance to World Angel, held out a cup seeking donations. Matt shook his head and then under his breath said, "Get a job." *I don't start playing humanitarian for another several hundred feet.*

The administrative offices were located on the second floor. Although the exterior was refurbished, the ornate, wood-paneled interior was reminiscent of a 1940s Humphrey Bogart movie. Matt made his way up the extra-wide staircase, trying to soften his footsteps on the hardwood floor. At the top of the stairs, he spied the door leading into the main office. Through the frosted glass he could see the reflection of the receptionist and walked in without knocking.

Matt was promptly greeted by a broad-shouldered brunette in her early twenties. Her pretty face was full, with dark, deep-set eyes, and she offered just a hint of a smile.

"Can I help you?"

"I've been reading about your organization and am looking for a volunteer activity so I thought I'd check it out personally," said Matt.

"We can always use more volunteers, but I'm not sure Dr. Mulumbo is available right now."

"No, I understand. I was in the neighborhood and thought maybe I could pick up some literature."

"I can get you that, but let me check with Dr. Mulumbo."

Spying the nameplate on her desk, Matt said, "Thanks, Kim."

Matt noted a softball team photo on the credenza behind her desk as she stood up.

"You play ball?"

"I played in junior college. Caught for two years, but that was before a couple of knee operations."

"I understand completely. My back put me out of work."

Kim excused herself and walked into Dr. Mulumbo's office. She returned in less than a minute. "He said if you could wait a few minutes, he would be glad to speak with you."

"Great."

The room was bright and comfortable, not ostentatious by any means but nicely decorated. Based upon what little Matt knew about the ministry, he assumed some professional, probably a doctor, donated the furniture when he modernized his own office.

Matt was drawn to the many pictures on the walls. The photos featured the various facilities overseas and the children who had been treated at the clinics.

One picture in particular caught Matt's eye. It was an eight-by-ten, black-and-white photo of an African boy, probably around nine or ten, with a huge grin, his face and arms badly scarred from burns and only one leg. He was standing with the aid of a wooden stick as a crutch. The left leg was amputated above the knee, and the youngster was clutching a Bible in his right hand. Matt swallowed trying to neutralize the lump forming in his throat.

"How long have you been with World Angel?" Matt asked Kim.

"Just a few months. I was going to start at UCLA this fall but can't decide on a major so I put it off at least a semester. I tell my parents I'm still trying to find myself. I don't want to waste time on classes I'll never use."

"Sounds reasonable to me."

"Maybe I should have you talk to my parents. The past two summers I went on some short-term mission projects sponsored by World Angel. When the job of administrative assistant opened up in August, I jumped on it."

Matt smiled and his eyes quickly scanned Kim's desk.

"Trying to cover all the bases?" asked Matt noting a Bible and the Koran.

"Huh?"

"The Bible and the Koran?"

"Yeah, I like studying world religions. I guess you could say I'm a seeker."

Matt paused. Lowering his voice a little, he said, "So was I."

Just then Dr. Mulumbo walked out of his office. His unassuming stature concealed his immense importance. He had very dark skin, close-cropped hair, and was maybe five feet four inches, if that. He was in his forties and had an undefined quality about him, an almost regal air exuding confidence.

Matt was ushered into the office. The furniture matched the furnishings in the reception area. When Matt complimented him on his choice of interior decorators, David Mulumbo laughed and said a doctor, who had supported the ministry for many years, donated the furnishings.

The pictures adorning the walls featured Dr. Mulumbo with a "who's who" of religion, politics, and Hollywood—Billy Graham, Presidents Bush, senior and George W., President Obama, former Secretary of State Madeline Albright, and assorted Tinseltown stars. Matt was a little embarrassed. Until an Internet search yesterday, he'd never heard of the organization. Matt spotted a medical degree from UCLA and numerous certifications in various fields of medicine.

Letters of appreciation cluttered the walls, some on presidential letterhead and some in crayon.

Matt began, "Doctor, it is a pleasure to meet you. I am so impressed by your ministry."

"Please, call me David," he said in a heavy English accent. "And thank you. So you are familiar with our ministry?"

"Oh yeah, of course, even long before I read the article in the *Times* several weeks ago. I pass by often and have been meaning to stop in but just haven't made the time to check it out personally."

"In a nutshell we are a nonprofit Christian relief organization providing medical assistance to children throughout Africa and the Eastern Mediterranean."

"The success of your organization is impressive," said Matt.

"What began in 1988 as a single trip with medical supplies to Kenya, my homeland, has evolved into twelve medical clinics. Since its inception, we have treated in excess of twenty-four thousand children."

"How do you finance all this?"

"God has provided us with generous corporate donors and dedicated medical personnel who work for salaries far below what they could earn elsewhere. We also have available to us doctors who volunteer hundreds of hours of their most valuable time."

Matt was captivated by the English accent.

"Our latest project is the clinic here in Santa Monica, just up the street. We are so excited about what God is allowing us to do. We have been able to purchase a nursing home that became available thanks to a corporate merger. We have remodeled the home into a sixteen-bed rehabilitation hospital. Now we will be able to bring some of our most severely injured children to the United States for the finest medical treatment in the world."

Nothing Dr. Mulumbo said or did demonstrated in any way he was connected with Saturday night's terrorist activity. If the doctor wasn't sincere, he possessed the skills of an Academy Award-winning actor.

"Where are most of the kids from?"

"Actually from all over. It really just depends on the most current political hot spot."

"I guess that means Afghanistan?"

David leaned closer, "We have both permanent and mobile facilities. Right now almost half of the children we treat are from Afghanistan and Iraq. But all of our clinics are full. We must turn away many children. I pray for forgiveness every day for the help we are not able to render to God's precious little ones."

"Are all of them Christian?"

David let out a hardy laugh. "Oh, heavens no. We treat the child regardless of religious affiliation. It would not be much of a ministry if we turned a child away because of religion."

"When will the new clinic open?"

"We hope to be fully operational in a few weeks. I need to get over there now and meet with a contractor. Would you like to join me?"

"Sure, I have time, and I'd love to see the facility."

Matt followed in his car as Dr. Mulumbo drove to the new clinic.

The clinic was a few miles east of the World Angel headquarters. The converted nursing home looked modern from the outside. A fresh coat of stucco, a newly landscaped front lawn, and a beautiful stone structure in front of the half-circle driveway announced, "World Angel Medical Clinic."

Matt was immediately impressed.

They parked in front of the complex and entered through the electronic sliding glass doors. David escorted Matt around the freshly painted complex. Although the facility was a hospital, the interior was designed to make it nonthreatening to children unfamiliar with the United States, the English language, and, in many cases, modern medical treatment.

Each room consisted of a state-of-the-art hospital bed and modern medical apparatus for ensuring the proper treatment of the most seriously injured child. Volunteers painted each room with cartoon Bible characters and carried that theme throughout the facility.

There was no surgical room. All of the surgeries were to be performed at Children's Hospital Los Angeles or the Ronald Reagan UCLA Medical Center, but a large room was created for physical therapy. David received donations from some of the nation's largest producers of PT equipment, and the clinic's department rivaled the finest facilities in Southern California. Many of the children treated would be amputation victims, and the PT room would be in near constant use. Two full-time physical therapists were on staff.

Omar was in the PT room, getting the equipment organized and preparing the room for the patients who would be arriving soon.

Matt and David walked over. "Matt, I'd like you to meet Omar Azia Khan."

Omar put down the clipboard he was using to inventory the

equipment and shook Matt's extended hand. He matched Matt in height and weight.

"Matt lives in Los Angeles and will be doing some volunteer work here at the clinic," said David.

Matt began, "Nice to meet you. Welcome to America. Dr. Mulumbo tells me you recently arrived."

Omar hesitated and responded with a curt, "Yes."

Matt paused and hoped for more of an exchange, but Omar seemed intent on limiting the conversation.

"The doctor also said you plan on taking classes at UCLA during your stay."

Omar looked at Mulumbo as if to say, "Minimize your discussion of my business with outsiders."

David sensed the awkwardness of the conversation. "Omar is a physical therapist who will be working with our amputees. He does excellent work. You will see how much the children love him."

Matt reached into his pocket and pulled out a package of Life Savers. He handed the package to Omar, who shook his head, refusing the offer. Matt then gestured toward David, who took the top candy in the roll. David smiled as he popped the cherry Life Saver into his mouth.

"Well, I'm sure I'll be seeing a lot of you. I plan on spending quite a bit of time here," said Matt.

Omar returned to his inventory duties without responding.

As Matt and David entered the hallway, walking toward the cafeteria, Matt asked David, "How was he selected?"

"He's been working at our clinic in Kandahar for the past several years. He has been most helpful. He was raised Muslim but never really practiced the religion and seems open to Christianity. He is a very skilled therapist. We thought this was a wonderful opportunity for his work and our witness."

As they continued the tour, David introduced Matt to several volunteers who were putting the finishing touches on some painting projects. All were Americans and failed to fit Matt's idea of the "terrorist" criteria.

David then knocked on the partially open door of a small office. A man in his early forties with a full beard and swarthy complexion was seated behind a desk reviewing medical records. He looked up as David and Matt entered.

"Matt, I'd like you to meet Dr. Ibrahim Saleh Mohammed al-Dirani." The words rolled off David's tongue in quick succession as if one elongated name. "We call him Dr. Ibrahim."

Ibrahim stood and shook Matt's hand.

Matt laughed. "I can understand why. I would have been in junior high before I could have spelled my name."

David smiled but Ibrahim remained stoic. The doctor was taller than Matt but much thinner.

"Matt is a volunteer paramedic who will be working with us at the clinic several afternoons a week," said David.

"That is good," said Ibrahim.

"Dr. Ibrahim is a gifted surgeon who worked with many of our patients throughout the Middle East," explained David.

"I've read a lot about the work of World Angel. You must be proud," said Matt.

"I don't do it for the pride," responded Ibrahim.

"I didn't mean it that way."

Ibrahim said nothing.

Once again David interceded during the awkward exchange. "Dr. Ibrahim is on rotation to help us set up the clinic. We are grateful for his services."

"I look forward to working with you," said Matt.

"Thank you."

Chapter Thirteen

For the foreseeable future Matt would avoid the FBI offices. He and Dwayne would speak regularly by phone and planned to meet personally every couple of days. At the conclusion of the first day, Matt called Dwayne on a "cold phone" in Dwayne's office.

"It went well, and it looks like I'm in. I met David and took the fifty-cent tour of the facility. He bought my act. I met several of the medical personnel and some of the volunteers."

Dwayne put Matt on hold and then came back to the phone. "Sorry, I wanted to shut my door. I guess I trust everybody but—"

Matt interrupted, "Trust no man 'til you have to."

"I like that. Can I use it?"

"Sure, it's not original. I think I read it in a fortune cookie I got from the paranoid owner of a Chinese restaurant."

Dwayne gave a slight chuckle. "We've already run background checks on some of the employees and volunteers. Did you meet an Omar?"

"Yeah, Omar, I think Khan was the last name. I also met a Dr. Ibrahim with about four other names attached. Neither gets my nomination for Mr. Congeniality. Both a little cold—actually, make that frozen."

"Good segue. I got a call from ICE. Omar is legal. It looks like he's got a brother, Rashid, who may have overstayed his visa. They're trying to find the file. They live together in Venice. We're trying to put together a package on everyone at the clinic."

"Anything on Dr. Ibrahim?" asked Matt.

"He's got a visa."

"So at least Omar and Ibrahim are here legally," said Matt.

"That doesn't mean their ambitions are legal."

"I understand. Do we have surveillance yet?"

"Yeah, I spoke with SOG. We'll get a couple of teams working later this evening. Thought I'd start with Omar and Rashid since the brother's status is questionable."

"If personality is a factor, don't forget the good doctor."

"You mean Mulumbo?" asked Dwayne.

"No, I mean Ibrahim."

"What's your take on Mulumbo?"

"He almost seems too good to be true. Besides, he's Christian."

"Don't eliminate anybody just yet," said Dwayne.

"Maybe he's a great actor, but he sold me on his sincerity. I wouldn't waste much time on him until we develop a reason."

"I'll keep you updated. And before you make any snap judgments, remember almost every 9/11 hijacker was described as polite, nothing suspicious or out of the ordinary."

"Yeah, I know," said Matt.

"Good job today. Call me if anything comes up."

"Or goes down."

"Huh? Oh yeah. Up or down, call me, wise guy," said Dwayne.

~~

Everything about the motel room cried out 1970s—dark wood veneer cabinets; worn green shag carpeting; variegated brown, striped foil wallpaper. The lone sixty-watt lightbulb in the ceiling fixture made the room depressingly dark. The hour was late.

Omar had the TV on but paid no attention to the syndicated game show being aired. He was relaxing in bed, fighting to keep his eyes open. When the phone rang, he jumped, startled out of a near sleep. He picked up the phone. Before he could even speak, the caller said, "*Allah Issalmak*."

Even though he spoke Pashto, Omar responded without thinking to the Arabic greeting, "God keep you safe."

The caller then said, "Tomorrow morning, precisely at eleven. Bank of America, 1430 Wilshire Boulevard, Santa Monica, male teller, Abu. He is prepared."

The caller abruptly hung up without waiting for a response.

Chapter Fourteen

The Special Operations Group or SOG, as it is known inside the Bureau, consists of specialized surveillance teams. Each team has six agents. All are specially trained, experienced, and highly dedicated. They dress and look the part, whatever that part might be for a particular assignment. They are not your Hoover-type, coat-and-tie agents, and they know L.A. better than the city planner. They are familiar with virtually every cul-de-sac and shortcut in the city, a task not easy in a town the size of Los Angeles. Even with the use of a plane overhead, the crowded skies and the crowded streets of the city make surveillance one of the most difficult assignments in the L.A. office.

Omar was staying in a small, nondescript residential motel on Lincoln Boulevard in Venice. His brother, Rashid, rented the room and both were driving Rashid's car, an older, green Ford Explorer in need of a paint job and new left fender. The right taillight was broken, which made surveillance at night simple. In the crowded

L.A. traffic, the white light, beaming through the damaged red plastic shield, hollered, "Here I am; follow me."

After several days of surveillance, nothing unusual had been observed. The teams concentrated on Omar. He shopped at the local Ralph's supermarket, ate once at a Bangladesh restaurant on Sixth Street and twice at a Chicken Kabob, a fast-food take-out place on Santa Monica Boulevard. Rashid went twice to a mosque near the airport, but Omar never accompanied him.

Today started uneventfully. The "forties" were assigned to the 7:00 a.m. to 3:00 p.m. shift, and in less than an hour the "fifties" would assume the surveillance responsibilities. Each member of the "forties" team had a number designation. They transmitted on a private, secure channel so typical radio protocol was unnecessary. The radio silence was broken with a question.

"Who was the goddess of peace?"

"Roman or Greek?"

"How should I know?"

"You asked the question."

A deep base voice responded, "Pax."

"Doesn't fit," was the response. "Six letters."

"Forty-one, you've got the point?" asked Forty, the team leader.

"Yeah. No problem. The brother is parked in front of the clinic, appears to be waiting for Omar. He's wearing a faded orange long-sleeve T-shirt, in case anyone cares. Wait. Here comes Omar now. Saddle up, boys."

Omar exited the clinic to the waiting car. Without even a greeting, Rashid, the older brother yet several inches shorter, began to question Omar as he opened the passenger door.

"Did I get a phone call last night?" asked Rashid.

"No."

"You mean nobody called last night?"

Omar thought for a second. "No . . . well, there was one call. It was very strange, something about a bank, but the caller did not ask for you. He then abruptly hung up."

Rashid's face reddened. "That call was for me! You should have said something."

"How was I to know? He never said your name. I didn't understand the call."

"You are my guest. No one knows you are staying with me. When you answered the phone, that person thought you were me. People are very upset. From now on do not answer the phone! Do you understand?"

Omar hung his head.

Forty-one relayed his observations to the others. "Rashid seems agitated about something. They're just sitting there. Rashid is pretty animated. . . . Okay, we're moving. We're eastbound on Wilshire. Right on 20th. . . . Red balled at Santa Monica. I'm two back."

The cars were stopped at a red light. The unit designated "forty-one" was two cars back, using those cars to shield him from Rashid's rearview mirror.

"We're moving. He's left on Santa Monica, eastbound. Thanks for the signal, jerk. This idiot ahead of me is parked, and I'm trapped. I need some help."

The team leader interceded. "Anyone got 'em?"

Forty-three jumped in. "I've got it. We're eastbound and red balled at 26th. Rashid is still in Omar's face. He's upset about something. . . . We're moving."

"Forty-three, we're right behind you. Give me a unit to parallel on Arizona," said the team leader.

"This is forty-two. I'm on Arizona."

"Forty-four is about two blocks ahead."

Forty-three had the point. "We're moving pretty well. He's catching all the greens. I'm three back in the number two lane, he's in the number one lane. Red balled at Bundy. . . . We're moving and Rashid is still talking. I don't think Omar has said a thing. He's just sitting there with his head down. Still eastbound Santa Monica. . . . Wait, he made a U. I can't get over."

Rashid made a U-turn in the middle of the block, almost causing an accident. Horns blared, and several drivers hollered obscenities at Rashid, who seemed oblivious to their tirades. Rashid suddenly stopped at the corner.

Omar exited the car in a hurry and walked over to the bus stop where he sat and waited.

Rashid drove off quickly westbound on Santa Monica Boulevard. He caught every green and ran several yellows. Within seconds he was gone, lost in traffic.

"This guy's gotta be no-good. Innocent people don't drive like that," said forty-three.

"You've never ridden with my wife," came a response.

The team turned when they could, but by the time they were able to get westbound on Santa Monica, the green Explorer was out of sight. The forties had been instructed to conduct a loose surveillance and not get burned. U-turns by the trailing agents in the middle of Santa Monica Boulevard would have been obvious.

The team leader radioed everyone to return to the bus stop. With a strong hint of sarcasm he said, "Nice try guys, but you don't get off that easily. The day's not over yet. Our focus is on Omar. Now we get to follow a bus. That's gonna be a little tougher to lose."

The deep bass voice said, "Eirene."

"What?" asked Forty.

"Eirene, six letters, E-i-r-e-n-e, the Greek goddess of peace," said the deep voice.

Someone responded, "And people think you're wasting an Ivy League education on the surveillance squad."

Omar boarded the westbound bus. It crawled along the road, stopping every other block for passengers. Just as the team leader was about to make a comment, the radio dispatcher came on the air.

"Attention all units. We have a good two-eleven at the Bank of America, 1430 Wilshire Boulevard, Santa Monica. The subject is described as a male, possibly Middle Eastern, five-six to five-eight, 130–150, wearing dark pants, gray hooded sweatshirt. Subject used a note. He was observed running eastbound on Wilshire. No further description. Santa Monica PD responding."

Several FBI bank robbery units radioed the dispatcher and responded they were en route.

"Forty, you think that was our boy?"

"I hope not. He's Middle Eastern, but there was no mention of the orange T-shirt. That seems pretty distinctive."

"He could have thrown on a hooded sweatshirt," interrupted forty-three.

"Don't think I wasn't thinking that. I'll let the bank robbery guys know. Forty-one and forty-two stick with the bus. Everyone else return to the motel. Let's go sit on that for awhile."

A lone gunman robbed the Bank of America. Witnesses said he had dark skin and an accent, possibly Middle Eastern. The clothing the robber wore did not match what Rashid was wearing while under surveillance. Witnesses described the sweatshirt as old with a green paint stain on the back of the right arm. The male teller, Abu al-Doori, was unable to activate the surveillance cameras until the robber had almost exited the bank. The agents would have to wait to determine if the surveillance photos could help in identifying the suspect.

At 2:43 p.m. Rashid returned alone to the motel. He was wearing the same clothes he wore when observed earlier in the day. He was not wearing the sweatshirt described by witnesses but was carrying what could have been a wadded up sweatshirt in his right hand when he exited the car.

Omar returned twelve minutes later. He got off a Santa Monica bus three blocks from the motel and stopped at a local mini-mart. When he exited a few minutes later, he was carrying a bag of groceries and a six-pack of Coke.

Chapter Fifteen

In the first-floor conference room, David greeted the medical personnel and volunteers attending the weekly staff meeting. A large oil painting of Jesus holding a small child covered the wall at the far end of the room. More photos of clinics, patients, and missionaries adorned the other walls.

Matt sat at the oblong conference table facing the windows looking out onto Wilshire Boulevard. Shoppers walking to and from Santa Monica's Third Street Promenade, an outdoor shopping mall three blocks from the ocean, continually passed in front of the windows. The homeless, pushing shopping carts filled with collections of papers and aluminum cans, also passed.

David opened with prayer. His strong English accent somehow made the prayer seem more spiritual. The meeting lasted several hours, mostly involving administrative matters concerning reimbursement of travel expenses for visiting medical personnel, travel restrictions, visa matters, and suggestions for fund-raising events.

Matt's enthusiasm for being an undercover humanitarian was waning. Whether working covert or overt, administrative matters were not his strong suit.

Finally David turned to Ibrahim and asked him to close the session with prayer. Ibrahim smiled, bowed his head, then went on and on and on. Some Hollywood marriages didn't last this long. The "amen" could not come quickly enough for Matt.

Kim, the receptionist, wheeled in a cart with snacks, coffee, and soft drinks, a reward for sitting through the staff meeting and Ibrahim's prayer.

Kim and Ibrahim were talking as Matt approached. Ibrahim, as Matt had learned, was a serious man of few words, except evidently when praying. He was uncharacteristically smiling as he spoke with Kim, who was pouring him a cup of coffee, a service she provided no other guest that morning. Ibrahim grabbed the cup and walked away.

Matt took a Dr. Pepper from the cart. "So I guess you two know each other?"

"Yeah, we met at one of the clinics last summer," said Kim.

Matt spoke briefly to several of those in attendance as he made his way toward Omar, trying not to be conspicuous in his efforts.

Omar seemed uncomfortable in the social setting and was attempting to exit when Matt reached him. Matt threw out his right hand, but Omar failed to return the gesture. Matt asked several polite questions in an effort to engage him in conversation, but Omar responded with one- or two-word answers and quickly excused himself.

The loud and annoying warning blared as the tractor and semitrailer backed into the Hollywood public storage facility. Wadi had arranged for the rental of three storage units to house the counterfeit cigarettes for the next week or so. By that time the cigarettes should be sold or at least spread to the next level in the distribution chain.

Wadi hired six Hispanic men who stood daily in front of The Home Depot on Sunset looking for day work. They were the perfect employees. They worked hard, spoke little English and no Arabic. The men were promised twenty-five dollars a piece for a two-hour job. Time was money to the men, and the sooner they completed this task, the sooner they could get back and pick up more work in the afternoon. They were told the container consisted of backpacks made in China, but the men had little cause or desire to question the contents.

The sealed container was scheduled to arrive about 10:00 a.m., but it was now almost eleven. A backup at the port caused a delay in the driver's getting clearance with his cargo. Traffic at the storage facility was still minimal at this hour, so few people would observe the master cases of counterfeit cigarettes being off-loaded into the storage unit.

As promised, Sammy arrived at the storage facility with the container. He showed Wadi the fraudulent bill of lading created by the export company in China. The contents were described as "backpacks" and "camping equipment," reducing the chance of U.S. Customs officials inquiring further. Wadi and Sammy compared the serial number on the metal tamper-proof seal to the one on the paperwork. The numbers matched, and Wadi was satisfied the container had not been opened since leaving China.

Sammy cut the seal with a pair of heavy duty wire cutters and opened the cumbersome blue steel doors of the forty-foot container. It was packed—one thousand fifty master cases, each case containing fifty cartons, each carton containing ten packs, twenty cigarettes to a pack. Wadi had successfully imported 10,500,000 counterfeit cigarettes, avoided federal and state taxes, and because of American vices, was generating a half-million-dollar profit for the cause.

Wholesalers, retailers, and consumers, some knowingly, many unknowingly, would support terrorism in the name of "saving a buck."

LATER THAT AFTERNOON MATT met with Dwayne at the Coffee Express on Ventura Boulevard in Studio City. There was a slight chill in the air, and the abandoned outdoor patio tables provided privacy. Both ordered the no-frills coffee, high octane, black.

Several wannabe starlets paraded in front of the café headed for an audition at the casting office next door.

Matt blew on his drink, the steam still rising. "Things seem to be going well, I guess."

"Great. What's your story?" asked Dwayne.

"I'm a former licensed paramedic from Indiana who was injured on a call several years ago. I received a medical retirement from the department and between some wise real estate investments I continue to manage and a small trust fund from my grandfather, I have time to volunteer."

Dwayne sipped his coffee. "Can you backstop that?"

"Yeah, I've used it before. HQ has phonied up my credit report to reflect the retirement and the trust fund. I'm pretty nebulous when it comes to the location of the real estate. I think I own a few porno shops in San Francisco and a cross-dressing bar in New Orleans. I'll be fine."

"The Queen Mother's going to love that. You really are trying to get me fired, aren't you?"

Matt laughed. "Don't worry. I'm only teasing about the cross-dressing bar. This cover gives me plenty of free time to work at the clinic. You got any news?"

Dwayne looked around to make sure no one had walked onto the patio. They were still alone. "The Agency is picking up chatter of some type of terrorist act planned for the West Coast soon but nothing more definitive."

"Someday you'll have to tell me what 'chatter' is."

Dwayne gave an anemic smile. "When I find out, I'll let you know. I worked there two years and still don't know exactly what they mean.

Just keep your ears open and your head down. Having a UC whacked is not career enhancing."

"Thanks for your heartfelt concern."

Matt took a drink. "Even if we limit the scope of the warning to Southern California, the targets are unlimited. It's a needle in the proverbial haystack."

"I can't argue with you. As we've seen in Israel and throughout the Middle East, indiscriminate attacks are just as effective as the destruction of a high-value target. Until we can narrow it down, be alert for anything that spells terrorism."

"You're not making this assignment any easier."

"We knew that going in."

As they were both finishing their coffee, Dwayne said, "Terrorist organizations don't quit; they have to be destroyed. Any group who believes it's sanctioned by God also believes it is freed from moral constraints." Dwayne gave Matt a moment to reflect on that; then he asked, "Any idea what we have at the clinic?"

"Not yet. We've identified the only two Middle Eastern employees, Omar and Dr. Ibrahim. I've got issues with Omar, but Ibrahim prayed this morning, and I expected a gospel choir to break out in 'Amazing Grace.'"

"Takin' it home, huh?"

"You'd have thought we were at a Billy Graham crusade. I think the only country he didn't pray for was Lithuania. My guess is World Angel was not created as a front for terrorism."

"I'm sure it wasn't. Terrorists typically wouldn't start an organization like this. They would infiltrate and exploit an existing charity."

"From what I've seen, it's hardly a sanctuary for the mujahideen."

"I'm not convinced the organization is our target. Our focus should be on an individual vulnerable to radicalization."

Matt laughed out loud. "Spoken like a true administrator fresh from a Behavioral Science Unit in-service. Any idea which individual is vulnerable to radicalization?"

"Of course not. That's why you're undercover," said Dwayne with a wide grin. "Focus on Omar and Ibrahim but eliminate no one until we can get a handle on this. Jihadists have been patient in pursuing terrorism, but we may not have the luxury of time. Do what you can, as fast as you can."

"You make it sound so simple," said Matt as both got up from the table.

"They teach us that at administrator's school. . . . Can't you find someplace a little closer to the office?"

"Sure, but this is closer to my house and gives me a head start on the commute home," said Matt, smiling as he walked away.

Chapter Sixteen

Matt went straight home from his meeting with Dwayne. Caitlin was already there and was preparing dinner. He slipped in quietly and approached her from behind as she was tossing a salad. He kissed her on the back of the neck.

"Oh, you know I love that, but please, my husband will be home any minute now. You better go."

"Very funny."

"Oh, is that you? I didn't hear you come in." She put down the wooden salad forks and turned to give Matt a kiss. "I love you."

Matt feigned indignation. "Who were you expecting?"

"Only you, Cowboy. I'm a one-man woman."

Caitlin spent the next several minutes in silence as she finished preparing dinner. Matt busied himself setting the table.

"You seem pretty quiet. Everything okay?" asked Matt.

Caitlin put down the cooking utensils and turned to him. "I worry about you. I'm not real thrilled with this new assignment. Terrorism just sounds so much more dangerous."

"Trust me, I know what I'm doing."

"What are you doing?"

"I have no idea."

She kissed him. "You are so reassuring."

"I'll be fine. It can't be any more dangerous than organized crime or gangs." He paused, then added, "I have to do this for them."

"I know you think you do. I wish you didn't feel that way."

"I owe it to Scott and the others."

"I know," said Caitlin, as she gave Matt another kiss. "Just be careful. I still have a few plans for us before I start collecting that retirement check."

"I'll be fine. I'm not checking out early and leaving you with a tax-free income the rest of your life so you can run off with some boy toy."

She pinched his cheek. "You are such a romantic. Did you remember we have bumper bowling tonight?"

Matt was confused. "Bumper bowling?"

"Matt, don't tell me you forgot. You promised. I told you the other night. Tonight we are bowling with my kids who read five books this month. Sound familiar?"

"Yeah, I'm beginning to remember." Matt looked to an empty chair. "Your honor, the prosecution would request permission to refresh the witness's recollection." Matt turned back. "Permission granted."

With that Caitlin walked over and threw her arms around his neck and gave him another kiss.

Matt smiled. "Now I remember. How many of these little darlings succeeded in the challenge?"

Caitlin winced, "All of them."

"What?"

"Next time remind me to make it ten books."

They finished dinner, changed into casual clothes, and headed to the bowling alley.

Twenty-one second-graders eagerly awaited Caitlin's arrival. Matt had been to her class one afternoon earlier in the school year. He knew names because almost every evening Caitlin came home with a school day tale. It was difficult putting faces from that one afternoon visit together with names, but he was thrilled to see how much his wife was loved. As Mrs. Hogan's husband or "sweetie" as one little girl called him, he enjoyed celebrity status.

The children came in all sizes and colors. It looked like an international children's enclave in the adult world of the bowling alley. Caitlin's class consisted of twelve girls and nine boys. Four children were born in Mexico, one in Afghanistan, one in Egypt, and one in China. Three girls and one boy were African-American. One father was a doctor. Two fathers were farm workers. One child was homeless and lived with her mother in government-subsidized motels for two-week intervals. Caitlin had quietly done a great deal for that family, and few people were aware of their circumstances. It was just one more reason Matt loved his wife; she had a compassionate heart full of love and hope.

The energy these twenty-one youngsters generated could power a small city. Factoring in the noise of a bowling alley with the noise of her overly enthusiastic class, it was at an earplug decibel level.

Three lanes had been set aside for Caitlin's class. Inflatable tubes were placed in the gutters of the alleys to prevent gutter balls, and eight-pound balls were brought out from under lock and key. The kids were more than ready. The only requirement now was to generate enough strength to power the ball down the alley so it would at least knock over a pin or two.

The kids had a blast. One girl, the largest in the class, was actually pretty good. Most of the time she was able to knock down a few pins without taking advantage of the bumpers.

Caitlin was at her best, encouraging the children, laughing with them, and celebrating their successes. Several mothers were also in attendance. Three mothers, all Hispanic, sat together in the back and watched. A fourth mother sat by herself.

Matt reluctantly joined the women in the back, believing he was obligated to play the dutiful husband. He introduced himself to each of the Hispanic mothers, who praised Caitlin and her work with the children. After a few minutes of small talk, he walked over to the lone mother, who was Middle Eastern. Ordinarily he wouldn't have even bothered, but in light of his undercover assignment, he thought he might at least learn something culturally beneficial.

"Hi, I'm Matt, Caitlin's husband."

"How do you do, Mr. Matt? I am Nahid Anwari. My daughter is Jaana. She is the one rolling the ball."

Matt turned and saw a little girl hobble as she tried to roll the ball down the alley. It was a weak two-handed effort. Jaana was one of the smaller students, which might explain her lack of strength. The ball bounced off the bumper several times before knocking down two pins. When the pins eventually fell, the seven-year-old pixie with raven black hair, big brown eyes, and a perfect olive complexion, let out a childish squeal.

"Your daughter's beautiful," said Matt.

"You are most kind. My daughter has not been well, but she insisted on coming. She probably should have stayed home and rest. She begged to come, so my husband and I agree. We love your wife. She is fine teacher and has welcomed us to your country."

Matt was always uncomfortable asking nationality questions in such a setting. He was never quite sure how to ask without offending. One time he asked someone with a heavy accent about his citizenship, and the person, who was highly offended by the question, had been born in the United States. But Nahid opened the door.

"Where's your family from?"

"We are from Afghanistan." She paused then added, "My husband came to your country in 2006, and we were able to join him two years ago."

Matt wanted to walk away. He had no desire to talk to anyone from Afghanistan, at least not on his own time. The bile churned in his stomach. *Man up and at least do it for Caitlin.*

Nahid smiled uncomfortably. "It was very difficult to stay behind, but I knew some day we would be together again. Your country is so great. We are very thankful to be here."

"Tell me about your country."

"It is about the size of your Texas. Our family lived in Kandahar, but I grew up in the Helmand province. In the spring time it is like a lush garden."

A lush garden . . . your poppies produce more opium than Colombia produces cocaine or coffee.

"The invasion by the Soviets changed our world. I was only two when that happened, but ever since we have been a country at war."

Yeah, you're a war-torn country transformed into a narco-state. You don't have black streams flowing up from the desert so you feed the world its other addiction, heroin.

"Our towns and villages have been destroyed."

At that moment a loud roar, from a group of men several lanes over, drew the attention of all. A large, overweight man with a few too many beers rolled a strike, capturing a victory for his team of drunks. Their yelps made it appear as though they were celebrating the destruction of Afghanistan. But Matt might celebrate that as well.

The yelling distracted Nahid momentarily, then she continued. "After the Soviets were driven from our country, civil war broke out between our many tribes. The Taliban came into power, but poverty and disease were everywhere. Then the United States attacked. My world, as I have known it, was destroyed first by years of war, then the Taliban, and then more war. Many members of my family died. All I have left are my husband and my Jaana."

Matt showed little reaction. "But it's been better for you in the United States?"

"Yes, of course. But I think many here are afraid because we are Muslims. They think we are terrorists. I see their looks."

Matt's eyes almost bored through her.

Nahid went on, "Many people have the wrong idea. Muslims are very traditional people. We oppose the use of alcohol. We believe in marriage. We oppose pornography and believe abortion is wrong. Those who did the attacks on your World Trade Center were not like most Muslims. They were the Wahhabi from Saudi Arabia. They were not even from my country. We are not terrorists. We do not know any terrorists. We came here for a better life. We hope someday to be Americans. I want someday to vote. I want to participate in your government. Do not hate me for my country or my accent."

Matt looked at her, shaking his head. "Nahid, I just met you."

"No, no, Mr. Matt, I did not mean you. I meant the people who look at me like I am bad. I say to them, 'Get to know me. I am like you.'"

"What kind of work does your family do?"

"In Afghanistan we were merchants, trading with many English companies."

"That explains why your English is so good," said Matt.

Nahid blushed. "Thank you. Sometime it is not so good."

"So what do you do now?"

"We are merchants in your country also. My country placed its hope in the Taliban, but it was still difficult to earn a living. They ruled under the sharia, the Islamic law. But that rule was harsh. Thieves' hands were cut off. Adulterers were stoned to death. Murderers were executed by their victim's families."

"It seems like a solution to the recidivism rate," said Matt, with a hint of sarcasm.

"I don't understand that word."

"It means the person will not repeat his crime."

"You are right. I know of no one who repeated their crime."

Matt's cynicism confused Nahid, and for a brief moment he was embarrassed he had taken advantage of her elementary language skills.

"The Taliban demanded so much. Hamid Karzai's government could not protect us either. I hoped by coming here we left that behind. But even in America, we get telephone calls from organizations wanting help. They want us to donate money or goods. Sometimes we do. I am afraid not to help. The callers sometimes are very frightening. But I tell them I have very little. I can only give a little. The callers then tell me about all the suffering in the Middle East because of the West and I should help. They say if I don't help, then I am on the side of Satan."

Just as the conversation began to touch on a subject of immediate interest to Matt, Caitlin announced it was time for the children to get ready to go home. The confusion taking place as the second-graders gathered up their belongings made it impossible for Matt and Nahid to continue their discussion. Nahid excused herself to make a phone call to her husband who was picking them up following the event. Matt thanked Nahid and went over to help Caitlin. He never told Nahid what he did; she never asked.

JAANA SAT ALONE ON the semicircular bench surrounding the lane, waiting for her mother to finish making the call. All the other students left.

Caitlin gathered up the usual forgotten items—a small purse, a pair of socks, and several scrunchies. They would go in the lost-and-found box in the classroom joining thirty other misplaced items.

Caitlin walked over and sat next to Jaana. "Did you have fun?"

"Yes, Mrs. Hogan, but the ball was very heavy. It really made me tired."

Caitlin laughed. "I imagine it did seem like a very heavy ball to you, but as you get older, it will seem light and easy to roll." Caitlin looked up and saw Jaana's mother standing by the tables. "I think your mother is ready to go."

Jaana stood up but just as quickly sat down.

"Are you okay?" asked Caitlin.

"I feel kind of dizzy. Sometimes tonight I have been cold and other times I felt hot."

Caitlin signaled for Mrs. Anwari and then put the back of her hand to Jaana's forehead. Her temperature seemed normal.

When Jaana's mother walked down the steps toward the alley, Caitlin stopped her. "Jaana just told me she felt dizzy and has been alternating between chills and a fever. It may just be the excitement of a night out with her classmates, but you might want to keep an eye on her. She may be coming down with something. At this age children are exposed to so much. Just about every bug comes through the school during the year."

"Thank you, Mrs. Hogan. Yes, she has been complaining for several weeks of not feeling well and that her leg hurts, but she insisted on coming tonight. We have taken her to the doctor, and he gave her some medicine. I think she is afraid to say too much because she thinks we will make her miss school."

As Nahid helped Jaana to her feet, Caitlin knelt down and gave her a hug. "Now, you take care of yourself. Listen to your mother and take your medicine. You're my best helper and I need you healthy. It's okay if you have to stay home in order to get better."

Nahid held Jaana's hand as they walked up the steps toward the large automatic sliding glass doors. Jaana had a slight limp and turned to wave as she exited the bowling alley. Caitlin returned the wave with a smile.

Chapter Seventeen

Matt survived the first few weeks of the undercover assignment and was beginning to reach a comfort level with the staff and volunteers. Since Omar and Ibrahim were the only two Middle Eastern workers at the clinic, he concentrated his efforts on them. Neither was receptive to Matt's overtures, but many successful undercover operations result from baby steps.

Most of Matt's work was more labor intensive than he assumed the assignment would entail—assisting the doctors and therapists. In fact, he was more a handyman than a medical practitioner. Had he been a true volunteer, he might have gone in to renegotiate his contract or simply quit, but he accepted a certain amount of garbage assignments to complete the mission successfully. Once the children arrived, he hoped the work might be more palatable.

Matt was standing by the loading dock waiting for a shipment that was several minutes late. The doctor delivering the supplies called the front desk stating he was a few minutes out, but that had been almost ten minutes ago. Just as Matt was about to go back inside, a dark blue 2008 Range Rover Sport pulled into the alley. The driver hopped out of the vehicle, extended his hand, and displayed an engaging smile.

"I am so sorry to be late. There was construction on Santa Monica Boulevard, and I had to take a detour. I am Dr. Ubadiah al-Banna, but please call me Dr. U. You must be Matt."

"I figured you got hung up in traffic. Nice to meet you."

Dr. Ubadiah al-Banna, Wadi's medical contact at Mount Sinai Medical Center, had short black hair, was clean shaven; and his long powerful fingers delivered a strong, impressive grip. Matt was surprised the doctor was Middle Eastern and assumed him to be Muslim. After the two shook hands, the doctor opened the rear hatch to the SUV.

"Everything goes," said the doctor, referring to the six large boxes in the back of the vehicle. "We were most fortunate to have two pharmaceutical salesmen donate many samples to the clinic. Do you know if the good doctor is in?"

"Dr. Ibrahim is at the Children's Hospital all day."

"No, I meant my friend David."

"He's here. I just saw him."

"Good. Then I must step inside and see my friend. Can you unload it yourself?"

Matt smiled, agreeing to the doctor's request, but Matt's motives were less than altruistic. Being alone with the car gave him the chance to copy down the license plate, check the vehicle registration in the glove compartment, and search the interior, all while appearing to unload the boxes.

"Sure, that's not a problem, but do you mind leaving the keys so I can move your car once it's unloaded? We're expecting a second delivery a little later this morning."

Dr. U tossed the keys to a smiling Matt. *I guess we can forego the consent to search form.*

Wadi, Rashid, and Babur were sitting around the lone table in the small, one-bedroom West Hollywood apartment. They were taking a break from the morning telephone solicitation efforts. Using Los Angeles as a base of operations made sense. The West Coast time differential allowed the men to contact merchants in the middle of an East Coast businessman's afternoon and still contact West Coast merchants throughout the day. The solicitations were a valuable vehicle for maintaining a connection with Middle Easterners living in the United States and for eliciting support for the cause. The telephone contacts allowed Wadi and his cell to assess U.S. residents who supported the efforts of those seeking to eradicate Israel and its allies. Even businessmen who refused to support terrorism supported the humanitarian charities the solicitors claimed to represent. In truth, all the donations aided the cause of the radical Muslim movement, a cause in which the three truly believed. Wadi, who initiated this venture, was successful in managing yet another avenue for raising much needed funds.

"Did you enjoy the basketball game last night?" asked Wadi.

"I am not a fan of basketball," said Rashid. "But I was able to get a seating chart and visited most of the restrooms." He handed Wadi the chart with the notes he made of the arena.

"Good, we may need this some day."

Babur's nicotine-stained fingers grabbed a cigarette from the Chinese-manufactured pack. The chain-smoking terrorist had been through half a pack, and it wasn't even ten. Just as he was about to light the counterfeit Marlboro, there was a knock at the door.

"I'll get it," offered Babur as he rose from his seat. He peered through the security peephole and turned toward Wadi, whispering, "It's Yasir."

"Wait, let me hide the doughnuts. Then let him in."

Wadi closed the lid on the box of Krispy Kremes and placed them on the shelf behind a stack of dishes. He closed the cabinet door just as Babur released the dead bolt and opened the door.

Yasir, who was well on his way to obesity, waddled in and headed straight for the scratched, compressed-wood cabinet over the sink. Opening the door, he reached behind the dishes and pulled out the box.

With a huge smile, Yasir said, "You hid them here the last time. You should be less predictable." He grabbed a glazed doughnut as he poured himself a cup of coffee. "The child will be here soon."

"That is most excellent," said Wadi.

"She is deserving of the best care, and I am glad to get her into this country," said Yasir.

Wadi took a cigarette from the pack lying on the table. After lighting it and taking several puffs, he said, "Her father served the cause well. He was a respected leader whose death was tragic, a wasted death for a man who should have been martyred. We are fortunate others have assumed his responsibilities. Did the doctor have many questions?"

"No," said Yasir. "He was most grateful for the donation and agreed the child was in need. As you suggested, we can exploit this situation in the future."

"Yes," said Wadi. "We will be able to use the children to bring in that which is needed for the cause. I did not want to attempt such, this first time."

"You are right. It is much too early," said Babur.

Wadi confirmed his initial plan. "Let us offer several more cash donations as we bring our children over. Let everyone in power become comfortable with our apparent concern, and then we will use this to our advantage."

The four men laughed.

Rising from his chair, Yasir took two more doughnuts from the box. "I have customers to see. I will call you later."

Chapter Eighteen

Caitlin pulled up to the small market and turned off her engine. She waited a few seconds before exiting her car. The extra moments gave her a chance to survey the scene. It was an action that became second nature being married to an FBI agent. She had to admit it wasn't a habit she employed when exiting her car in Thousand Oaks or Beverly Hills, but this neighborhood screamed "rising crime rate." A quick look around revealed the residents agreed. Wrought-iron bars on the windows and doors of every house in sight were not installed because a recent issue of *Home and Garden* called it "a must-have decorative item."

Hearing and seeing nothing out of the ordinary, she hopped out of the car and headed up the sidewalk toward the partially opened steel grate door marking the entrance to the neighborhood convenience store. The door, as well as the exterior of the stucco building, needed a coat of paint if for no other reason than to cover the graffiti.

Caitlin had been to the market once before to speak with Jaana's mother when Nahid had been unable to attend the parent-teacher conference. She was hoping Nahid was working this afternoon.

The store was small with only a few rows of shelves filled with a limited selection of grocery items. Behind the counter were every brand of cigarettes and cheap liquor desired by the neighborhood. Had it not been for liquor advertisements, the walls would have been bare.

The store appeared empty. There were no customers, and no one was behind the counter. A chill ran down Caitlin's spine, and fear began to envelope her. She turned her back to the front counter as she looked around, seeking any sign of life in the dimly lit market.

"Yes, can I help you?"

The gruff, heavily accented voice startled Caitlin, who jumped and turned to see a short, Middle Eastern man with dark hair, leathery skin, and a full beard, entering from a doorway behind the counter.

"Oh, you scared me," said Caitlin.

The man offered no apology and repeated the question, "Can I help you?"

"Yes, I am looking for Nahid," said Caitlin.

"She is not here. What is this about?" His penetrating, dark, deep-set eyes were less than welcoming.

"I am Caitlin Hogan, Jaana's teacher, and I was hoping to speak with Nahid."

Zerak wiped his hands on his worn apron and extended his right hand across the counter. His hardened demeanor softened immediately. "Oh, yes, Mrs. Hogan. My wife and my Jaana speak of you often. I am Zerak, Jaana's father. I am so glad to meet you."

Caitlin, still trying to compose herself, shook his hand and hesitated briefly. "Jaana hasn't been to school for the past week, and I wanted to make sure she was okay."

"You seem very nervous, Mrs. Hogan."

"When I walked in and saw no one in the store, I was afraid something was wrong," said Caitlin.

"It is okay. I was just in the back for a minute. I saw you through my office window."

Zerak pointed to a small pane of one-way glass, not much larger than a basketball.

"How kind of you to check on my Jaana. She has not been well. The doctors are running many tests. The medicine is not working. I know she would love to talk with you. Let me call her and you two can talk."

"I would love to speak with her, but I would hate for you to wake her if she is napping."

"No, no. I am sure she is awake. Step back into my office and we will call."

Zerak pushed a button next to the register. The harsh buzz signaled the security gate was unlocked. Zerak opened the gate, and Caitlin walked through the narrow opening.

"I hope someday to put in a glass plate to protect me from the robbers. I have the gate, but the last time the robber just jumped over the counter and took the money out of my cash register. It can be very dangerous. Maybe someday I will open a boutique in Beverly Hills." Zerak let out a big laugh. "Until that day I will keep selling liquor and cigarettes to the neighborhood."

"The last time?" asked Caitlin. "How many times have you been robbed?"

"I have lost count. I believe four times." He paused for a second, adding up the felonies in his mind. "No, it has been five. But that does not count the times the children or the people who use drugs steal from the shelves and run out the door."

Caitlin could only shake her head in amazement. She thought Matt's job was dangerous; at least he carried a gun.

An elderly Russian woman wearing a muted multicolored babushka shuffled into the store just as Zerak escorted Caitlin into the office.

"Please have a seat. This will just take a minute."

Zerak excused himself and left Caitlin in the office. She watched the customer through the one-way mirror. The woman's grocery list was minimal, a gallon of whole milk, white bread, cheap Vodka, and two packs of cigarettes. She paid cash for the Vodka and smokes and used food stamps for the milk and bread.

Zerak returned to the office after completing the transaction. "I am sorry for that."

"Don't be sorry. You have a business to run and I am interfering."

"Please, don't ever say that. You have been so kind to my Jaana. She speaks of you all the time. I am pleased to welcome you to my store."

Zerak picked up the phone and called his home number. Jaana picked up on the second ring.

"Jaana, I have someone special at my store who wishes to speak to you."

Caitlin was focused on Zerak's face as he spoke to his daughter, and she saw his attention diverted to a customer who had just entered the store. A look of concern registered in Zerak's eyes.

Zerak excused himself as he handed the phone to Caitlin and walked back out to the store.

Caitlin turned in the worn office swivel chair and peered through the one-way mirror. A rotund, causally dressed, olive-skinned, bald man who looked like an Arab Humpty Dumpty was carrying a brown paper bag. He waddled through the store looking over the merchandise. His breathing was labored, and his chest heaved in and out with every breath. He walked toward the mirror, and Caitlin instinctively retreated, fearing she could be seen through the modified glass. The man bared his teeth and with a toothpick began to remove a rather large chunk of unidentified food material caught between his tobacco-stained incisors. Caitlin was repulsed by the sight but relaxed a bit, knowing she was concealed behind the coated glass.

All this time Caitlin had been carrying on a rather quiet conversation with Jaana. The seven-year-old sounded weak, and Caitlin tried to be reassuring, but it was hard to concentrate on the conversation.

As the customer walked back toward the counter, he stopped and with great difficulty bent over to tie his shoe. Caitlin noticed a very distinct bulge in his lower back, similar to what she had seen when Matt was carrying his back-up weapon. She worried this might be a robbery. Without scaring Jaana, Caitlin quickly ended the conversation, promising to visit her at home.

Keeping her composure, Caitlin prepared to dial 911 and took a long hard look at "Humpty Dumpty." She began jotting down the particulars of his description—height, weight, age, clothing. Just as she started to dial, she heard Zerak greet the man.

"Welcome back to my store, Yasir. How can I help you?"

"So, how much are you paying for a carton?" bellowed the "salesman," pulling a carton of "American made" cigarettes from the paper bag. Before Zerak could respond, Yasir said, "These'll only cost you $11.50 per carton. I have the best price and best quality counterfeits on the market."

Yasir Mehsud had been to the store before. Each time the salesman brought counterfeit cigarettes. The fifty-three-year-old Afghan national regularly tried to peddle his wares to the various merchants in the area.

Caitlin could see Zerak give Yasir a look demanding he terminate the conversation immediately, then said, "Just one moment. I have a visitor in the back."

Zerak returned to his office.

Caitlin saw he was coming, stuffed the notes in her purse, and started to rise just as Zerak entered the tiny room.

"Thank you for letting me speak to Jaana," said Caitlin. "I promised her I would visit soon. Maybe tomorrow I'll bring her some assignments. If she is up to it, she can complete them so she won't fall too far behind." Caitlin was nervous and afraid her voice was betraying fear.

Zerak did not appear to notice and escorted her out of the office back into the store.

Caitlin could feel her entire body beginning to shake as the adrenaline pulsated through her veins.

"Yasir, this is Mrs. Hogan, my Jaana's teacher. She came here to check on my little girl."

Caitlin thought Zerak took deliberate pains to introduce her. He could have just as easily escorted her out of the store without the formal introductions.

Yasir gave Caitlin an ear-to-ear grin. His yellow teeth made his appearance even more ominous. "This is what makes America great, free education and teachers who look like this. Why would anyone miss school?"

Coming from any other source, Caitlin might have appreciated the compliment. Suspecting Humpty Dumpty carried a gun and knowing he was selling counterfeit cigarettes made her even more anxious. Caitlin returned the smile and exited the store as quickly as possible, hoping she did not arouse suspicion.

Once on the street she took a deep breath and welcomed the cool autumn air on her face. As she approached her car, she reached into her purse for the keys. They had fallen to the bottom of her bag, and the extra seconds it took to fish them out seemed like an eternity. Finally she found them. She pressed the remote and the car doors unlocked. She quickly slid behind the wheel. With her hands now shaking almost uncontrollably, she managed on the third or fourth try to insert the key in the ignition. The car started without a problem and she drove off.

As soon as she was a safe distance from the store, she called Matt's cell phone.

Chapter Nineteen

When Matt opened the door to the condo, he was greeted by a hug, an extended kiss, and then a two-handed push to the chest. "Where have you been?" demanded a frustrated Caitlin.

"Good evening. So nice to see you, too."

"No, I'm serious. Where have you been? I've been trying to call you all afternoon. I even sent you a text message."

Matt looked at his cell phone. The phone was off. He tried to turn it on but the battery was dead.

"I'm sorry, honey. The battery's dead. I didn't even realize it. No wonder Dwayne didn't bug me all afternoon."

Matt walked toward the bedroom where he plugged the phone into the charger. Caitlin followed closely.

"What's up? What's so important I get passion and a push?" asked Matt.

Caitlin spent the next several minutes describing her experience at the store. She retrieved the notes from her purse and provided details of Yasir's description, telling Matt of Zerak's reaction to Humpty Dumpty's presence.

"Could these be terrorists?" she asked.

"I think that's a pretty big leap. I spoke with Jaana's mother at the bowling alley. She seemed sincere."

"Matt, you didn't see Zerak's eyes when Yasir walked in. Zerak did not want me there."

"If that's the case, he wouldn't have introduced you."

"I think he wanted Yasir to know my name. Matt, I'm sure he had a gun. I saw the bulge, the same bulge when your carry a backup. He's selling counterfeit cigarettes. I'm scared. Do you think he knows I'm married to an FBI agent?"

"Honey, that's only something you can answer. I never told Jaana's mother I'm with the FBI. Have you said anything?"

"No, I've never said anything to the children or their parents about what you do."

Matt took both of Caitlin's hands. He looked her in the eyes, "Then I don't think you have anything to worry about. But if it will make you feel better, I'll look into it."

"Please, Matt. I'm serious. I think this is important."

"I do, too. I'll look into it. I promise." Matt kissed her on her forehead.

Matt tried to be reassuring, but he, too, was uncomfortable with the events Caitlin described. Nahid's sincerity notwithstanding, he wanted to learn more about Zerak and the storybook visitor who waddled into the store.

On the way to the clinic the next morning, Matt called the office and spoke with Abby Briones, an analyst with the Joint Terrorism Task Force. He relayed as much information as Caitlin provided regarding Jaana's family, the store, and the incident at the market.

Abby promised to do her magic, work up a package, and get back to Matt as soon as she learned anything.

Before arriving at the clinic, Matt stopped at the 7-Eleven just down the street and purchased a six-pack of Coke and more Life Savers.

Three children had already arrived from overseas and were beginning treatment and rehabilitation. A nine-year-old boy from Liberia had been severely burned in a fire caused by a school bombing. Two girls from Afghanistan, one a burn victim and another who lost a leg, were also being treated. More children were scheduled to arrive on Saturday.

Matt helped other volunteers prepare the clinic for the new arrivals. The cafeteria required a second coat of paint, and shelves in the laundry room needed to be built. Matt grabbed a roller and painted most of the afternoon. He smiled as he thought how much he disliked working around the house, and now he was doing what he hated most in the name of God and country. He would have to conceal this part of the assignment from Caitlin. She had been bugging him for months to paint the living room, and he was running out of excuses. Matt and two others finished around 4:00 p.m.

After cleaning up, he walked down the hallway toward the physical therapy room. Omar was working with Shahla, a nine-year-old from Afghanistan, who lost her leg when a land mine exploded.

Afghanistan was a nation at war for three decades. In December 1979, the Soviet Union, in an unprovoked attack, invaded the country. The news shook the Islamic world. The mujahideen or "holy warriors" numbering tens of thousands from such Muslim countries as Saudi Arabia, Yemen, Pakistan, and Algeria rallied to defend the country against the "godless" communists. Before the Soviet withdrawal nearly a decade later, in February 1989, an estimated one million Afghans had been killed and more than five million fled the country. But far from bringing peace, the Soviet withdrawal threw the country into a chaotic state of civil war in which competing ethnic factions sought control. In 1994 Mullah Omar started the Taliban movement in an effort to restore order and bring sharia or Islamic law to Afghanistan. The Taliban, which is translated as "seekers" or "those who study the Koran," sought to make a pure Islamic society. To date the experiment has failed.

Matt stood in the doorway and watched Omar as he worked. Matt said nothing and Omar was oblivious to his presence. Omar was very gentle with Shahla. He labored in love as he exercised what was left of her leg, trying to help her maintain mobility and regain strength. Shahla was a good candidate for an artificial limb, and Omar was helping her prepare for that day.

Within a short time Omar turned, as if sensing a presence, and looked at Matt. Almost with contempt in his voice, Omar asked, "Can I help you?"

"No, I'm sorry. I wasn't spying," said Matt. As soon as he said it, Matt regretted his use of the word *spying*. "You are very gentle with your young friend."

"She has been through a lot. She needs the gentle hand."

Matt walked in uninvited.

Omar continued to exercise the limb.

"Who is your friend?" asked Matt.

Omar said, "Her name is Shahla. It means 'beautiful eyes' in my country."

Matt smiled and extended his hand to her, but she did not respond. Omar spoke to her in Pashto, one of two official languages in Afghanistan. She extended her hand and Matt took it. But there was little beauty in her dark brown eyes, nor a smile on her cherub-like face.

Matt tried to engage Omar in conversation, but he ignored the overture. Omar spoke in near whispers to Shahla, offering her words of encouragement. She sat there as Omar manipulated her limb. Her vacant stare showed no fear. In fact, she showed no emotion.

Matt opened the Life Savers and handed her the roll thinking she would take the top candy. She merely looked at him. He smiled, but there was no response. He took the top one and put it in his mouth, then handed her the roll again. She did nothing. He removed the top candy and handed it to her. She placed it in her mouth and sucked on the candy, still showing no emotion.

Omar watched carefully as Matt showed kindness, then Omar spoke. "She lost not only her leg but her family when the land mine exploded. She was brought to my clinic in Kandahar. We began treatment there, and now we are going to complete it in your country."

"That explains why she's so sad. Maybe she can find hope here. It must be frightening for her."

"It is frightening for me to leave my country and come here as well."

Matt sat down next to the table where Shahla was being treated. "But I would think the United States has a lot more to offer than what is available in your country."

Omar continued manipulating Shahla's leg. "That may be true now. The Taliban brought stability, but the invasion by the United States changed all that."

"You prefer the Taliban to democracy?"

"The Taliban's dream was to make a pure Islamic state where the Koran was the only rule."

"Did it work?" said Matt.

"The Koran has many good rules the Western world does not understand. We had little crime under the Taliban."

"Isn't that because the consequences were so severe?"

"You talk of deterrent in your legal system, yet murderers go free because your police did not follow the rules. Is that justice? We had no such problems in my country. Those who violated the sharia were punished. You were taught the rules and knew the consequences if you chose not to follow the Islamic law."

"I think it was difficult for the outside world to see that the Taliban was accomplishing good for your people."

Omar continued speaking softly, as he educated Matt. "According to the Western world, the most important accomplishment of the Taliban was banning the growing of the poppy, a source of heroin the rest of the world craves. As a reward for reducing the production of opium, your President Bush gave millions of dollars to my country in May of 2001. Only Mullah Omar could not control the Northern Alliance, your ally, who continued to grow the poppy. So you see the Taliban was not all bad."

"The protection of Osama bin Laden and his terrorist training camps in your country is what caused the greatest opposition for the Taliban by the rest of the world."

For the first time Omar made eye contact. "I know my history. Your country wanted to get back at the Soviet Union for their support of the North Vietnamese. When the Soviets invaded my country, America encouraged the recruitment of Muslims from throughout the world to fight the Soviets. You supported training camps in Pakistan and my country. You supplied us. Not directly, that might cause embarrassment if caught, but you supported us through the Pakistan military intelligence. You supported Osama bin Laden when he was fighting the Soviets, but once the Soviets left, the United States cared little about what happened in Afghanistan."

Just then David entered the room. Omar abruptly stopped his discussion. David inquired about the progress of Shahla, and the discussion became medical in nature. Matt excused himself but knew he and Omar would one day continue their discussion.

Chapter Twenty

The sun had already set and Matt was driving home. Because the newest World Angel clinic was located within a few miles of the ocean, he had two choices for the route home. He could take the ever-crowded 405 Freeway north to the 101 and suffer through eight lanes of traffic his entire commute or take the Pacific Coast Highway to Malibu Canyon and over to the 101 Freeway. Tonight Matt chose the latter. Traffic was moving slowly, but at least he could look at the ocean rather than disgruntled commuters as they inched their way home in all directions.

Matt had the window down, the music up, and a Big Gulp from 7-Eleven to tide him over until he arrived at the condo. It had been a long day, and at least a drive in his "new" Mercedes ML 500 made the commute more tolerable. The Mercedes was a "gift" from a drug dealer, seized by the Bureau the previous year following a sting operation in Las Vegas. Matt could keep the vehicle for the duration of the case, and he wanted to enjoy all the accoutrements while he had the opportunity. The sound system was second to none, thanks to the meth dealer's expensive tastes.

He attended a training session at the World Angel building in the morning and spent the rest of the day at the clinic. He cut the grass, trimmed the bushes, and moved boxes of supplies from one end of the clinic to the other. He laughed as he was performing the manual labor. This was precisely why he went to college—to avoid heavy lifting.

Although Matt did not have the experience of a twenty-year veteran, this UC assignment was unique and the type most agents never encounter. Typical undercover assignments involve spending an hour or two with the target in an effort to engage him in a criminal act—a drug buy, a fraudulent transaction, or negotiations for a contract killing. Even if the criminal act required numerous meetings, those individual meetings seldom lasted more than a lunch, a dinner, or a few drinks. This assignment, however, required Matt to remain in his role for eight to ten hours a day, with target and nontarget alike. It was difficult staying in character that long. Too many times a topic of conversation might arise, and Matt wanted to contribute with a humorous anecdote from the FBI, only to catch himself before the words escaped his mouth.

Today one of the nurses returned late from lunch. She walked into a bank, a few blocks from the clinic, just as a robber was racing out the door. The robber shoved her aside, pushed open the door, and escaped into the street. The nurse was able to point to the exact spot where the robber touched the door. FBI agents "dusted" the door and lifted a set of latent fingerprints from the glass surface.

She enjoyed playing junior G-man if only for a few minutes. The Agent in Charge of the investigation let her examine the prints before they were lifted by tape and placed on a plain white card. She could see every loop and whirl left behind by the touch of the fingers and understood what a valuable piece of evidence she had identified.

Matt wanted to tell her a story he often told at dinner parties. In his first year in the Bureau, he bagged a transvestite bank robber who, while exiting the bank, ran directly into a plate glass window, thinking it was a door. The well-attired male robber in a dress and fishnet stockings, wearing "Sunset Orange" lipstick left a clear set of lip prints on the window. Matt was able to lift the lipstick and the prints from the glass. The FBI lab identified the Sunset Orange, and the latent prints boys were able to discern some unique characteristics of the lips. Once Matt identified the robber, with the help of an informant, Matt got his conviction. The most damaging pieces of evidence at court were lip prints that matched and the three tubes of Sunset Orange lipstick found when searching the robber's residence. Matt was proud of that victory, but today was not the time to brag about investigative successes.

A cool ocean breeze was blowing through the open driver's side window. It felt good. As Matt slowly moved through the traffic, he could see the waves breaking against the shore. *I wish Caitlin and I were walking along that shore.* As he finished the thought, his cell phone rang.

"Hello."

He could hear crying on the other end and a weak "Matt."

"Caitlin, is that you?"

"Matt, I'm sorry to bother you, but I just had to call."

"Honey, what's the matter?"

"I just got a call from Mrs. Anwari, Jaana's mom. Matt, Jaana has cancer."

"Oh, Caitlin, I'm so sorry."

"I need to go to the hospital tonight."

"Honey, I'll be home in about an hour. Wait and I'll go with you."

Matt fought his way through traffic and arrived home in forty-five minutes. Caitlin was waiting, her eyes red and swollen. The news of Jaana's cancer hit hard.

Caitlin loved all her children, but there was a special place in her heart for Jaana. Notwithstanding the troubling incident at the family convenience store, Caitlin knew how hard the family struggled to make ends meet.

Despite sixteen-hour workdays Jaana's mother attended almost every class function.

Caitlin engaged in nervous chatter the entire drive to the hospital. "Thanks for coming with me. I love this little girl so much, but her father frightens me. I hope he's not there, but maybe if you meet him, you'll understand."

"Let me worry about him. I'm here to support you," said Matt.

"Have you learned any more about the father?"

"I'm still waiting to hear back. I've got one of our analysts running a complete profile on the family. I should hear something in the next day or two."

Almost as if she did not hear him, Caitlin changed the subject. "Once she brought me a box of macaroni and cheese."

"I guess that's an immigrant store owner's equivalent of an apple."

Although Matt had heard it before, he let Caitlin continue. "Jaana is my hardest worker and my top student."

"I know."

"She's at least a grade level ahead of all my other students, and she's a voracious reader. She's reading at a fourth-grade level."

Matt said nothing.

"She stays after school almost every day and helps around the classroom, cleaning up, emptying trash, putting away books, projects, and supplies. The last day she was at school she told me when she grew up she wanted to be a teacher, just like me, and go back to Afghanistan and teach little girls all the things she was learning in America."

The words choked and could no longer come. Tears rolled down Caitlin's cheek.

Matt reached over and grabbed her hand. They finished the trip in silence.

Chapter Twenty-One

As Caitlin and Matt were about to enter the hospital room, Caitlin stopped. She grabbed both of Matt's hands, bowed her head, and said quietly, "God, give me the power to be strong for you and brave for Jaana."

When Caitlin and Matt entered the warmly lit single-bed room, a giant smile came over Jaana's face. She was delighted to see her teacher. Caitlin ran over to the bed and gave her star pupil a long hug. Caitlin worked hard to fight back the tears that came so easily just minutes before.

"I've missed you in school and didn't know until this afternoon you were in the hospital. I'm so glad your mother called me."

"I'm sorry I missed school."

"Oh honey, that's okay. You just get better real soon and hurry back. Our room is a mess, and you're my best helper. I can't make it nearly as neat as you can. Besides, who's going to help Stephen with his reading? You're the best teacher he has."

Stephen McCormick was a second-grader who had little interest in schoolwork or reading. He did, however, have an interest in Jaana. Every couple of days, Caitlin let Jaana and Stephen read together in the corner. Stephen always did better then, more concerned with impressing Jaana than Mrs. Hogan.

After a few more minutes of conversation about classmates, Caitlin and Matt excused themselves to the hallway to discuss Jaana's condition with her mother. The bright, crowded hallway contrasted with the soft lighting of Jaana's room. She could only live in the shadows of her room a little longer. The hallway was reality, where the light exposed all that was wrong with the world Jaana knew.

"My husband must work many extra hours at the market. We have so little money. I do not know how we will ever pay the doctors," said Nahid.

"Let's just concentrate on getting her better," said Caitlin.

"It is difficult for me to explain about my daughter. Let me get the nurse."

Nahid excused herself to the nurse's station and returned a minute later with Jennifer Horner, a tall blonde with a caring smile.

After the introductions, Nahid said, "Could you explain to them what is wrong with my Jaana?"

The prognosis was not good. A little girl, whose family fled a war-torn country where dying from the enemy's attack was commonplace, was now confronting death from within.

Jennifer's demeanor turned serious and professional. "There is no way to soften the news. A pediatric hematologist and an oncologist saw Jaana this morning. Over the past several days she has had X-rays, bone scans, blood tests, and a biopsy. I'm afraid the testing confirmed our worst fears. She has Ewing's sarcoma, a fast-spreading cancer."

Caitlin let out an audible gasp.

Jennifer lowered her voice and almost whispered. "At the very least she may lose her leg, but Ewing's can be fatal if it has metastasized."

"Why did it take so long to discover? She's been complaining for weeks about a sore leg," asked Caitlin.

Jennifer paused before answering, "Ewing's is difficult to diagnose. It's often confused with less serious ailments. We just hope it hasn't spread."

Caitlin could only shake her head in disbelief at the devastating news. A wave of emotions swept over her, and it took her several minutes to compose herself.

Matt, Caitlin, and Nahid returned to the room.

"Jaana, Matt and I have to go, but I'll be back to visit often."

"Tell my friends I said hi."

"Oh honey, I'll certainly tell them."

Caitlin paused. Matt thought she was going to cry; instead she spoke. Looking at Jaana's mother, she said, "Is it okay if I pray for your daughter?"

Nahid did not immediately respond to the request. Just as Caitlin began to say something, Nahid responded, "It is okay."

Caitlin walked over to the bed and held Jaana's tender, young hand.

"Dear God, there are so many difficult questions at a time like this. The main question is why. Why is this happening? I don't know the answer, but you do. We know everything happens for a reason. Help us to understand. Help us to find your will in our lives. God, I commit this little girl to you. Touch her heart, her soul, and her body. Bring healing and understanding. Bring hope, dear Lord. She is one of your precious children. You know how much I love her. Let her know my love for her is so small compared to the love you have for her and her family. Jesus, thank you in advance for the blessings you are going to give my precious little friend and her family. It's in your name we ask these things. Amen."

Caitlin leaned over and kissed Jaana on the forehead, then hugged Nahid. No words were exchanged. No words were necessary.

A dull ache formed in Matt's throat. He grabbed Caitlin's hand as they walked in silence down the hall toward the elevator.

Chapter Twenty-Two

The air was still but the action heavy on Ventura Boulevard, the most traveled road in Los Angeles's San Fernando Valley. Almost any night the traffic up and down the east-west boulevard was nonstop, and tonight was no exception.

The Russian Veil was a popular bar nestled among the Valley's upscale restaurants. It was one of the few on the boulevard targeting a lower middle-class clientele. In polite company it was referred to as a gentlemen's club. In reality, it was just a strip joint where female immigrants from the former Soviet states catered to bikers and blue-collar workers. Most recently, the girls were from the Ukraine and escaped a life of poverty by agreeing to take off their clothes in front of drunken Americans.

The empty garage in the rear of the bar was ideal for tonight's cargo—counterfeit cigarettes. Wadi was delivering five hundred master cases to the owner. Boris Gregorian was a former Russian military intelligence officer who could now be better described as a gangster capitalist. He came to the United States soon after the breakup of the Soviet Union in 1991. He parlayed his military and intelligence contacts into a lucrative criminal enterprise spanning the greater Los Angeles area.

Gregorian was a huge man. At six feet four inches and well over three hundred pounds, he was built like a bear and had a matching disposition. There was nothing cuddly about Boris, whose contempt for the United States was almost as great as the Islamic radicals with whom he did business. Boris blamed the West for every perceived wrong in the world and welcomed any opportunity to help destroy the very fabric of the capitalistic society he now called home. In fact, Boris believed every criminal act he committed was an act of patriotism for Mother Russia. His introduction to Wadi provided one more chance to profit from the vices of an overindulgent America. He welcomed the delivery of the five hundred cases of cigarettes, especially since the product came at no cost to him. Wadi's bosses bartered the cigarettes in exchange for a service the big Russian would soon provide. Every future cigarette sale Boris made was pure profit.

Wadi quietly objected to whatever business arrangement Boris made with Wadi's superiors, but as the consummate soldier, he did as ordered. Tonight those orders meant the delivery of the master cases to the vacant Ventura Boulevard garage.

Even though Boris paid nothing for the counterfeit merchandise and had some undisclosed relationship with the Islamofascist leadership, Wadi was not about to reveal any more than he had to about the business. Wadi viewed the Russian as just a little too slick and did not trust him. Only a select few were allowed at Wadi's Hollywood storage facility. For the others, and that included Boris, each sale followed a precise protocol. The buyer rented a box truck and left the vehicle at a predetermined location with the keys hidden under the floor mat. A trusted cell member picked up the truck and drove it to the storage facility where it was loaded and driven to the buyer's designated locale. Wadi always remained a safe distance from the delivery location and watched the completed transaction.

Wadi wasn't pleased with tonight's operation. The box truck Boris rented ran with the speed of a gentle laxative. Twice the vehicle stalled as it attempted to make it over the Hollywood Hills.

Once the vehicle arrived at the warehouse, Boris stopped traffic, allowing the truck to back into the Ventura Boulevard facility. As the driver, Rashid Kahn, attempted to back the truck in, the vehicle stalled, blocking both lanes of eastbound traffic. It took only a few minutes for traffic to back up several blocks, and impatient motorists honked long and loud, as if that would make the truck start.

Wadi sat in his car and watched in vain. The organization was covered. Rashid had an invoice identifying the contents of the boxes as backpacks made in China. Should a problem arise, Rashid had an alibi, but any blip on the distribution radar screen could mean potential problems.

Boris was in the middle of the street with the hood of the truck raised, desperately seeking to identify the problem. Rashid continued to grind the starter to no avail.

The officer hit the "yelp" toggle switch once, and the loud noise signaled their arrival. The red lights on top of the black-and-white patrol unit flashed brightly, and the two-man patrol team westbound on the boulevard stopped. The LAPD officers exited the car.

"What seems to be the problem?" asked the lead officer.

"If I knew that, I wouldn't be sitting in the middle of Ventura Boulevard," said the defiant Russian with a thick accent.

The probationary police officer, accompanying the lead officer, removed the nightstick from his utility belt in anticipation of a problem.

"You're tying up traffic. I need this vehicle moved now, or I'm going to have to cite you," said the lead officer.

"Unless you plan on helping me push this up the driveway, it's not going anywhere," said Boris, who remained cool when confronted by the police.

Rashid continued to grind the starter in an effort to start the engine. Just as the lead officer pulled out his citation book, the engine started. Boris slammed the hood of the truck down.

Rashid quickly threw the truck into reverse and backed into the driveway. The officer closed the book, and the unit left without citing anyone and without further inquiry.

All concerned breathed a collective sigh of relief. Any law enforcement action at any level was problematic. Counterfeit cigarettes were a productive enterprise for the cause, and everyone connected with the operation wanted to maintain the free-flowing profits.

They began the ride home in silence. The freeway traffic was steady. The evening rush hour was over. Matt was used to having noise, any kind of noise blasting from the car radio. It could be a ball game, a book on tape, or his favorite country and western CD, but to drive in silence was an anomaly.

The night was clear and unseasonably warm. He rested his elbow on the open window. The steady whine of tires racing along the paved freeways created a white noise that almost seemed soothing.

Matt kept his eyes on the car ahead, but his mind was elsewhere. He was sorting out what he just witnessed. A seven-year-old was facing death, and he had no satisfactory explanation. Somehow a senseless war made sense. An act of terrorism was easy to understand. Any violation of the Ten Commandments could be explained. All were acts of evil, hatred, or greed. All were conscious decisions by those choosing to violate the laws of order and common decency. But this was different. How do you combat cancer? What evil do you attack? What undercover operation will successfully eradicate the iniquity of malignant cells spreading throughout a child's body? Matt had questions but no answers.

Matt met Caitlin ten years earlier while he was still a Marine. For Matt it was love at first sight. For Caitlin it took a little longer but not much. Will Hoffman was Matt's executive officer when the two were stationed at Camp Pendleton. Will and his wife attended a Bible study with Caitlin's parents. After graduating from college, Caitlin returned home and attended the study one evening. The next day Will raved about this beautiful, unattached, and employed female. What was not to like? Will and Caitlin's parents arranged for a barbecue the next weekend, inviting Matt and Caitlin. The relationship grew out of that Saturday afternoon encounter. Matt was drawn not only to her beauty and strength but ironically to her faith. Matt was a seeker. She never preached or pushed, but she listened as no one he had ever met. He thought he was finding answers, but then Christmas Day 2005 shattered what little faith he had. Still Caitlin was his tether to a world in constant chaos.

They drove several miles before Caitlin spoke. She reached over and put her hand on Matt's thigh. She looked at him, and he gave her a quick glance. "Thanks for going with me."

Matt hesitated with a response. "Why?"

"Why, what?"

"Why does God allow such things? After all that girl and her family have been through, why would a loving God do this?"

Caitlin paused before answering. "Matt, that's a tough question, and I'm not sure I have an answer. I don't know that it's my place to question God. Why this would happen to Jaana is something I can't answer either. Someday when we are face-to-face, I'll ask him. I do know I want to use this opportunity to show her and her family the love of Jesus Christ. I don't know what tomorrow holds, but I know who holds it. That's my faith and that sustains me."

Matt started to say something but didn't. He was attempting to formulate his thoughts. About a mile down the freeway he responded. "Caitlin, I watched you in that room this evening. I wish I had your faith."

"Matt, I believe and I trust. That's my faith."

Matt shook his head. "That's just it . . . trust. What does that mean? Does that mean I don't prepare, I don't study, I don't practice? As an undercover agent, I've gone toe-to-toe with some of the worst society has to offer. Every group I have ever infiltrated has a history of violence. If ever one of those groups discovered I was an agent, death would be almost certain. One slip of the tongue, one casual friend who spots me at the wrong time, or corruption within the Bureau could mean disaster. But I prepare for that. I practice those scenarios. That's why I have trouble sleeping the night before an undercover meeting. I try to plan for every contingency. I know the enemy, and I think I know what it takes to defeat him. I don't dwell on death because I trust in my preparation."

Caitlin said, "And I trust in your preparation as well. Of course you prepare. God has given you certain skills and talents, and he wants you to use them for his kingdom. But beyond your preparation, I'm on my knees every day asking God to protect you. Your successes aren't just coincidental blessings. You, me, Jaana—we're part of God's plan."

Matt continued to question, "But I still don't understand why this little girl must have her life cut short? Why she may never be able to enjoy all life has to offer? It's the same questions I had when Scott died."

"Matt, God can heal her, and maybe that is in his plans. But remember, every person Jesus healed eventually died. The most life has to offer is the promise of eternity with God. I want her to know that promise, and I pray God will give me the opening and courage to present her with that hope. If she has that, does it matter whether she lives on this earth for a day or for a hundred years? If Scott had that faith, would another thirty or forty years matter? Eternity is forever. I want to do everything I can to make Jaana's life on this earth as joyous and hopeful as I can. I want her to know this cancer will not destroy God's love for her. It will not conquer our friendship or take the promise of eternal life from her and her family. I will be there for her. But I would not be loving her if I did not share the hope of Jesus Christ."

Matt smiled and took her hand. "You're a strong lady, Caitlin Hogan. I'm glad you are on my side."

Chapter Twenty-Three

It took several days, but FBI analyst Abby Briones worked up an intelligence profile on the Anwari family. There was little specific adverse information about any of the three family members, and there were no apparent relatives in the United States. They were legally in this country, had consistently filed their taxes, and had no criminal records. Their income, modest as it was, placed them just above the poverty line. Zerak had several moving traffic violations; however, poor driving habits were not indicators of terrorism. If that were so, Caitlin would be one of the Task Force's major targets.

Abby ordered toll records for the residence and the market telephones and prepared an analysis of the incoming and outgoing calls. The tolls showed a great deal of activity on the market phone but little, if any, on the home phone. There was, however, some cause for concern. Not all the subscribers had been identified, but most of the outgoing calls were to phones registered in Middle Eastern names. At least two of the subscribers were on the FAA No-Fly Watch List. Due to the confusion and controversy as to how those names were obtained and placed on the list, it was uncertain if the subscribers were, in fact, the same people listed. Three overseas numbers in Afghanistan were identified by the CIA as having strong connections to known Taliban supporters. Although the probable cause was weak, the information Abby obtained provided sufficient facts to warrant a wiretap on the market phone.

Known in the Bureau as a FISUR, the authority for the court-ordered telephone surveillance was issued under the auspices of the Foreign Intelligence Surveillance Act of 1978. Through headquarters, the Los Angeles FBI would seek an order from the seven-member FISA Court to commence electronic surveillance. The purpose of the wiretap is solely to gather intelligence, and the requirements for obtaining such an order are less restrictive than the criminal wiretaps issued under Title III authority. Since the court only meets twice a month, coverage of the phones would not begin for several weeks. Once in place, Matt and Dwayne would be privy to the conversations taking place over the market phone.

The quiet outdoor café in Brentwood provided a perfect cover for Matt's meetings with Dwayne. The café was only a mile from the Federal Building so it was convenient for Dwayne to slip away from his deskbound supervisory duties for a few minutes and return almost without being missed. L.A. traffic made it impossible to judge the driving time for any trip, so a meeting spot beyond a one-mile radius could interfere with Dwayne's administrative responsibilities.

Matt discovered the café several years before when he was watching a then mob-run restaurant across the street. Once Matt sized up the activity at the restaurant, he began to frequent the place at lunchtime. Eventually he purchased a kilo of cocaine from the owner of Mama Lucci's Trattoria. The feds seized the restaurant and sold it at public auction. It was now a barbecue joint complete with country and western music and sawdust on the floors. It seemed out of place in trendy, upscale Brentwood, but the eatery was getting rave reviews by local restaurant critics. Matt was only too happy to improve the cuisine and the music in the neighborhood.

There was no morning crowd at the café. A retired couple sat at one of the outdoor tables and two elderly ladies at another. They were the only patrons when Matt arrived. He sat beneath a large eucalyptus tree and awaited Dwayne's arrival.

Stuck on a conference call with headquarters, New York, and Detroit on an unrelated matter, Dwayne arrived fifteen minutes late with apologies.

When Matt worked organized crime and gangs, everyone talked among themselves about their cases, sharing intelligence and ideas. On more than one occasion something someone said in one of those informal "chats" proved useful in a case. Terrorism, however, was a need-to-know basis. The supervisor served as a filter, dispersing intelligence as he deemed appropriate. Matt knew it would serve no purpose even to ask what the "unrelated matter" was.

The waitress walked over and refilled Matt's coffee cup. Dwayne ordered a Diet Pepsi.

"Diet Pepsi? At 10:15 in the morning?" asked Matt.

"I've been in the office since 5:30 so it's practically afternoon for me. Besides, I've already had three cups of coffee."

After some small talk and a brief discussion of a new administrative directive, Dwayne said, "Abby did a great workup on the market. We've applied for a FISA order and should be up within a few weeks."

"Great," said Matt. "From everything Caitlin's said, the family is very close, but they just got blindsided. The daughter has cancer so I'm not sure how dedicated the father might be to the cause."

"That's horrible. How old is she?"

"Seven."

Dwayne shook his head in disbelief. "We'll be on the phones soon so maybe we can determine his involvement with any cause, be it his daughter's health or terrorism."

"I'm not sure I'm making any headway at the clinic," said Matt. "I've spent some time with Omar and Ibrahim, but so far I have nothing concrete. I guess part of my problem is not knowing what to look for and what to expect."

"It is a completely different culture, and it's important you understand how it differs from the life you knew growing up in the Midwest."

"Anderson, Indiana, wasn't exactly a hotbed of Muslim activity."

"Well, this is not a crusade against Islam."

"Yeah, right, and the 9/11 hijackers were Baptists," said Matt sarcastically.

"Matt, this is a war against terrorism, a terrorism created by a radical religious element. It is no more part of mainstream Islam than the Aryan Nation is to Christianity."

"Those crowds I see protesting in the Middle East on FOX News every night look a lot larger than some Montana militia group."

"They are, but it's a clash of cultures not religions. And realize it is not limited to the Middle East. There is a small segment of the radical Muslim community living right here in the United States. Our prisons have become breeding grounds for extremists. We have radical mosques, even in L.A., all financed by Saudi petrodollars. They would celebrate another 9/11. They're angry and are out to destroy Israel and its principal supporter, the United States. But peaceful Muslims who are accepting of our democratic society are not the enemy."

The waitress brought Dwayne's Diet Pepsi, and he waited for her to leave before he continued.

"So how am I supposed to identify the radical element?" asked Matt.

"There's no easy answer. They come from all economic strata. Many cell members in the United States are college educated or are attending our universities. Some have infiltrated legitimate charities and are diverting funds for terrorist purposes. Some have taken leadership roles in certain mosques and from there are radicalizing the youth. They may have even been born here. We have our own homegrown terrorists: Jose Padilla, John Walker Lindh, and probably hundreds if not thousands of others. Three of the four London bombers in 2005 were born in England. By all accounts they were normal young men, described as polite and helpful. One was a special ed teacher. They played cricket, for crying out loud. You can't get much more normal than that in England. They were on no one's radar."

"You're not much help trying to pick the terrorist behind door number three."

Dwayne shrugged his shoulders and threw open his hands. "We haven't created the perfect profile. Continue to get close, as close as you can to everyone at the clinic. Probe and listen. How do they feel about the United States? What's their opinion of our foreign policy? Jihad? How religious are they? Talk about beliefs. Be a citizen of the world. And certainly do not support Israel. In fact, you might even express some favorable Palestinian views and suggest they deserve an independent nation status."

"I was hoping you could be a little more specific, you know, the mark of the beast tattooed on the forehead," said Matt.

"If only it were that easy. Let's move on to something else. It's important you understand the difference between being a guilt-based society and a shame-based society."

Matt wrinkled his brow. "I don't understand."

Dwayne sipped his Diet Pepsi and explained, "In the West, our Judeo-Christian beliefs cause us to feel guilty about our sins. We emphasize individual responsibility and accountability. Your success in interrogations is based on the fact a person feels the need to confess, to cleanse his soul, so to speak. The Middle Eastern culture is shame based. The family is of prime importance. Above all else, bring no shame upon the family. An admission of guilt acknowledges fault and shames the family. Many will never admit guilt. To do so dishonors the individual and his family. Lying can even be viewed as a virtue."

Matt smiled. "It's certainly a virtue when working undercover or dealing with OPR."

Dwayne returned the smile. "We'll talk about your virtues another time."

The waitress returned and refilled Matt's cup.

"You're not making this any easier," said Matt.

"If it were easy, anyone could do it," replied Dwayne.

"That sounds as if it comes straight out of the supervisor's handbook."

Dwayne smiled. "It does. You better get to the clinic. Can't fight crime sitting around drinking coffee. Oh, by the way, Omar and Rashid went to the Clippers game the other night. Omar say anything about that?"

"No, but it's not exactly like he's my BFF. What's unusual about going to Staples Center?"

"Rashid went to almost every restroom in the place."

"My guess: an enlarged prostate."

"Gee, you are so intuitive. I'll add that to my report to the Director."

Chapter Twenty-Four

The children of Mrs. Hogan's second-grade class worked hard to prepare their surprises for Jaana. Each child brought a canned good or other food item for the family. Several of the girls helped their mothers bake muffins or cookies. Caitlin had a large wicker basket she decorated, and the children filled the basket with gifts for Jaana and her family.

They spent the better part of the afternoon making paper flowers that became part of a large bouquet. Each child also made a card individually decorated with a personalized message. The cards ranged from Hallmark quality to the barely legible, but each was made with genuine love for a gravely ill classmate.

Caitlin had to answer a lot of questions, and the answers did not come easy. She wanted to be honest but not instill fear. Yes, Jaana is sick. No, you cannot visit her; only adults are allowed in that part of the hospital. Yes, she will be in the hospital for a long time. No, she probably won't be back to school before Christmas. Yes, the doctors are doing all they can for her. Yes, it is okay to pray for her; and if you want to pray for her right now, God will hear those prayers. Yes, I am praying for Jaana, and I will continue to pray for her every night, just as I pray for each of you every night.

Caitlin knew the discussion of prayer might cause her problems. When news of the attacks of 9/11 hit the classroom in 2001, the children were very scared. Caitlin tried to reassure her students and even prayed with them. The word of her praying in the classroom reached a school board member, and Caitlin received a letter of reprimand in her personnel file. "A further violation of school policy will result in a more severe punishment."

Matt joked she was still several reprimands behind him, but it bothered her that she was criticized for doing something that brought comfort to the children in a time of panic.

She carefully avoided leading a prayer on behalf of Jaana but allowed the children to pray if they wanted. Several mothers were in the classroom, so at least she had witnesses should a problem arise.

As the school day ended, Caitlin gathered up all the presents and prepared to drive over to visit Jaana.

MATT WAS IN THE physical therapy room and surprised by Caitlin's call. Caitlin seldom bothered him at work, especially when she knew he was on an undercover assignment. "Oh, hi. This is a surprise. Is everything okay?"

"Yeah, I'm on my way to visit Jaana and just thought I'd check in."

"Same old same old. Been at the clinic most of the day. Helping Omar with some of the patients and doing my usual janitorial chores."

"Well, don't quit your day job," said Caitlin.

"You okay? You sound a little down."

"I'm not down, just a little nervous. Not quite sure what to say when I get over there and hope I don't run into Jaana's father."

"I wouldn't worry about him being there. He's spending almost all his time at the market, trying to make ends meet, but if you want to wait, I'll go with you."

"No, I'm fine."

Matt had his back turned when Omar slipped into the room.

"If you need me, I'll come, but as to what to say, don't try to make the conversation happen. Jaana will love just seeing her favorite teacher. The opportunity will come. Your actions speak volumes. Remember what you always tell me: people don't care what you know until they know you care. You care, Caitlin. She knows that. Listen, I better go. I don't want to get fired from a volunteer job. Won't look good on the résumé. You'll do just fine. I love you, and I'll see you tonight."

"Thanks. I just needed a little pep talk. I love you, too."

Matt turned to see Omar a few feet away.

"I could not help but overhear your call. I am sorry. You said the name Jaana."

Matt reluctantly answered, "Yes, Jaana."

"Is she from Afghanistan? That is a popular name in my country. Jaana means Allah is gracious."

"Well, this little Afghan needs God's grace. She is very sick and is in the hospital."

"I am sorry to hear that," said Omar. "What is wrong with her?"

"She has a rare form of cancer. The doctors aren't sure she'll make it."

"Wouldn't it be wonderful if I could help her? I am registered with the Bone Marrow Donor Program. I am so hoping someday I can help. It can be very difficult to find a match. Maybe I am her match."

Matt was struck by the incongruity of that statement. *Do terrorists register to be bone marrow donors?* "That would be a miracle if you were."

"That is wonderful of your wife to visit her. She must be a very nice woman. She is a teacher?"

"Yes," replied Matt.

"Teaching is an honorable profession in your country. We actually had two different systems of education in my country. Prior to the civil war, we had a public school system providing free and mandatory schooling. We had many universities. I attended the University of Nangarhar in Jalalabad. That is where I learned physical therapy and studied English. When the Taliban took over, much changed. Women and girls could no longer go to school unless they did so in secret."

Omar opened the small refrigerator behind his desk and removed two cans of Coke. He handed one to Matt.

"Thanks," said Matt, who was stunned by the gesture.

Omar continued, "The Taliban returned to the school system that existed throughout many of the villages. It was a religious system taught by the mullahs who conducted the religious services on Fridays. They would teach the men and the boys in the mosques. Although most of my country is Muslim, you could not get an education unless you attended mosque. To go to school, you would have to attend services. So much was different from what I find in your country. That is why I have a great deal of respect for the teachers in your country. Will I ever get to meet your wife?"

Matt hesitated and ran his fingers through his hair. He popped the top on the can of Coke and took a sip, waiting as if the answer could be avoided if he stalled long enough. Omar continued to look at him, anticipating an answer. "Sure, one of these days."

Omar smiled. *A genuine smile,* thought Matt. Not the kind Matt often offered while working undercover as a practiced liar. Omar, at least today, seemed sincere, but Matt was reluctant to bring Caitlin any further into the investigation. The situation at Zerak's market was troubling enough. Matt had no plans of purposely introducing her to someone who might be a terrorist. He was being paid to risk his life, but the job description did not call for risking the lives of his loved ones.

It was perfectly normal for him to be married in his undercover persona. In fact, it was usually preferable. When working undercover, it was best not to lie too much; otherwise, you could get caught in your lies.

Early in Matt's undercover career, he told a target, a Mafia drug dealer, he was single. In a subsequent conversation, Matt happened to mention something about his "wife." The elderly Mafioso picked up on the comment and confronted Matt about the inconsistency. Quickly thinking, Matt said he was married but separated from his wife and was in the process of filing for divorce. He still had a wife; he just didn't like talking too much about the "witch" because her attorney was trying to squeeze him for all he was worth. The target laughed at Matt's marital problems because he too had been through a costly divorce. Matt hastily changed the conversation back to a criminal discussion on drugs but learned a lesson: lie as little as possible. No sense getting killed over marital status or some other mundane fact.

"Please, when you know more, tell me about the little girl. I know very few people from my country, and maybe I could visit her someday," said Omar.

Matt agreed to keep Omar informed but was extremely uncomfortable with the prospect of introducing Omar to nontargets, especially fellow countrymen who might share a common belief system. Possibly with time the issue would pass. Matt vowed not to bring the topic up and hoped to avoid discussing Jaana again in Omar's presence.

Caitlin arrived at the hospital at five o'clock, just as dinner was being served. Jaana was asleep, and her mother chose not to wake her for the meal. The nurse on duty agreed to take the meal and return when Jaana awakened.

Nahid Anwari welcomed Caitlin and was so pleased with the gifts and cards from the second-graders.

"My daughter will be pleased. The flowers the children made are beautiful. She will like the cards very much."

"The gift basket is for the entire family. All the students and their families brought things your family might need while Jaana is in the hospital. There are several gift certificates for meals at restaurants in the area."

"You are most kind," said Jaana's mother.

"How's she doing?"

"She had more tests today. A new doctor saw her. They talk of taking away her leg to stop the cancer. She does not know that yet. Tomorrow the doctors will talk with all of us about our choices. It will be a very hard day."

Caitlin sat down next to Jaana and touched her hand as the mother continued to look at her suffering little girl. "I am so sorry. I wish I had all the right answers for you. What can I do to make this a little easier for her and your family?"

"You have been so kind already. You have done much just coming here. Jaana loves you very much."

"Well, I love her. She's special to me."

"Jaana says besides her family, she loves you and her kitten the most. She misses her kitten. We told her it is not allowed in the hospital. She is anxious to go home and be with her Palwasha. That means 'spark of light' in our language."

A tear fell from Mrs. Anwari's cheek, and Caitlin's eyes began to mist.

"I am afraid for my daughter. Would you please pray again for my daughter?"

Caitlin looked at the mother. "I have never stopped praying for her, and I will continue to do so. I meant it when I said God has special plans for your daughter. I don't know what those plans are, but they are special plans for a special little girl."

Chapter Twenty-Five

As Matt wheeled the pail out into the alley, his cell phone rang.

"This is Matt."

"Matt, it's Steve."

"Hey, what's up?"

"Sorry to bother you. I hope I didn't call at a bad time?"

"I wouldn't have answered if you had. I'm participating in a highly technical, advanced hydromedical research protocol to eliminate nosocomial prodromal symptoms."

"Huh?"

"I'm dumping the water I used to wash the floor of the physical therapy room."

"Wow! I hope someday when I grow up, I can be an undercover agent. Listen, I know you probably don't have much time to talk. Not sure if this is important or not. I tried to get a hold of SOG, but they're working a kidnapping in Orange County."

"What you got?"

"Somebody named Yasir called Zerak on the target phone. This Yasir is bringing two cases of reds and lights later this afternoon. Any idea what that means?"

"Yeah, thanks Steve. I'm afraid it's not the nuclear football, but I think it's counterfeit cigarettes."

"Oh, guess it wasn't important."

"No, thanks for calling. I'm about done here. I may run over there and sit on the place for awhile. See if I can see anything."

"Need help?" asked Steve.

"No, it's no big deal. If I need help, I'll give you a call. Thanks for the heads up."

"Good luck with your medical experimentation program," said Steve as he hung up the phone.

From down the block and on the opposite side of the street, Matt watched Yasir exit the store and waddle toward the late-model Cadillac. Yasir's distinct stride made him easy to follow even in a crowd. A toddler with a loaded diaper walks with as much precision.

Yasir popped the trunk to the Cadillac, and Matt could see two boxes of what he guessed to be master cases of counterfeit cigarettes. Zerak came out of the market just as Yasir was lifting the first of the two cases from the trunk. The two men returned to the store, each carrying a box. Within two minutes Yasir was back on the street.

Normally Matt would never attempt a one-man surveillance, but because the sun had set, the darkness provided a perfect cover. He decided to try a loose tail. He had already copied down the license plate, so his main goal was accomplished.

Yasir made his way toward the front of the Cadillac and worked his corpulent body into the driver's seat. Matt could see him on his cell phone.

Yasir completed his phone call and began driving south with Matt following from a safe distance.

After driving less than three miles, Yasir pulled into the parking lot of Valley College just off Burbank Boulevard. A yellow rental box truck, parked directly under a light pole, waited near the baseball field. Yasir backed his vehicle to the rear of the box truck.

The well-lit lot provided all the illumination Matt needed. He parked across the street and from this vantage point watched a Middle Eastern male exit the truck.

Matt quickly got on his cell phone and attempted to reach Dwayne but was only successful at reaching his voice mail. Matt left a message but sensed by the time Dwayne received it, it would be too late to muster the necessary manpower to conduct an adequate surveillance. Matt also sent a text message but knew that wouldn't increase the chances of reaching Dwayne any sooner.

As Matt watched, the two men greeted each other with a traditional hug. Then Yasir counted out currency in front of the driver and handed it to him. In a move that spelled a less than confident belief in either Yasir's math or his honesty, the driver counted the money again. With the financial transaction complete, the driver opened the rear of the truck for only a brief moment. It was long enough, however, for Yasir to remove four cases from the truck and put them into the backseat of his car.

When the two quickly parted, Matt had two choices. He chose the easier. He would follow the box truck.

The truck made its way out of the parking lot and headed east on Burbank. At Laurel Canyon Boulevard, the driver turned right. Matt was hoping he would eventually hop on the freeway, but when he continued past the on-ramp toward the Hollywood Hills, Matt assumed they were in for a long journey somewhere.

The congested winding canyon road linking the San Fernando Valley to Hollywood provided little relief for drivers caught behind the slow moving box truck. The route chosen proved ideal for Matt. He remained a safe distance behind, often as many as four or five vehicles, and had no fear of the box truck racing away at the next intersection. As the truck crawled through the canyon, Matt tried in vain to phone Dwayne. But now he was outside the coverage of the service provider and unable to obtain a signal.

Once they reached the summit, the pace picked up a little. On the other side Hollywood awaited. The night-lights made for a beautiful view.

The box truck eventually arrived at its destination, the self-storage facility in Hollywood.

Matt was amazed at the ease with which he was able to follow the truck, apparently undetected. The driver did nothing to evade a surveillance unit and, as far as Matt could tell, was not married to the rearview mirror. Even when he was within a car length, Matt never saw the driver checking the mirrors for a tail.

It really is better to be lucky than good.

The driver pulled up to the entrance of the facility and punched in the security code at the gate. The chain link gate opened, and the truck drove through. Parked just outside the gate was a metallic black Porsche Boxster containing a male occupant. When the gate opened, the man exited the car and walked through, following the truck.

Matt parked a safe distance from the facility and made his way on foot around the storage units. Giant oleanders surrounded the entire complex, providing perfect cover.

By the time Matt was able to wind his way surreptitiously through the brush, he was able to get within twenty-five feet of locker 270. The red steel door of the storage unit was up, and the two men were standing in front. Matt guessed the two were speaking in Arabic since he could understand nothing of their conversation. He tried to memorize faces and descriptions of the duo. The Porsche driver was dressed in designer jeans, a black cashmere sweater, and expensive-looking shoes—a walking advertisement for *Gentlemen's Quarterly.*

The storage facility had at least three hundred master cases of what Matt assumed to be counterfeit cigarettes based on the actions of Humpty Dumpty at Zerak's store. The driver of the truck took a white business-sized envelope from his jacket pocket, opened it, and began counting out currency for *GQ*. Matt guessed the payoff to be several thousand dollars.

The truck driver then began loading cases from the storage unit into the truck. In less than five minutes, Matt's suspicions about the contents of the cases were confirmed. As the man was loading a case into the back of the truck, the box slipped from his hands, crashed to the ground and split open. About a dozen cartons of Marlboro Lights packaged professionally in shrink-wrap slid across the asphalt driveway. The man yelled an obvious Arab obscenity and rushed over to pick up the contraband. He quickly surveyed the scene to make sure only his criminal associate witnessed the transgression and returned the cartons to the case.

Matt's phone vibrated. He breathed a sigh of relief, realizing he had put the phone on vibrate earlier in the day. Matt looked at the caller ID. Dwayne was returning his call.

Matt quietly retraced his steps and returned to the car. He called Dwayne immediately. It took several minutes to explain the situation to Dwayne, who promised to send help. Just as Matt was completing the conversation, the security gate opened. *GQ* walked out of the facility and returned to the Porsche. The truck followed. The driver gave an obligatory nod to *GQ* and drove off.

Matt remained at the facility and watched the Porsche leave. He grabbed a plate as the Porsche passed, hoping to identify the registered owner of the vehicle.

Matt began to scribble notes as fast as he could write, outlining probable cause for a search warrant of the storage locker. He closed his eyes and replayed the surveillance in his head, visualizing all he observed and then wrote vigorously. He repeated the process several times until he had an extensive rough draft affidavit.

Chapter Twenty-Six

Caitlin arrived home from the hospital and was surprised to find the condo empty. The smell of vegetable soup simmering in the Crock-Pot was all that greeted her.

She checked for voice-mail messages. One was from her mother and a second from her sister but nothing from Matt. It wasn't that late, so she assumed he would be home shortly. Actually, she welcomed a little bit of quiet time.

She opened her Bible and turned to 1 Thessalonians 4, smiling as she recalled the sermon on death several weeks before. The pastor quoted soul singer Ray Charles: "Ain't none of us getting out of here alive," then went on to say death is difficult for Christians just as it is for nonbelievers. As Christians we grieve, but not like those who have no hope.

Hope is what she wanted to give Jaana and her family. Hope in a medical miracle but confidence in life everlasting as well. She struggled with how to present the message of eternal hope and sought

God's guidance in finding the right opportunity. She closed her eyes and started to pray.

The phone rang and interrupted her conversation with God.

"Hello."

"Hey, Babe, I don't have much time. Something's come up, and it looks like I may be stuck here most of the night."

"Is everything okay?"

"Oh yeah, your Humpty Dumpty look-alike showed up at Zerak's store, and now I'm writing a search warrant affidavit. Just time-consuming, that's all."

"Matt, you aren't going to search the market, are you?"

"No, I followed Yasir from the store, and he led me indirectly to here."

"Matt, that family has enough problems now. I hope I haven't made more for them."

"Don't worry yet. Let me run out these leads, and we'll see where they take us. Right now Zerak's not on my radar, but that's not saying he won't be. He's buying their product, but I'm not convinced that makes him a terrorist. Gotta go."

"Well, be careful. I love you, Cowboy."

"I love you, too. Don't wait up. It could be a late one."

WITHIN A HALF HOUR Dwayne arrived at the scene. Matt filled him in on the details, and Dwayne looked over the rough draft.

"You missed your calling," said Dwayne.

"What do you mean?"

"You should've been a doctor. I can hardly read this scribble."

Matt was experiencing a variety of emotions—excitement, fatigue, satisfaction—and refused to reward Dwayne's attempt at humor with any type of acknowledgment, including a laugh.

As Dwayne continued to review the affidavit, Matt asked, "Should we go to the manager and find out who rented unit 270? Do you think the judge will require it?"

"Yeah." Dwayne thought for a moment then said, "No, let's not. We have no idea who owns this facility or who the manager is. They may be part of the conspiracy. I think you've got enough here. I would add a paragraph explaining why we did not contact the manager. That should be sufficient."

Dwayne continued to read, then added, "Let's do this. I'll stay here for now. Go back to the office and finish typing up the affidavit. I'll call out the cavalry and get a couple of rookies to sit on this place until you can get the warrant signed. When the judge looks it over, if he has a problem, then we can interview the manager. No sense alerting anyone if we don't have to."

Matt looked at his watch. It was only 6:45 but seemed much later. With any luck they could have the affidavit signed by nine or ten, and they would be done by midnight or one. It almost made him sorry he followed the box truck. *Too bad this wasn't TV, and it could all be done during a commercial break.*

Brian Weinstein and Liz Chavez arrived within a half hour of Dwayne Washington's call. Both were probationary agents with less than a year on the job. Their mission this evening was to watch the storage unit and ensure no one removed any items until Matt could obtain a search warrant.

Matt drove over to the Hollywood Division of the Los Angeles Police Department and met Detective Pete Garcia, a member of the Joint Terrorism Task Force. From there, both men used the LAPD computers to access as much information as possible about the storage facility, the owner, and any of the tenants. Pete also arranged for an LAPD truck to be available for the search. As soon as Matt obtained the warrant and they were able to enter the unit, backbreaking work would be the order of the evening. That event might still be several hours away.

Property records determined the storage facility was owned by a real estate investment trust with corporate headquarters in Delaware. A further check revealed no known link to terrorism. In fact, the REIT owned property throughout the greater Los Angeles area as well as a casino in Atlantic City and a riverboat on the Ohio River. Matt laughed out loud when he pulled up the property records and said it looked like a Mafia front. He might have been correct, but this evening wasn't the time to follow up on mob leads.

Matt also ran the plate on the Porsche. It came back to a leasing company in Detroit, Michigan—another dead end, at least this evening.

Pete found several police reports filed from the address of the facility, but all involved theft from the various units. Pete was able to identify the manager and ran a background check on him. He lived on site and had no criminal history. Task force officers could talk with him after the warrant was signed.

Matt finished drafting the warrant and affidavit and e-mailed a copy to the duty Assistant United States Attorney who would have to approve it prior to Matt's submitting it to the evening magistrate. The affidavit was nearly nine pages double-spaced. About half of it pertained to the actual observations Matt made earlier in the evening, and the remaining half concerned his opinions as to why he believed contraband would be found in the unit. Considering the speed with which he drafted the affidavit, Matt was more than satisfied with his final product.

With approvals from the AUSA in place, Matt headed to the Beverly Hills home of the federal magistrate for her signature. Matt was lucky. Judith McKean, the duty magistrate this week, was always accommodating. On the federal judicial totem pole, magistrates were one step below district court judges. They handled search and arrest warrants, misdemeanor trials, some civil actions, and most of the criminal procedural steps prior to the case being assigned a district court judge. Judith McKean was the most thoughtful of all the magistrates and usually made the agents share a cold drink with her as the affidavit was being reviewed. Sometimes, when time was of the essence, the extra bit of geniality was nerve-racking, but the judge never made unnecessary modifications to the affidavit, so an agent's patience was a virtue. Tonight should be smooth sailing.

Chapter Twenty-Seven

The upscale Beverly Hills restaurant was more suited to Wadi's newly cultivated tastes for exquisite cuisine. Sammy Chu, who was more suited for his brother's hole-in-the-wall storefront, grabbed the waiter's sleeve as he passed by the table. "More bread and bring the dessert menu."

Wadi and his Chinese criminal associate were celebrating their continued triumph at profiting from American vices. Counterfeit cigarettes proved a most lucrative venture in supporting the cause and far less dangerous than narcotics. Sammy's overwhelming success these past several years demonstrated the lack of enforcement efforts at thwarting the sale of the contraband. Untaxed cigarette sales of counterfeit U.S. brands took a backseat to what law enforcement agencies perceived as more dangerous criminal problems. Wadi and Sammy hoped that perception would continue for the foreseeable future.

"Can we use a fifty-three-foot container the next time?" asked Wadi.

Sammy laughed and spoke as he ate. Small chunks of food were expelled with every other word Sammy uttered. "My dear Middle Eastern friend, you are getting greedy. The forty-foot container no longer suits you?"

"It is not greed; it is wise business sense. We venture the same risk for a twenty-foot container as we do for the forty or fifty-three footer. It makes sense to maximize our profits with each importation."

"I will check with my associates in China. It should not be a problem, but the price of importing will be reflected in the larger container."

"As long as it is proportional, I will pay. Order me another container, the fifty-three footer, if possible. If not, we will take the forty," said Wadi. "Can you also assist me in getting the cigarettes into Toronto?"

"That can be done. We will still bring the package into Long Beach. Our drivers will take it across the border in Buffalo. That, however, carries a much larger price tag because of the difficulty in guaranteeing success. Our people at the border only work certain times so we must often wait several days just outside the crossing point before we attempt to move the product," said Sammy.

"I understand," said Wadi. "As long as you are fair in your dealings, I am sure we can do business."

"I will get you a price, and you can make a decision as to whether it is worth the effort," said Sammy.

They finished their meal in silence. Knowing Wadi was picking up the tab, Sammy ordered two desserts.

Matt left Judge McKean's residence and called Dwayne.

"It's a go. No problem with the warrant. I should be there in a half hour."

"Great, the troops are ready. It shouldn't take long to load up the truck once we get in. I'm assuming it's all cigarettes. We can inventory everything tomorrow," said Dwayne.

"From what I could tell, it was all cases of cigarettes, stacked from floor to ceiling. With enough help, it should go quickly."

"I've got a couple of rookies watching the place. Thought we'd just give them the bolt cutters and let them break the unit open. Is that okay with you?"

Matt appreciated Dwayne's asking. It was always irritating to put together a case and then have SWAT or probationers or, worse yet, a supervisor seeking publicity steal the glory by cuffing a suspect, escorting him for the media perp walk, and taking credit for the score. But this was merely a search, no big deal. "Yeah, that's fine. In fact, they can load the truck all by themselves for all I care. I joined this outfit to avoid heavy lifting."

"From the way you described the unit, I'm sure there is plenty of work to go around. Get here as soon as you can."

The team gathered just down the street from the entrance to the storage facility. Seven members of the task force, including the supervisor, were present. Dwayne briefed the team and then assigned responsibilities.

"Brian, we'll let you do the honors." With that Dwayne handed Brian a massive pair of bolt cutters. "Liz, you can pop the door. Pete will drive the truck in. We'll load it as quickly as possible and inventory it tomorrow. It's getting late. Let's just get in and out. No one has been to the unit since Matt saw the two subjects leave, so it should be a nice quick hit."

This was no midnight raid on a Hell's Angels clubhouse, so the task force members left their cars parked on the street and walked toward the facility. As fate would have it, just as Pete drove the truck toward the entrance, a late-model station wagon was pulling out. The now opened gate precluded the need to announce their presence to the facility manager until they were inside and ready to initiate the search.

Dwayne headed toward the office as the team made their way to unit 270.

Dwayne rang the doorbell several times to the manager's office, but there was no response. With that he radioed the command to cut the lock.

Brian applied the bolt cutters to the lock and used every bit of strength he could muster to effect the ultimate outcome.

"Too bad we don't have video. This would make a great commercial for Master Lock," chimed an agent.

"Or YouTube," said another.

Brian continued to apply pressure, and his failure to cut through the steel was becoming a personal embarrassment. He was making some headway but very little.

The more experienced agents were less than kind in their remarks, questioning Brian's manhood. Each snide remark caused the probationer's face to redden even more and his will to intensify. With Dwayne's arrival the catcalls subsided.

Applying some technique he must have learned from watching professional wrestling on television, Brian performed a series of rapid grunts and groans, and the blades of the tool penetrated the lock. A huge smile came over his face, but the agents ignored him, demanding instead that Liz open the door so they could finish what had become a very late evening.

Liz reached down, grasping the handle of the metal sectional roll-up door. As she pulled upward, it began to move smoothly along the roller tracks. The door reached a height of about three feet when an audible click and sizzle could be heard.

Matt and Dwayne looked at each other, puzzlement registered on both their faces. Fate was about to confront the team.

Before either could shout a warning, Liz continued to lift the door, and an explosion ripped through the metal object, throwing Liz to the ground. Her shrill screams could be heard over the roar of the flames as her nylon raid jacket burned brightly.

Controlled chaos prevailed.

Matt ripped off his shirt and jumped on Liz as she rolled on the ground, her screams continuing. Using his shirt as a blanket, he managed to smother the flames. His stomach knotted when he saw her hand was now a charred extremity where there was soft tan skin just seconds before; her nylon jacket melded onto her skin. Liz lapsed in and out of consciousness.

Pete Garcia threw the truck into reverse and moved the potential explosive hazard well away from the flames shooting out from the concrete storage unit. The pungent smell of burning flesh and sulfur permeated the air.

Dwayne dialed 911, summoning medical and fire assistance.

Matt, with the help of others, moved Liz safely from the front of the storage unit and administered what aid he could before the paramedics arrived.

The entire contents of the unit continued to fuel a sea of orange and red flames as smoke billowed out of the storage locker.

The agents could only watch as the evidence was destroyed by a series of ignition traps set throughout the unit designed to explode with any unauthorized entrance. The task force's lackadaisical approach to the search and their carelessness cost them a team member.

Emergency personnel arrived within minutes. Matt provided the first response treatment, preventing shock and minimizing damage to Liz. His quick thinking probably prevented a greater tragedy, but with Liz safely en route to the hospital, he reflected on the serious mistakes made this evening.

Never in his career had he been faced with a booby-trapped search venue. He faulted himself for not watching *GQ* and his associate secure the unit. He was so eager to call Dwayne that his enthusiasm clouded wisdom. These were terrorists, not white-collar criminals seeking to evade taxes. His cavalier approach to tonight's work was inexcusable. The war had become even more personal.

Chapter Twenty-Eight

Wadi sat on the gray, concrete park bench at the entrance to the Santa Monica Pier. Even though it was a chilly autumn weekday, the pier was a popular place. Teenage couples and poorer families with small children dominated the crowd. Wadi watched as he waited for Ismad to arrive. The sounds of the carousel and the laughter of children enjoying the afternoon were in sharp contrast to the life Wadi knew in his country. He looked at his watch. Ismad was late, but Wadi enjoyed the opportunity to relax, so he didn't mind the extra minutes alone.

Wadi learned early that morning the FBI had raided the storage unit and 325 master cases of counterfeit cigarettes were destroyed—3,250,000 cigarettes went up in smoke. At least, all the evidence was consumed in the fire. The preparations for a possible intrusion proved useful. It was another loss for the cause but a small one that should have no repercussions in the organization's overall plans.

The facility was chosen because it had no exterior video surveillance system. A Saudi female from Detroit with false California identification rented the unit. Wadi doubted there was any link to him; otherwise, he would be in custody. It was problematic as to how the feds identified the storage locker, but the cause would move forward. He and Sammy had already negotiated for the next container, and it would be en route from China shortly. Next time they would be more careful.

Wadi walked over to the concession stand and purchased a cotton candy. As he returned to the still empty bench, he spotted Ismad walking down the pier behind a teenager on Rollerblades. The boy was wearing ragged cutoffs, with green spiked hair and more piercings than Custer at the Last Stand. Ismad was dressed in black and glared in disgust at the young man's appearance.

Wadi greeted Ismad with a traditional hug, but Wadi sensed Ismad was returning the greeting more out of duty than respect. Ismad had difficulty hiding his belief that Wadi had assimilated too much of the Western ways. Wadi deliberately smiled as he pulled off a piece of cotton candy and placed it on his tongue, realizing the action further incensed his associate. Wadi knew Ismad understood the importance of Wadi's position and believed enough in the cause to meet with the cell leader. Besides, Ismad needed Wadi if he were to be successful.

They sat on the bench, eyes forward, looking across the pier. Ismad referenced several overweight people walking past. Their heavy footsteps clomped loudly on the concrete, like the Budweiser Clydesdales in the Macy's Thanksgiving Day Parade. Without looking at Wadi, Ismad said, "Americans are soft." He paused, then added, "And stupid. In the name of tolerance and diversity they will allow us to win. They will hand over their country and realize it only at the eleventh hour, even as we continue to bring terror to their shores."

Wadi slowly nodded in agreement. "With Allah's help it will be done."

"The names of the infidels I meet in this country are listed in the Sijjin. They are destined for hell just as the scroll records," said Ismad.

They continued with inconsequential small talk for several minutes before Wadi asked, "Why did you wish to meet today?"

Ismad said, "I am waiting for you to tell me of your latest failure."

"I don't understand."

"Of course, you do. I am well aware of what happened at the storage facility last night."

"That is not your problem."

"Oh, but it is. Every mistake you make potentially impacts my mission. I have only one opportunity to succeed," said Ismad.

"This is the purpose of our meeting, so you can hurl more accusations?"

"You deny you failed?"

"Failure is a strong word, implying my mission has failed. Last night was a small setback. Throughout my stay in this country, we have seen small setbacks, but we will continue, and we will succeed."

"Your work is more a tragedy of errors."

"At the Yaumud-Deen, I will be rewarded."

Ismad turned to Wadi and looking him in the eye said, "The day of judgment may come sooner than you expect, if you continue to lead as a fool."

Ismad rose from the bench and walked back toward the parking lot.

"It's my fault," said Matt.

"Listen, I don't wanna hear any of that!" Dwayne's response was almost angry. "The only people to blame for Liz's accident are the people responsible for setting the devices. You did your absolute best under the circumstances. I was on the scene. I have the experience. If anyone in the Bureau takes a fall, it will be me. But this was unforeseeable. It's the first time they have used such devices in the United States. We all have to learn from this."

Matt sat there for a few moments, then said, "I stopped by the hospital this morning to see her."

"I know. I was just there, and she said you stopped by. The flowers you brought her were very nice. I bet you wouldn't have done that for me."

"You're right. You're more a cold six-pack and nachos type of guy."

"The doctor was there when I arrived," said Dwayne. "The damage wasn't nearly as bad as they first feared. He's confident they saved the hand. There will be lots of scarring on the hand and arm, but skin grafts may cosmetically cover the worst of the problem areas."

"Will she be able to come back to the job?"

"Too early to tell, but based upon what Liz was saying, she's not too confident the hand will ever be fully functional, at least, not in terms of law enforcement. She's not sure she wants to come back, even if there is a complete recovery. She's serious about a guy, and he was never too thrilled dating someone who carries a Glock. I think she may pack it in."

Matt slammed his fist on the table.

Dwayne let him vent and then said, "It could have been a lot worse. You saved her life."

"Yeah, well, I don't feel like much of a hero."

The two sat in silence as the waitress filled both of their iced-tea glasses. Matt and Dwayne were the only two on the outdoor patio, and the mid-afternoon sun provided warmth on an otherwise chilly day.

Dwayne handed Matt an al-Qaeda intelligence briefing. "Thought you might like to look this over. It's a pretty good overview of the organization."

Matt began to peruse the report.

"You don't have to read it here. Just keep it from falling into the wrong hands."

"I'll shred it when I'm done. I just have trouble remembering all these names. It really is confusing," said Matt.

"I know it is. Even our people can't keep the names straight. Heck, we spelled Osama bin Laden with a 'U' until after 9/11."

"Yeah, I noticed that on the wanted posters."

"There are no vowels in Arabic so spelling can be a problem. Mohammad when translated into English sometimes appears as Muhamad, other times it is Mohammad, other times Mohammed. It just goes on and on. One time we figured out a terrorist by the name of Mohammad al-Ghamdi could actually have fifty-six different spelling possibilities," said Dwayne.

"And I thought my spelling was bad."

"Also wanted to let you know, we've had a series of bank robberies on the Westside. Some of the witnesses have described the robber as Middle Eastern."

"So."

"One took place just after SOG lost Rashid while they were watching Omar."

"You suspect Rashid and Omar?" asked Matt.

"I suspect everybody, but look for something indicating their possible involvement."

"You mean, like if Omar comes in with purple all over his face from an exploding dye pack?"

"Yeah, something like that," said Dwayne. "Did Omar come to work this week wearing mouse ears?"

Matt gave him a confused look.

"Omar and Rashid went to Disneyland last weekend. Rashid took a ton of pictures."

"Dwayne, it's the happiest place on earth. You can't really indict them for visiting an amusement park."

"No, but I'd feel better if they limited their weekend treks to the mosque and back." Dwayne looked at his watch. "Listen, I have to run. I've got a meeting with the Queen Mother. Don't worry about Liz. She's gonna be fine."

Chapter Twenty-Nine

Jaana's hospital room was beginning to take on the character of a second-grader. The walls were covered with get-well cards made by her classmates. A large bouquet of handmade paper flowers sat on top of the television. For a place that knew only suffering, a ray of hope emanated from each thoughtful gesture represented by the flowers and cards. This morning a life-changing decision had been made.

Three doctors and Jaana's parents arrived at the same conclusion. These five adults now crowded into the room to announce the decision that would change a seven-year-old girl's life forever.

A weary little girl greeted them with a warm smile as they entered the room. "This is the most visitors I have ever had. Hi, Dr. Paul."

"Hi, Jaana. I think you remember these other two doctors. They have had a chance to meet you and talk to you about your sickness."

"Yes, I remember." Her smile turned downward, the corners of her mouth extending below the lips. It was not quite a frown, but it certainly portended the information she was about to receive. Even at seven, she knew this many doctors along with her parents were not harbingers of good news.

Dr. Paul Conway, the pediatric oncologist, had drawn the short straw. He would be the one to tell Jaana about the operation. Dr. Conway was a tall man whose colorful smock and consistently rumpled hair betrayed the fact he was one of the nation's finest pediatric physicians. The other doctors stood somber faced as Dr. Conway pulled up a chair next to Jaana. Her parents stood on the other side of the bed, and both reached down to touch their daughter's hand.

"Jaana, we have spent many hours studying your sickness, and we have looked at all the tests. Your body is sick."

"I have cancer."

"Yes, Jaana, you have cancer. Right now the cancer is in your leg, but it may spread throughout your body. Do you understand?"

She nodded, "I think so."

Dr. Conway continued, "We need to remove the bad cancer in your leg, or you will never get better. Honey, the only way to remove the cancer in your leg is to remove your leg. We need to get all that cancer out of you. We need to take off your leg to do that."

Jaana remained surprisingly calm as Dr. Conway delivered the news. "When will you do that?"

"The sooner the better. We would like to do it tomorrow."

"Okay," said Jaana. She hesitated and looked at her parents who were stunned by their daughter's reaction. "After you take out the cancer, when will you put my leg back on?"

The doctors looked at each other and then at her parents.

Dr. Conway reached down and ever so gently touched her arm. "Honey, we won't be able to put your leg back on. We'll be able to give you a new leg, but it won't be a real leg like you have. It will be what we call an artificial leg, and if you work real hard, it will be almost like a real leg."

Jaana looked at the doctor and then at her parents. Tears began to flood her cheeks. "You mean you are going to take off my leg, and I will never get it back?"

Zerak leaned over and wiped away the tears. "Jaana, your leg is very sick. It will never work again. The doctors have to take it away, or you may never get to come home."

The doctors slowly walked from the room. Hope seemed to be caught in the draft.

Jaana cried softly for hours until no tears remained. Her parents sat by her side through the afternoon. At one point Nahid slipped out of the room to call Caitlin.

Matt finished early at the clinic and was looking forward to a workout at Gallo's. It had been several weeks since his last trip to the gym, and he needed to exact his frustrations on something or someone.

Rock Gallo, the seventy-nine-year-old owner, was great about letting Matt drop in anytime. The gym wasn't open to the public, and it wasn't some "chrome and mirrored foo foo gym" as Rock referred to those membership clubs flooding the TV with advertisements right after the New Year.

Gallo's was no aerobic workout, punching imaginary foes or heavy bags that never hit back. Gallo's was real boxing with real boxers who were trying to escape the poverty of the streets by seeking fame in the ring, fame that never came easy.

Matt met Rock seven years before while covering a lead for the Las Vegas office on an alleged fixed fight at Caesars Palace. Rock loved the fact an FBI agent knew a peanut bag wasn't just something kids bought at a circus. The two became fast friends. Rock was the only one at the gym who knew what Matt did for a living, and Rock jealously guarded the secret.

To date the undercover assignment was unsuccessful. His relationships with Omar and Ibrahim were progressing slowly, but he was no closer to identifying either as a terrorist than he was the day he walked into World Angel headquarters. It was frustrating. It had never taken him this long to size up a target. Typically, this far into an investigation, he had at least confirmed the target was a drug trafficker, child pornographer, or an organized crime figure worthy of further investigation. More often than not, with this amount of time invested, he had already engaged the target in criminal conversations, if not criminal acts. But so far, he "could neither confirm nor deny" Omar or Ibrahim had ulterior motives for visiting the United States. Like his CIA counterparts overseas, Matt seemed to be chasing shadows.

He was meeting regularly with Dwayne, reporting his observations and opinions. Dwayne was sharing with Matt everything coming across the wire, but that, too, was of little consequence. The CIA, NSA, DIA, and every other alphabet organization of the federal government could only verify that "chatter" reported the planning of an unspecified terrorist act in Los Angeles. The who, what, when, and where remained a mystery.

Matt parked his car on the street, carefully noting the "no parking" restrictions. He certainly didn't need his undercover car towed. That happened to him once before, and he learned the hard way the Bureau did not reimburse towing charges.

He grabbed his gear and walked down the alley to the entrance. There was no sign marking the location, nothing to direct outsiders to Matt's secret haven.

He climbed the wooden stairs creaking with almost every stride. The dark stairwell added to the mystique of the secluded gym, known only to a select few. A young fighter who had recently turned pro was making his way down the stairs. He greeted Matt with a semi-toothless smile. "Ain't seen you in a while."

"Hey, Big Thad! How you been? When's your next fight?"

"Got one scheduled for next month in Bakersfield. Just waitin' for the phone to jingle, know what I'm sayin'? There's a card down in Dago in two weeks, and Rock says he heard one of the fighters busted his hand the other day. Hopin' to fill in. I'm ready."

"I know you're ready. Let me know, I'll buy a couple tickets."

"Thanks, Matt. I'll see you."

Matt was a fight fan and knew it wasn't easy for a young fighter to make it on the purses area promoters paid. Local fighters were called because they had a following, and their body in the ring meant fannies in the seats. The fighters were often given tickets to sell and could keep a percentage of everything sold. It was a way of encouraging young fighters to promote the fight game and themselves. Few fighters received the fat paydays reported in the media. Promoters offering million-dollar purses were as plentiful as cheering liberals at a pro-life rally.

Matt walked through the double doors and knew he was where he wanted to be. There was no mistaking the sights and smells of Gallo's. "Eau de dirty socks and jocks." Stale sweat permeated the air, and the showers had fungi that could compete with any junior high science project. But it was Matt's second home.

Rock greeted Matt and then hollered at him to get ready. With an unlit cigar clenched between his teeth, Rock barked out commands like a gravely voiced Parris Island drill instructor. He had to, if he expected to be heard over the resounding patter of the speed bags and the whine of the half-dozen boxers skipping rope. Even though he was a septuagenarian, Rock wasn't above climbing into the ring and pounding skills into his young protégées. His bald head glistened from sweat, frustrated he wasn't able to convince his student to protect the body.

"Hey, Fernando, I got somebody who can go to the body with the best of 'em. Matt, get ready! Quit standing around. Champions aren't made in the locker room; they're made in the ring."

That was pure Rock. He could have been a contender. He was undefeated in the ring, but when the Korean War heated up, he enlisted in the Marines. He was part of the landing at Inchon and the drive to the Yalu River. He returned to the States twenty-two months later. The injuries he received earning a Silver Star and two Purple Hearts did not heal sufficiently to make a comeback. The "sweet science," as the old-timers called boxing, was his love and his education. He knew little else. Starting with almost nothing, he opened a gym that gained popularity quickly. In a short time he built a stable of excellent boxers keeping him busy for five decades.

Rock was a man's man, and Matt was proud to call him a friend. He could be coarse and crude, and the night Matt reluctantly introduced him to Caitlin, Matt held his breath. But Rock was pure gentleman. He spoke of classical music and quoted Scripture. Matt was speechless that evening. Caitlin fell in love with this crusty old Marine whose family had long since died. Rock was a fixture ever since at every holiday gathering.

Matt entered the ring and viewed his opponent in the far corner.

Fernando Perez had a dozen professional fights under his belt and a scheduled eight rounder next month in Bakersfield. The light heavyweight was undefeated, and the boxing establishment was beginning to take notice.

Matt had watched Fernando work, and the young Panamanian had lightning quick hands and the stamina to last well into the night. Matt was not interested in a pummeling. He wanted to be the "pummeler," not the "pummelee."

Rock climbed into the ring. "Matt, Fernando needs work defending the body. I want you to go hard. Go everywhere but work the body. Fernando, keep him honest but you need work protecting the ribs. I want you slipping punches to the head and body. You both understand?"

Matt and Fernando put in their mouthpieces, touched gloves, and Rock made the sound of an imaginary bell. At three-minute intervals for the next fifteen minutes, Matt was focused and alive. Any frustrations he had were being meted out on Fernando's body. It was an exhilarating workout and worth every ounce of sweat he expended.

Matt loved to work the body. He had been trained as a boxer to headhunt. The hands were held at shoulder level, and the shortest distance between two points was a straight line. It made sense to learn to jab and cross effectively.

But the ring differed in one major aspect from the street. In the ring you wore gloves. On the street you did not. The hands were unprotected. The bones of the skull were almost always stronger and denser than those of the hands. In a street fight, a shot to the face might mean a knockout, but it could just as easily result in a broken hand.

Matt learned the hard way. Several years ago on an arrest, the suspect struggled and took a swing. Matt instinctively responded with a left jab and a right cross. Both punches landed solidly to the chin. The suspect was unconscious, but Matt broke the knuckle of his right pinkie finger. Called a "boxer's knuckle," it's common around the gym. It is lower than the other knuckles and is almost invisible even when making a fist. Every time Matt wrapped his hands before entering the ring, the "missing knuckle" on his right hand reminded him to work the body.

"Time!" shouted Rock as he climbed into the ring to towel off Fernando. He put his arms around both fighters. "That's it. Great workout, kid! Thanks, Matt. That's just what he needed."

"It's what I needed, Rock. Thanks."

Matt wiped the sweat from his face and climbed out of the ring. His shirt was soaked. He removed the gloves and headgear, put his mouthpiece back in the plastic protective case, and began to unwrap the two-inch wide strips of cloth protecting his hands. He walked over to his gym bag and glanced down at his cell phone. Caitlin had left a message. She needed Matt for a "mission" and wanted Matt to call her right away. Jaana was scheduled for surgery in the morning.

Chapter Thirty

As they exited their car in the hospital parking lot, Caitlin turned to Matt. "I feel a lot better knowing Zerak won't be here."

"Congress wouldn't approve, but the wiretap's paying off. At least, we know his plans for this evening. Since Jaana's hospitalization, he's been there every night, allowing Nahid to spend time here."

"Do you think he's a terrorist?"

"The phones at the market have been pretty active. We're still waiting for transcripts from the calls in Pashto. I can't say he's not a terrorist. You can't prove a negative, but other than the cigarette deal, he seems pretty clean."

"I guess that's good news."

Caitlin and Matt walked through the double automatic sliding glass doors of the hospital entrance. The well-lit sterile lobby was empty of visitors. The white, nondescript walls were in sharp contrast to the warm, colorful, inviting entrance to the World Angel clinic.

Everything about this place said "medicinal." A middle-aged security guard, working a second job, sat near the door but didn't even glance up from his newspaper as the two entered. Two elderly female volunteers dressed in pink smocks sat at the large desk beneath the sign reading "Patient Information." Caitlin knew their destination and, at least for this evening, wanted to limit her contacts with the hospital staff.

Matt walked by her side, wearing an oversized jacket, his hand inside the coat, Napoleon style.

Caitlin had a coy smile on her face, but Matt was stoic. He was used to such adventures and did not want a smile to betray his mission.

Caitlin whispered out of the side of her mouth as they waited for the elevator. "This is so exciting. Now I see why you get into this cloak and dagger subterfuge."

With a slight grin, Matt said, "Quiet. You'll blow our cover."

Two young candy stripers walked toward the elevator as the doors opened. They entered ahead of Matt and Caitlin into the cavernous stainless steel cage, deep enough to hold a gurney and the requisite medical personnel. Caitlin pushed the fifth-floor button, and the girls pushed three.

"Good evening, ladies," said Matt.

They both giggled a nervous, "Hi."

"Do you enjoy working here?"

The shorter of the two, the brunette, said, "Oh, yeah, everybody's great."

"I assume you want to be nurses?" asked Matt.

Caitlin joined the conversation. "Well, of course they do. That's why they're volunteering here."

The blonde with shoulder length hair answered. "We're both going to nurses' school next fall."

The girls seemed uncomfortable with conversing on the elevator and kept their eyes on the lights above the door signaling the approaching floors. The elevator seemed to take an inordinate amount of time to reach the third floor. When the doors opened, the two girls quickly exited. The doors slowly closed, and the elevator inched up toward the fifth floor. Caitlin looked at Matt and laughed. "What was that all about, Mr. Undercover?"

"Remember, Love, the walls may have ears." Matt nodded to what appeared to be a surveillance microphone in the upper corner of the elevator and the sign that read, "For Your Safety and Security These Elevators Are Monitored." "A good offense is the best defense. I needed to take the enemy off their game. I was afraid my stomach might start growling."

Caitlin rolled her eyes. "Oh, okay, 007. Maybe at the next stop we could get you something to calm your stomach. Shaken not stirred, of course."

The doors opened, and they exited past an orderly waiting to push an empty bed onto the elevator. They were face-to-face with the nurses' station, a modern technological marvel with machines monitoring every patient in every room. At least from a medical standpoint, Jaana was in the best of care. An older, overweight nurse was chastising two younger nurses over a paperwork oversight and paid no attention to Matt and Caitlin.

Jaana's room was at the far end of the corridor. Caitlin sidestepped the "wet floor" signs as Matt trailed. Just prior to entering Jaana's room, Caitlin whispered a prayer. "Father, please give me wisdom and strength."

Caitlin knocked on the partially opened door, and they walked into the dimly lit room. Nahid Anwari was sitting next to the bed. Jaana had her eyes closed but opened them as soon as she heard Caitlin's voice.

In a weakened voice, Jaana said, "Hi, Mrs. Hogan. Thanks for coming."

Caitlin walked over and kissed her on the forehead. "Hi, Jaana. I brought a friend."

"Yes, I see Mr. Hogan."

"No, honey, I brought you another friend."

With that, Matt pulled her kitten from beneath his jacket.

Jaana squealed, "Palwasha! Oh thank you, Mrs. Hogan!"

Caitlin winced. "We have to be very quiet. I don't think the nurses would allow Palwasha in here. She just came for a short visit."

Jaana's mother smiled. This was just what her daughter needed to lift her shattered spirits.

Palwasha snuggled next to Jaana as she gently stroked the kitten's soft golden fur.

"Mrs. Hogan, I'm going to have an operation tomorrow morning."

"I know, Honey. Your mother told me."

"They're going to take off my leg."

"I know."

As a tear began to race down her cheek, Jaana said, "I'm scared."

With Nahid seated on the other side of the bed and the lights casting a soft glow over the room, Caitlin pulled up a chair next to the bed. Matt stood in the background next to the door, on guard, blocking the entrance of any other visitor until Palwasha could be concealed. Caitlin gently ran her finger down Jaana's cheek drying the tear. "Can I tell you a story?"

"Of course, I love your stories."

In a soft voice Caitlin began. "Once there was a small kitten, maybe a little smaller than Palwasha. In fact, the kitten's name was Palwasha."

Jaana smiled. "That means 'spark of light' in my country."

"I know, Jaana. Your mommy told me. Well, this Palwasha lived on a farm with her owner. It was a big farm with lots of land and plenty of places to play. Every morning the farmer put out food and milk for Palwasha, just like you do for your kitten. And every night the farmer held the little kitten and rubbed her back, just as you are doing now. Palwasha loved to run in the fields and play around the house and the barn. There was so much to see. Every day she explored new areas of the farm.

"One day when Palwasha was playing in the field, the skies got very dark. It was the middle of the day, but black rain clouds covered the sun. Soon there was thunder and lightning. Palwasha got scared, and she didn't know where to go. She had been exploring all day and didn't know how to return home.

"Then it began to rain. The loud thunder was frightening, and the quick strokes of lightning provided the only light to find the trail home. Palwasha was cold and wet and afraid.

"The farmer went out into the rain to find her. But every time the farmer got close, Palwasha would run away. It was so dark and the rain was falling so hard she couldn't actually see the farmer. She just saw this large shadow calling her name. The farmer was very sad. He loved his kitten as much as you love your kitten. The farmer had to figure a way to get Palwasha to trust him so she would come into the warm farmhouse where he could dry her off and feed her and love her. What could he do?"

Caitlin paused and looked to Jaana for an answer. Jaana wrinkled her nose trying to think of a solution. Then Caitlin said, "What if the farmer sent another kitten, one that knew the way home?"

Jaana said, "Yeah, that would work. If the farmer sent another kitten, who knew how to return home, then Palwasha would trust that kitten and follow her home."

Caitlin smiled. "That's exactly what the farmer did. The farmer sent another kitten out into the rain. The kitten found Palwasha and said, 'Palwasha, trust me and follow me. The rain may not stop, but if you follow me, I will lead you home.' Soon both kittens were back at the farmhouse. The farmer was so happy. Palwasha was lost but by following the special kitten, Palwasha was home safely with the farmer."

Caitlin moved a little closer. "Jaana, God is even greater than the farmer. He has a beautiful home for all of us. He wants us to join him in that home, called heaven. Sometimes we get lost in the rainstorms, even when it isn't our fault. And God calls our name, but we don't listen, because we are afraid. So God became a man. That man was Jesus. And like the kitten who Palwasha followed, Jesus walked among men and women. He said to them, 'Follow me and I will take you home.' Jesus promises to take us to God's home. All we have to do is ask Jesus to live in our hearts, and Jesus will guide us home to God. And when it is time, we can go to God's house and live forever. No matter what happens tomorrow, Jesus will be with you. You don't have to be afraid."

Jaana smiled. For the first time since the doctors met with her earlier in the day, she was at peace.

Matt interrupted the tender moment when he blurted out, "Nurse alert! Quick! Give me the kitten!" Matt rushed to the bed and tucked Palwasha under his coat just as the nurse entered the room.

"I'm sorry. Everyone but family will have to leave. This little girl needs her rest. She has a big day ahead of her tomorrow. I'm going to have to ask you two to go."

Jaana grinned. "You mean three."

The nurse looked confused as she ushered Caitlin and Matt out the door.

With a still weakened voice, Jaana said, "I love you, Mrs. Hogan."

Caitlin turned back around toward the bed. She bent over and gave Jaana a kiss on the forehead and held her fragile little hand. "I love you, too, Jaana. I'm going to be praying for you all night."

The nurse continued to guide them out of the room.

"Good night, Mr. Hogan. Good night, Palwasha."

As Rashid started to pull into the motel parking lot, he saw two LAPD units camped near the motel room; a uniformed officer was standing near one of the vehicles. Rashid quickly swung the Explorer back onto the street and parked a few blocks north of the motel. He wanted to phone Omar but feared calling the room in case the police answered. He broke into a cold sweat, worried his activities had been discovered. Rashid chose to wait out the police, but he didn't have to wait long. Within a few minutes both patrol units left, heading south on Lincoln.

Rashid left his car parked on the street and headed toward the back of the motel, ducking in and out of the bushes concealing his activities. When he reached the back of his unit, he ripped the screen from the window and pulled himself up through the narrow opening.

He was greeted by Omar, who heard the noises and grabbed a small lamp from the table. His arm cocked.

"Were you going to hit me with that or provide light?" said Rashid, climbing down inside the bathroom.

"Between the police and the strange noises, I didn't know what I was going to do."

"Why were the police here?"

"They were next door. One of the girls had a problem with a customer. The police arrested both of them."

"America is a nation of whores. Do they believe taking one off the street will make it any better?"

Chapter Thirty-One

Jaana's operation was scheduled for 6:00 a.m. Caitlin stopped by the hospital before going to school, hoping to see her before she went into surgery. Caitlin was about five minutes too late. Jaana was already under the effects of the anesthesia when Caitlin arrived. She spoke briefly with Nahid and promised to return that afternoon. Because the Anwaris could not afford a cell phone, Caitlin left hers with Nahid so she could periodically call to check on Jaana's progress.

Caitlin taught that day, but her mind was at the hospital. The children were worried about their classmate, and everyone wanted to make more cards. Caitlin had a difficult time concentrating and welcomed the opportunity to do an art project rather than reading or writing. ABCs could wait one more day.

Three times during the day, Caitlin called the hospital to check on Jaana. She was still in surgery the first time Caitlin called, and Nahid had nothing to report. They had been waiting several hours and still no word from the doctors when Caitlin called the second time. Caitlin knew God was in control, but the uncertainty of Jaana's condition was unsettling. Results came with the third call.

Nahid said the surgery took longer than expected because the cancer had spread beyond just the bone and affected the blood vessels and soft tissue surrounding the knee. The doctors removed the left leg at mid thigh. They were thankful they were able to preserve a portion of the leg so the transition to a prosthesis would be easier.

Dr. Conway spoke with Zerak and Nahid following the surgery. He was confident they removed the entire tumor. Jaana was expected to remain in the recovery room for several more hours. In a few days they would begin chemotherapy to destroy any tumors that might have spread throughout the body. She still had a long battle ahead.

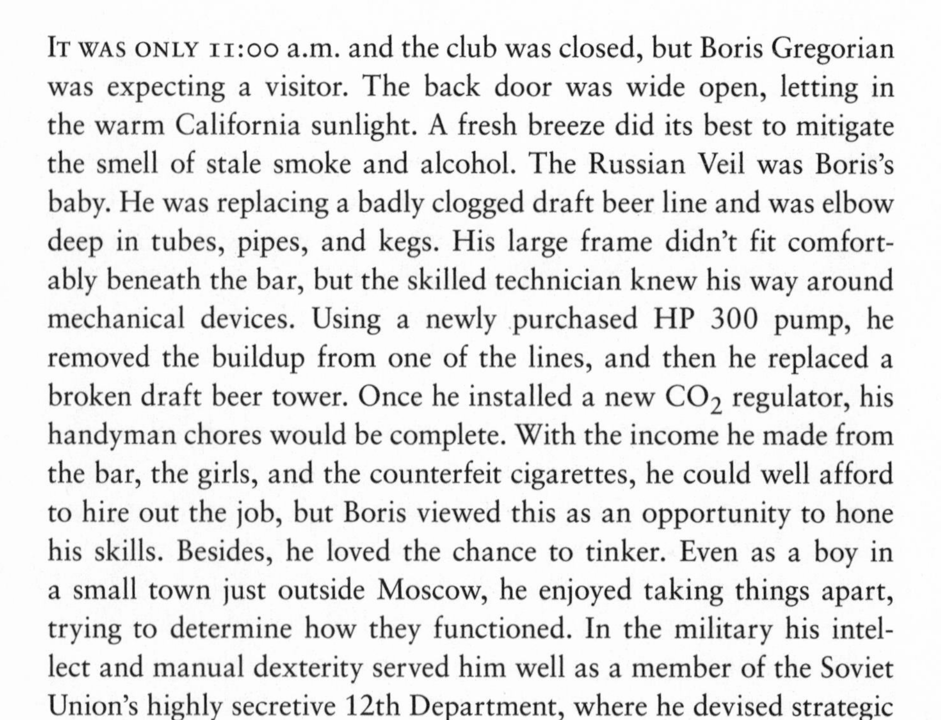

It was only 11:00 a.m. and the club was closed, but Boris Gregorian was expecting a visitor. The back door was wide open, letting in the warm California sunlight. A fresh breeze did its best to mitigate the smell of stale smoke and alcohol. The Russian Veil was Boris's baby. He was replacing a badly clogged draft beer line and was elbow deep in tubes, pipes, and kegs. His large frame didn't fit comfortably beneath the bar, but the skilled technician knew his way around mechanical devices. Using a newly purchased HP 300 pump, he removed the buildup from one of the lines, and then he replaced a broken draft beer tower. Once he installed a new CO_2 regulator, his handyman chores would be complete. With the income he made from the bar, the girls, and the counterfeit cigarettes, he could well afford to hire out the job, but Boris viewed this as an opportunity to hone his skills. Besides, he loved the chance to tinker. Even as a boy in a small town just outside Moscow, he enjoyed taking things apart, trying to determine how they functioned. In the military his intellect and manual dexterity served him well as a member of the Soviet Union's highly secretive 12th Department, where he devised strategic weapons for the "godless Communists," which his expected visitor jokingly called Boris's previous employer.

He heard a car pull up and park in the back alley. The engine sputtered as the driver turned off the motor, and Boris rose to his feet in time to greet his guest.

"Dr. U, right on time as always. Maybe I should look at that engine. All that knocking and pinging can't be good for your gas mileage."

Dr. Ubadiah al-Banna smiled. "Since when have you worried about my bottom line?"

"If you want, I'll take a look," said Boris.

"Maybe some other time. I'm sure it is just cheap Russian gas smuggled into America without the proper additives to prevent global warming." He smiled. "We have business to discuss."

Caitlin said she would go over as soon as school was out. She had been visiting almost daily and wanted to be there for Jaana. She and Matt wanted to have children but wondered if that day would ever come. Caitlin miscarried twice, both experiences painful and traumatic. Caitlin was also aware how much suffering the Anwaris had been through with their children.

Their first child, Matteen, was four years older than Jaana. He died at the age of five when he stepped on a land mine while visiting family at a small village near the Pakistan border. Nahid cried as she described the horrors of losing a son that way. Now her other child was also facing death.

Nahid understood death in her country. It was more difficult to understand it in the United States. She thought she had escaped the daily fear of death when she and her family came here. She was wrong.

When Caitlin arrived, Jaana had just been returned to her room. She was still tired and continued to sleep through the evening. The room was dark except for the light given off by the medical monitoring equipment and the hallway lights wedged through the partially opened door. Caitlin waited with Nahid.

Under the circumstances Jaana seemed to be doing well. For the time being the pain medication was reducing the expected discomfort.

After several hours Caitlin encouraged Nahid to go downstairs to the cafeteria for dinner. She agreed, leaving Caitlin alone with her favorite student.

Caitlin sat next to the bed stroking Jaana's hand. Jaana's soft features and near-perfect complexion betrayed her suffering over the past several months. Caitlin closed her eyes and began to pray. Before she was able to formulate a complete thought, Jaana whispered.

"Hi, Mrs. Hogan."

"Oh, Jaana, honey, I'm so thankful you are okay. Your mother just went downstairs for a few minutes to get something to eat. She'll be back up soon and will be so happy to talk to you."

"Mrs. Hogan, I saw Jesus."

"What?"

"When I was in the room with the doctors, I saw Jesus. He was right by my side. He held my hand during the whole operation and told me not to be afraid. He was there just like you said."

Jaana closed her eyes and fell back asleep. Caitlin wasn't sure what to say or what to think. Was a child's faith greater than hers? Caitlin looked toward heaven and whispered, "Thank you."

Chapter Thirty-Two

Westwood Village is one of the finest college communities in the country. Just outside the UCLA campus, the village contains everything a student thinks he needs—food, fun, and fast times. You can buy pizza by the slice or enjoy the finest cuisine at sky-high prices.

It is also home to the Fox Westwood Village Theater where many movies premiere. The red carpet is rolled out for Hollywood's stars and starlets. On those special nights the corner of Broxton and Weyburn is closed to all but pedestrian traffic, and roving spotlights brighten the night skies. Even a nonpremiere Saturday night is a crowded affair with university students celebrating another weekend of freedom from the confines of parental-imposed curfews.

The Nocturnal Bruin is a popular college hangout for UCLA students. The walls are decorated with museum-quality oversized photos of UCLA's athletic heroes in action. Autographed photos of such Hall of Famers as then Lew Alcindor, now Kareem Abdul-Jabbar, Olympic decathlon champion Rafer Johnson, basketball coach John Wooden, Dallas Cowboy QB Troy Aikman, as well as others cover the two-story walls from floor to ceiling. Behind the bar is a replica of Gary Beban's Heisman Trophy and autographed basketballs of all eleven NCAA men's basketball championship teams.

Tonight, as most nights, the music was pulsating and deafening, making it difficult to carry on a conversation.

Wadi had several drinks under his belt when Ismad walked in the front door and elbowed his way past college students waiting for a table. He spotted Wadi at the end of the bar.

Ismad walked directly to him. He kept his eyes straight ahead, locked on his target. He felt out of place, and he was. He was old enough to have fathered many of the patrons and was uncomfortable being around the alcohol, the loud music, and the suggestive dancing. He wore a cheap, black-flannel, long-sleeve shirt and black pants. His black shoes were practical if you were walking the yard at San Quentin, but they hardly measured up to the quality and style being worn by the college-age partiers.

Wadi was the complete opposite in his multicolored Tommy Bahama shirt and Italian designer jeans.

Most of the coeds who frequented the bar were absolutely beautiful—thin, tan bodies, and engaging smiles. A plunging neckline and a bared midriff were requisites for the uniform of the day.

Wadi noticed, as did every other testosterone-driven man in the bar.

Wadi greeted Ismad with a hug and handed him a beer. Ismad set the glass in front of him but didn't take a drink. When the bartender walked over to them, Ismad ordered soda water.

Although Wadi was younger by more than a decade, he was Ismad's unofficial superior. Wadi's most recent assignment from his overseas administrator was to support Ismad in his singular mission. Only three people in the United States knew what that mission was. Two of them were present at the Nocturnal Bruin.

Ismad, still uncomfortable with the meeting place, looked Wadi in the eye. With anger he asked, "Why are we meeting here? I see young women who appear to be Muslim yet are in public, unaccompanied by their male relatives. They make no effort to cover their faces. In fact, they make no effort to cover their bodies. Allah cannot be pleased with such lewdness, and you are a part of it all."

"Relax, my friend. It is important we blend into the American society. Can you think of a better place to blend?"

Ismad looked at him with incredulity. "I can think of hundreds of places better than this in which to conduct our business. I do not need to see this debauchery in order to carry out my mission. I do not need to learn about American society from you or your friends. I know what I am to do, and I will do it. You supply my needs, and I will be successful. I ask nothing more of you."

A well-endowed blonde beauty reached between them to grab a beer from the bartender. Wadi gave her an enormous smile. As she walked away, Wadi said, "In America, they say those are store-bought."

Even Ismad caught the reference, "You are a vile man who deserves no reward."

Wadi was oblivious to Ismad's tirade. Just as Ismad finished his sentence, a young, dark-haired Lebanese coed ran up to Wadi from behind, grabbed him around the neck, and kissed his cheek. "Wadi, you did come! Let's dance!"

She led Wadi to the dance floor. The two engaged in conduct Ismad deemed unacceptable in the eyes of Allah.

Ismad turned his back to the dance floor but saw the "decadence" in the reflection of the mirror covering the wall behind the bar. Ismad's anger deepened with each passing minute as Wadi spent what seemed like hours on the dance floor with his Americanized female friend. In reality it was only two songs. When Wadi returned to the bar, he quickly ordered another beer.

With disgust Ismad shouted above the undulating music, "You have my number. Call me when you want to discuss our business. I will not discuss it now."

As Ismad stepped from the bar stool and started toward the door, Wadi grabbed him by the shoulder. Wadi smiled a wicked smile and said, "This is L.A. Lose the flannel."

Ismad twisted quickly and headed for the door.

On the way back to his West Hollywood apartment, Wadi raced through Bel Air along the winding Sunset Boulevard. He slammed through the Porsche's six-speed manual transmission, taking the curves with precision. Wadi had consumed several drinks, and although not legally intoxicated, he was "drunk angry."

It wasn't the first time he had been confronted by older soldiers who questioned his ways and his loyalty to the movement. Wadi considered himself just as dedicated to the cause as anyone. Who was this Ismad to display such contempt?

It was Wadi's mission to coordinate cell activities throughout Southern California, and in order to be successful he had to blend into American society, just as the 9/11 hijackers did. They drank. They smoked. They went to strip bars and avoided mosques. Yet no one questioned their dedication. Even loyal Americans had to admit the hijackers willingly gave their lives for a cause in which they believed. How many Americans were willing to do that? How dare this Ismad, who are only here for one mission, question the tactics that have brought success for the Southern California cells.

Wadi joined the cause while still a teenager when he came under the influence of a charismatic Muslim cleric who espoused a militant line. What he said made sense, and Wadi pledged to embark on a holy jihad, as the cleric defined it.

Not every terrorist belongs to al-Qaeda, but all militants, including Wadi, share a common link: the respect and admiration for the organization's poster child, Osama bin Laden, the one they call the Emir. They view him as an inspiration, a symbol of resistance to Israel and its Western supporters.

Bin Laden met members of the Muslim Brotherhood while a student at the King Abdul-Aziz University. There he was introduced to the concept of "offensive jihad." In 1979, during his college days, the Soviets invaded Afghanistan. Bin Laden was twenty-two at the time and immediately began raising support for the Afghan guerrillas. That support continued through the war.

He is credited with recruiting almost fifteen thousand Muslims from throughout the world to fight the Soviets. A different caliber of Muslim recruit chose to follow bin Laden. They were doctors, engineers, and businessmen rather than clerics or impoverished Palestinians.

When the Soviets departed in defeat, bin Laden's followers returned to their homelands with a new fire and a new cause, the establishment of the Caliphate, a pure Islamic state. Many believed the Taliban in Afghanistan would be that hope, a model for the Muslim world.

Bin Laden's father served as the minister of public works and became a billionaire contractor who assisted in the renovations of the mosques in Mecca, Medina, and the al-Aqsa mosque in Jerusalem.

When Saddam Hussein invaded Kuwait in 1990, the Saudi government, fearing their country might be next, sought the help of the United States, rejecting the offer of bin Laden and his followers. Ironically, the bin Laden construction company built the military base in Saudi Arabia that housed more than four thousand U.S. servicemen. It is this continuing U.S. presence bin Laden and his followers, including Wadi, vehemently oppose.

The Prophet Muhammad from his deathbed said, "Let there be no two religions in Arabia." Islamic militants view any presence of non-Muslims in the Middle East as being in opposition to the Prophet's declaration.

Wadi attended the al-Badr terrorist training camp in Afghanistan during the Taliban rule. Those in attendance represented more than fifteen nations. Most returned to their own countries, bringing with them the terrorism taught at the camp. Wadi learned military as well as organizational skills during that training. He did well and impressed those in leadership. He was selected to go to the United States and coordinate the activities of support teams and strike teams.

A master's degree program served as a perfect cover. As a part-time student he could socialize with other Muslim students and recruit them for the cause. He could use his new business and organizational skills to successfully coordinate the cells' activities.

It was a responsibility he took seriously. Had he applied these skills in the private sector, he would be wealthy. Was it wrong to purchase goods that maintained his cover and allowed him to move freely in a consumer-oriented American society? Overseas leaders praised his efforts and expressed no concerns.

The support cells reporting to Wadi raised hundreds of thousands of dollars for the cause. His cells in the United States were self-supporting, and each month money and supplies were sent to the Middle East for distribution to other cells throughout the world. Wadi alone developed the Chinese counterfeit cigarette connection. The cause profited directly from the sale of these cigarettes. In addition, many of the wholesale buyers who owned small mom-and-pop-type convenience stores independently supported organizations overseas, such as Hizbullah or Hamas, with the profits from their cigarette sales—a "trickle-down" profit for terrorism.

Wadi also coordinated the sales of Afghan heroin and ran a "boiler room" soliciting funds for the cause. He provided support for people like Ismad who came to the United States for a specific mission, yet Ismad dared to criticize Wadi's "decadent" behavior!

Wadi rolled down the window of his Porsche and let the cool night breeze blow on his face. The bright lights of Sunset Boulevard lit up the skies. The women were beautiful and so obtainable. "Only through prayer can I block out the temptation of America's seduction," said Wadi out loud, to be heard only by Allah. Then Wadi smiled. He yielded to America's temptation many times since coming to the United States, those memories fresh in his mind.

He still believed in the cause, but the longer he stayed in America, the more reluctant he was to return to his country. Freedom brought excesses and abuse, but it also brought a level of happiness he never experienced in his country. Israel was wrong; it stole the Palestinian homeland. But encountering again someone like Ismad made him question the true value of supporting those with such a critical spirit.

Chapter Thirty-Three

Matt parked his car down the street and entered the clinic through a side door. The weekend staff was never at full strength, but if he could slip in and out of the clinic without being noticed, it would be better. There was no need to advertise he was there.

He walked down the hallway and unlocked the door to the physical therapy room. He grabbed a clipboard and set it near the cabinet where the supplies were stored. For the past week he had been taking supplies from the cabinet and storing them in a closet in the storage room. His only purpose for doing this was to provide an excuse for conducting this Saturday morning inventory.

In reality he wanted to break into Omar's desk and see if there was any evidence pointing to a terrorist mission. During the week Omar, the other therapist, and other employees were in and out of the room, never providing enough time to accomplish the task.

Matt sat at the gray steel desk with his lock-picking equipment. The desk was vintage government surplus. He imagined at one time an agent like himself probably "bagged" this desk because it belonged to a Bureau administrator and the agent needed to know just what incriminating items were secreted in the drawers. Matt perfected his skills with similar missions. Supervisors' desks always housed valuable tidbits of personnel intelligence. Then, like now, it was illegal.

The lock was easy, and Matt had it picked in a matter of seconds. He began to rummage through the top two drawers. Mostly he found equipment brochures and medical training manuals. Buried beneath the manuals were several articles from the Internet on terrorism in the United States and a lengthy article from *Playboy* on al-Qaeda. Matt smiled as he looked at the article. Matt read the article when it circulated around the office shortly after it appeared on the newsstands. Matt distinctly remembered the cartoons on the same pages as the article. Someone, apparently Omar, cut out the cartoons. *A modest terrorist!*

Matt read several handwritten letters and memos, but they were innocuous. He was hoping to find a diary, phone book, operations orders, the address of bin Laden's hideout, *he could use the twenty-five million-dollar reward*, anything that spelled terrorism. A few articles did not constitute a smoking gun. Matt's illegal activity raised more questions than it answered. Why would someone who trained at a terrorist camp, if Omar did, need informational articles on the subject?

He attempted to open the bottom drawer, but it was stuck. Matt pulled on it several times before finally dislodging it. He found more magazines, some in English and some in a foreign language. Matt assumed the language was either an Afghan dialect or Arabic. In any event, they didn't seem to be terrorist primers.

One item, however, was shocking in appearance. It was a cheap pamphlet that looked like an Arab religious tract. The cover featured a grainy photo of a Middle Eastern man holding an automatic weapon over his head. Unable to read its contents, Matt stuffed the document in his shirt, closed the drawer, and locked the desk just as he spotted Omar walking down the corridor. Several seconds later and Matt would have been caught. Matt quickly picked up the phone and punched in his home number. Omar entered the room as Matt began his conversation.

"I'll be home soon. . . . No, I couldn't sleep and thought I'd finish the inventory so we could go to lunch at that seaside restaurant in Malibu. Glad you got to sleep in. I love you."

No one was on the other end. Caitlin was at an all-day teacher's conference, and Matt hoped Omar bought the idea he was sitting at the desk merely to use the phone.

"Didn't expect to see you here this morning," said Matt.

"I could say the same thing."

"I noticed we were short on some supplies and wanted to take an inventory. I may not be here on Monday and didn't want you to run out."

Omar glared but said nothing.

"What brings you here? I thought you had weekends off," asked Matt.

"I do. I was just checking on the children and needed to use the phone."

Matt got up from the desk. "It's all yours."

Omar said nothing.

Matt was doing a poor job of selling his presence in the room.

The autumn sun set as Rashid drove east on Wilshire Boulevard, winding his way through Westwood. He turned left on Santa Monica, continuing through Beverly Hills into West Hollywood. Traffic was heavy but flowing. The gray hooded sweatshirt fended off the chill of the night air. The multimillion-dollar condos on Wilshire and the homes in Beverly Hills were unlike anything he saw in his country, but America's opulence was far from enticing.

Once he got into the West Hollywood business district, he saw all that America had and his country did not—bars, nightclubs, restaurants, and strip joints. Decadence may have been a better word. At Havenhurst, he slowly turned the corner. Wadi was waiting.

Wadi cautiously looked around and waited for several cars to pass, ensuring they were not part of any surveillance effort, before entering the Explorer. He jumped in the passenger side and ordered Rashid to continue driving south on Havenhurst. When they reached Fountain, Wadi barked out orders. "Turn left. When we get to Fairfax, turn right. We will pick up two more at the Farmer's Market."

"It's a little late to be robbing banks, isn't it?" asked Rashid.

"Tonight our work is different. We will discuss it later."

Rashid asked no more questions.

As they neared the CBS studios and Farmer's Market, Wadi said, "Slow down."

The Explorer was crawling along Fairfax when Wadi spied the two associates. "There on the bench."

Rashid pulled to the curb.

Two men, both dressed casually, were sitting on the bench. Wadi got out of the car and spoke to them outside Rashid's hearing. One of the men had a black gym bag.

The two men hopped into the back of the car as Wadi climbed into the passenger seat. He ordered Rashid to continue driving south on Fairfax to Wilshire. The two in the backseat said nothing—no introductions, no pleasantries.

Although the Explorer was old and needed some body work, it still had plenty of pep. Rashid gunned the accelerator as he pulled from the curb into traffic. The driver of a black Mercedes slammed on his brakes, sounded his horn, and quickly changed lanes to avoid hitting the Explorer. Rashid continued driving as if nothing happened. Wadi looked at him but said nothing.

Rashid raced to the intersection where traffic was stopped waiting for the light to change. The Mercedes was waiting. Rashid looked over. The driver of the Mercedes returned the look, saying something; but since the windows were up, his words could not be heard. Rashid continued to glare. The driver of the Mercedes was older and alone, unable or unwilling to take on four men. When the light changed, Rashid again gunned the accelerator leaving the Mercedes behind.

Wadi continued to stare at Rashid as he drove south on Fairfax, roaring to every light.

"Slow down," barked Wadi.

Rashid slowed, but as he came to the next light, it turned yellow well before the Explorer entered the intersection. Rashid sped up and ran the light. Again a motorist attempting to turn left into the intersection honked long and loud at Rashid.

A black-and-white LAPD patrol unit was sitting two cars back at the light. The police officer obviously saw the indiscretion but chose not to react. Maybe it was "end of watch," and he determined it wasn't worth the effort to turn on the lights, swing in and around traffic, and write up the paperwork. Besides, the *Los Angeles Times* had once again recently skewered local law enforcement for profiling Arab Americans. *Let it go.*

"Turn at the next right and pull over," demanded Wadi.

Rashid did as directed. When he stopped, Wadi ordered him out of the car. They both walked to the curb. Like any good leader, Wadi chose to criticize in private. "You must not draw attention to us. Do you understand me? Why are you driving like this?"

Rashid was humble in his explanation. "I am sorry. I do this to prevent us from being followed. I was taught to drive this way so the police cannot follow. I am also nervous. What are we doing tonight?"

Wadi looked at him, realizing fear plus obedience accounted for the driving pattern. "Let's get back in the car. Soon, very soon, we will discuss tonight."

Wadi and Rashid returned to the Explorer. Rashid made a U-turn on the residential street and continued south on Fairfax.

Rashid drove three more blocks before he was told to turn right on Sixth Street and stop. Wadi explained tonight's mission. "The Israeli Consulate is located in an office building on Wilshire Boulevard. The management office for that building is in the basement. In a file cabinet are the plans for every office in the building. We are going to photograph every document pertaining to the consulate, the ventilation system, and power plant in that building. We can access the basement from the entrance in the alley."

Rashid asked, "Someday, will we attack the consulate, striking a glorious blow for Allah?"

"That is not for you to know. Our mission tonight is as I described. If someday we are ordered to attack, we will," said Wadi.

Wadi opened the gym bag. He pulled out a Sony Cybershot digital camera and showed it to Rashid and the others.

Wadi said, "I will take the photos."

Wadi then pointed to the smaller of the two men in the back. "He works for the alarm company that maintains the security for the building. He will override the alarm system. Then we will enter the building and go directly to the basement. The stairwell is on the right as we enter through the alley door."

The alarm technician then added, "The exterior perimeter alarm system to the alley door is a low-voltage, electrical stand-alone with multiple sensors. It will take me several minutes to disarm each sensor. There is a rather simple interior perimeter sensor alarm on the door to the maintenance office. It will only take me a minute to bypass. The system is monitored at the first floor guard desk."

Wadi said, "After we complete the search, then we will leave. The consulate is in suite 1700. We are concerned with both the office plans as well as the overall plans to the building."

The alarm technician looked at all three. "I will rearm the alarms as we exit. But it is very important you do not touch anything once we enter the building and as we are leaving. I cannot disarm everything. Each alarm is on a separate system to prevent the failure of one system from affecting the entire building."

Wadi asked the technician, "Once inside the office, will we be able to touch anything without setting off an alarm?"

"Yes, once inside the building maintenance office, there are no more alarms. The only alarm is to the door. The security guard only checks the basement twice a night, usually when he first comes on around four in the afternoon and then later in the evening around ten or eleven. We will have plenty of time if we are quiet and careful."

Wadi interjected, "We can afford no mistakes. This is important to the cause. Let's go."

Chapter Thirty-Four

Rashid drove west one block on Sixth and turned left, crossing Wilshire Boulevard. He parked the Explorer less than a hundred feet from the dark alley leading to the rear of the building.

Earlier in the week Wadi ordered a cell member, unknown to anyone but Wadi, to shoot out the lights.

Someone in the neighborhood reported hearing shots fired but could not be specific about the location. By the time the police arrived, the cell member had accomplished his mission and escaped. Gangs from LAPD's Wilshire District had been moving north, and the police, unaware the lights were damaged, assumed gang members were responsible for the shooting. They quickly dismissed the call when they found no evidence of a weapon having been discharged.

Prior to exiting the Explorer, Wadi reached into the gym bag and pulled out four pairs of surgical gloves.

Rashid was the last to leave the car and struggled to put on the gloves. The cheap latex glove ripped as Rashid attempted to pull it over his right hand. Two of his fingers were sticking out, unprotected by the glove. Frustrated, Rashid ripped off both gloves and threw them into a nearby trash can. The others kept walking as Rashid ran to catch up.

The four moved slowly through the alley and came upon the rear entrance. The technician took several tools from the gym bag. The other man held the flashlight as the technician began disabling the exterior door alarm. He worked quickly and with precision. It took him less time than he expected, and the four were in the building within two and a half minutes.

They moved down the stairwell to the basement. Wadi led the way down a long corridor past several closed doors. Behind each door the loud rumblings of heating and air-conditioning units could be heard. Wadi had previously been in the basement and went directly to the building maintenance office.

The technician opened his bag a second time and within seconds bypassed the alarm to the interior door. They were in.

The room was larger than one would have expected. It consisted of a small reception area and two separate offices for the building administrators. Two large file cabinets were against the far wall. The technician easily picked both locked cabinets then stood guard at the door. The other man walked through the two offices.

Rashid searched the file cabinet on the left. Wadi searched the cabinet on the right. Within a few minutes Rashid found the documents pertaining to the consulate.

Rashid whispered, "I have it."

Wadi looked over at him. "Do you have the file?"

"Yes, I think it is all here."

Wadi looked at Rashid's hands. "Where are your gloves?"

Rashid offered a nervous smile as he answered. "They tore as I tried to put them on. It is fine. I have never been arrested."

Angered, Wadi said, "No, but you were fingerprinted when you applied for a visa. Do you think the Americans are stupid? I had extra pairs of gloves in the gym bag. You should have said something."

Rashid's smile faded. "It is too late; I will wipe it clean before we leave."

The papers Rashid pulled from the folder included an extensive floor plan of the seventeenth floor detailing each office in the consulate. Wadi began photographing the blueprints for the individual offices, conference room, restrooms, kitchen, library, and storage room. The blueprints for the technical services room detailed the phone and secure teletype systems.

Within minutes they found every document they wanted. Wadi was able to photograph everything. In fewer than ten minutes, the four accomplished their mission. They disturbed very little in the office, and the cleanup was minimal. Rashid hoped he redeemed himself by finding the plans.

The four walked into the hallway. As the technician was resetting the alarm to the interior door, Rashid leaned against a door across the way. Wadi saw him and glared. Rashid quickly stood up straight.

The other man heard footsteps. "Someone is coming."

The technician finished and grabbed his bag. The four ran down the hallway and escaped through the rear door. They were down the alley and out to the car before the security guard exited the building.

Rashid sped down the side street. No one in the car said a word as Rashid drove north on Fairfax. Finally Wadi ordered him to turn right on Santa Monica Boulevard. As they approached Plummer Park in West Hollywood, Wadi directed Rashid to drive behind the park.

It was dark and the park was empty. Rashid stopped the vehicle and all four exited. Wadi was still wearing the surgical gloves as they walked toward some thick shrubs near the restrooms.

Wadi stopped. "This is good. We will talk here."

Wadi faced Rashid. "Tonight you have almost cost us our mission. The cause cannot tolerate your mistakes."

With that Wadi pulled a .32 caliber automatic from behind his back and fired one shot. The round struck Rashid just above the right eye and penetrated deep into the skull and brain.

Rashid dropped immediately. His body convulsed on the pavement as if protesting a death that should have been reserved for martyrdom. Then all movement ceased.

Neither the technician nor the other man seemed affected by the cold-blooded murder of a coconspirator.

Wadi reached over and grabbed the keys to the Explorer from Rashid's right hand and shoved them into Rashid's pants pocket. He replaced the keys with the .32 caliber auto. Wadi carefully wrapped Rashid's fingers around the gun and pulled the trigger a second time. Wadi picked up one of the two shell casings. The technician bent over to pick up the second casing.

"Leave it for the Americans," ordered Wadi.

"Is it wise to leave your gun?" asked the technician.

"It is not mine. I purchased it off the street from a skinny hype with a serious addiction. He needed to sell me the gun he stole in order to buy the heroin we imported." Wadi shook his head in disgust. "In a democracy they allow even him to vote."

All three laughed.

Wadi gave each man a twenty-dollar bill and told them to take separate cabs back to Farmer's Market where their car was waiting. He walked west on Fountain and headed back to the apartment on Havenhurst, ten blocks away.

Chapter Thirty-Five

Plummer Park is in West Hollywood, an incorporated city. The park consumes a small city block and serves as a focal point for the neighborhood, now predominantly Russian immigrants. By big city standards it was rather simple, consisting of tennis courts, block-wall restrooms, and picnic tables. If the grass were carpet, it would be described as threadbare. But the residents of the multilevel apartment complexes surrounding the area appreciated a place to congregate.

Rather than create its own police department, the West Hollywood city government contracted with the Los Angeles County Sheriff's Department for protection.

A sheriff's patrol car pulled into the park around 10:30 p.m. The deputy, working as a one-man unit, exited his car and began to walk the perimeter of the park, a routine he performed at least once every shift. Sounds of the city could be heard—cars traveling up and down Santa Monica Boulevard, dogs barking, the wind blowing through the trees—but the park was unusually quiet.

Typically the park was crowded with newly arrived Russian immigrants. This night the temperature dipped below forty-five, and most people chose to stay indoors.

Several men were sitting at a table at the far end of the park smoking a strong brand of Russian cigarette. In all likelihood they had also been drinking, but they seemed docile so the deputy reasoned, "Why be confrontational?" The deputy nodded to them as he walked past. Each returned the greeting with a nod or a wave.

As the deputy approached the restrooms, he noticed what he first thought was a man sleeping under the bushes. The deputy's immediate reaction was "too much vodka." As the deputy closed in on the body, he saw a puddle of blood. He then saw the .32 caliber pistol in the right hand. The deputy instinctively drew his weapon and pointed it toward the body. He quickly scanned the area looking for others but at the same time maintained his attention on the body fifteen feet away. Using his shoulder-attached radio mike, he called for assistance.

The deputy carefully approached Rashid. After determining it was safe, he bent over the body and felt for a carotid pulse. There was none.

Within seconds two additional units arrived. A paramedic unit from the nearby fire station also responded to the "officer needs assistance—possible 187" call; "187" was a reference to the state criminal code for murder. It was a designation with which law enforcement officers in L.A. were all too familiar. The deputy knew it was too late for the ambulance, but since only a paramedic unit or the coroner could declare a person dead, their presence was welcomed. It really didn't take medical training to confirm the deputy's assessment.

Soon a uniformed sergeant rolled up on the scene and took control until homicide detectives and investigators from the coroner's office arrived. Dead bodies were nothing new for the sergeant, and he quickly put into action the protocol he had followed many times: secure the area, prevent anyone but authorized personnel from entering the crime scene, begin a grid search for evidence, and dispatch deputies to canvas the area seeking witnesses.

Even though it looked initially like a suicide, the homicide unit was always called to conduct the investigation. Homicide detectives determine who did it. The coroner's office determines the cause and manner of death.

The men sitting at the picnic table at the far end of the park remained throughout the police activity. The three men were Russian, and only one spoke passable English. All three had been drinking as the initial deputy suspected. They tried to hide the bottle of vodka secreted in a brown paper bag as the two-man team of deputies approached. One of the Russians put the bottle at his foot and kicked it next to the table leg, hoping to hide it from the deputies.

The two deputies arrived and identified themselves, as if the Russians needed an introduction. The deputies wore uniforms. They were the police. That was all the Russians needed to know. They came from a police state and understood uniforms.

The one deputy reached down and picked up the brown paper bag. He showed the contents to his partner. The deputies could have cited the men for possession of an open container in a public park, but tonight a dead body took priority.

The deputy returned the paper bag with a slight grin then tried to engage the men in conversation. The initial efforts were fruitless until one man who spoke no English said something in Russian to the "interpreter."

Normally the Russians at Plummer Park did not volunteer information to law enforcement personnel. The interpreter hesitated and then looked at the deputies. "My friend lives in the street across." He pointed to an apartment complex directly across the street from the park.

The interpreter continued, "Before we meet here at the park, he hear what he think was cracker bomb. Then he hear second cracker bomb."

The deputies looked at him with confusion. The taller of the two deputies questioned, "A what?"

"Cracker bomb, like what you do on holidays with the lighter."

After a brief pause the deputy said, "Oh, you mean a firecracker."

"Yes, my English not so good."

"No, it's just fine. It's a lot better than our Russian. When was this? What time?"

The interpreter looked to his friend and asked the question in Russian. After getting a response, the interpreter said, "It was just a few minutes before we came to the park. My friend thought nothing of it. It was two pops. Maybe it is nothing."

The deputy followed up with several questions, but the answers were not all that helpful. The Russian saw nothing, and when he arrived at the park, no one was present. The other two Russians joined him a few minutes after he arrived. No one else had been in the park since the three men gathered, and no one heard anything unusual. Based upon further questioning and assuming the pop sounds were shots, the deputies surmised the time of the incident was between 9:00 and 9:15.

A canvas of the neighborhood was negative. No witnesses. No answers.

The homicide detectives arrived within thirty minutes, but for investigators from the coroner's office, it took almost two hours. The coroner's team came on duty at 4:00 p.m., and this was their third call of the evening. On some summer nights in L.A., that would be interpreted as a slow evening. Tonight it was just steady work.

A decision had not been made about the call. At first glance the evidence pointed to suicide. But a careful analysis of the scene made the investigators think twice. Was this a homicide meant to look like a suicide? The gun was in the deceased's right hand with the fingers wrapped around the weapon and the index finger outside the trigger guard. There was no evidence of a struggle—no evidence the body was dragged, no evidence of broken branches on the bushes, and the blood pooled in one location. One expended .32 caliber shell casing was discovered a few feet from the body, a little too far based on the location of the weapon, but it could have bounced that far after being automatically ejected following the firing.

But there was no suicide note. The deceased was carrying no identification. Most suicides aren't looking to hide their identity, just end their life. The gunshot was above the right eye, and the angle of trajectory appeared to be straight in. The autopsy would identify the exact angle, but most suicide victims put the gun to their temple at an angle and pull the trigger leaving a tattoo of charred gases and unburned powder surrounding the entry wound. The pattern on the deceased was broad and nearly faded, demonstrating a shot more distant than next to the temple.

One of the investigators conducted a gunshot residue test on the victim's right hand. He swabbed the web and palm with a diluted solution of nitric acid. The swab tested positive for barium and antimony, evidence of GSR (gun shot residue).

Conflicting evidence stemmed from the fact the weapon remained in the clinched hand of the victim. Experienced investigators knew most victims drop the gun once it is fired. This evening wasn't going to end with a quick check of the appropriate box on a crime report.

The victim appeared to be Middle Eastern not Russian. The sergeant ordered one of the deputies to run vehicle registrations on the six cars parked along the road next to the park. It was a good hunch. Five of the cars came back registered to Russian-Armenian names. The sixth, a 2001 Ford Explorer, was registered to Rashid Aziz Khan in Venice. The sergeant guessed Khan was his victim. He called the station and ordered a computerized driver's license photo, and a deputy rushed it over.

The photo confirmed the identity. They had their victim identified, but now more questions arose. Why would Rashid Aziz Khan chance driving a car without identification? Why drive from Venice to commit suicide in West Hollywood? He was carrying no identification, maybe it was a robbery. But if that were the case, why leave a gun wrapped in the fingers of the deceased? Maybe he got off a shot as well? Hence the GSR and two "pops." Could someone have come after the "suicide" and stolen the wallet from a dead man? There were many questions for the homicide detectives.

Photographs of the crime scene were taken before the coroner's investigators arrived, and white tape outlined the location where the body was discovered. The coroner's investigators obtained much of their preliminary information from the homicide detectives with whom they worked on numerous cases. Like the homicide detectives, the investigators had the authority to interview witnesses, follow up on leads, collect evidence, make identification, and notify the next of kin. Typically, though, in a homicide all of the work was done by the detectives.

Based on body temperature, lividity, and rigor, the time of death was placed between 8:30 and 9:30 p.m. The investigators could not be any more precise.

The investigators placed Rashid in a black body bag and zipped it. He was placed on a gurney, loaded into the coroner's wagon, and transported to the main facility of the County Coroner's office on Mission Road near the County USC Medical Center. An autopsy would be conducted the next morning.

The L.A. County coroner's office investigates more than six thousand deaths annually; more than one thousand of them are suspected homicides. This death fell within the "suspected homicide" category. The law required an autopsy, the cost of which, nearly $5,000 if privately requested, would be borne by the county.

Chapter Thirty-Six

The security guard at the Wilshire Boulevard office building notified LAPD. Two young uniform patrol officers arrived within fifteen minutes. The guard was a retired small-town cop from Missouri. He and his wife moved to Los Angeles years before when their children relocated to the West Coast. By all appearances he had consumed a few too many free doughnuts throughout his career.

He took the guard job after his wife died the previous year. He was old but effective enough behind the lobby security desk. All that was required of him was to monitor the alarm system, log in after-hours visitors, and at least twice a shift ensure every exterior door was locked.

The guard enjoyed talking with the young officers who responded. He always loved sharing war stories about the "good old days," especially before the Supreme Court gave these "barnyard wastes" more rights than they deserve. The officers were kind, listened to a few stories, and took a report, but the security guard provided little substance.

"This here board lit up like a Christmas tree. Something triggered the alarm. Had a cat set it off a few weeks ago so I headed down to the basement for a look-see. When I opened the door, I heard footsteps; and by the time I got down there, I seen four men running. They got out the back before I could catch up. I think I scared 'em off. I checked all the doors. Nothin' disturbed. I think I got to 'em before they was able to pull any crap."

"Sir, did you get a good look at them. Can you give us a description?"

"They was runnin', son. All I seen was their backs. They was all medium build, medium height. Couldn't tell you their age. Never seen any faces, but they ran pretty fast. Must be younger than me."

The young officer laughed.

"Pretty sure they was all white or at least brown. I could see hands, and they weren't black. You know, maybe Mexican."

"What about clothes, sir. Can you describe what they were wearing?"

"They was all wearing jeans, I think. . . . Wait, one guy, the slowest one, or at least the one pullin' up the rear, was wearin' a gray sweatshirt with green paint on the back of the right sleeve."

"Anything else?"

"That's about it."

There was little more the officers could do but take a report. They checked every door in the basement. All were locked. Nothing seemed disturbed and nothing was missing.

As they started back up the stairs, dispatch reported a drive-by shooting a few blocks south of Wilshire. The officers raced to their unit, leaving the guard at the bottom of the steps, who hollered, "You guys be safe."

Trespassing at an office building was low on the crime priority list. The officers were back in service within twelve minutes of going "10–7." They would complete the report at the end of watch and submit it to the watch commander along with dozens of others filed that evening.

Nothing much would be done about the intruders. The watch commander might increase patrols in the area for the next few evenings, but short of that there was little he could or would do.

The phone rang. The sound startled Matt and Caitlin. Both were in a deep sleep. Matt rolled over to answer the phone. The bedroom shutters were slightly opened, and Matt noticed it was dark outside. He was disoriented and couldn't figure out when this interruption was occurring. He looked over at the digital alarm clock on the nightstand. When his eyes finally focused, he saw it was 2:43 a.m.

Matt's first thoughts were something had happened to his mother.

He picked up the receiver. "Hello."

"Matt, sorry to call at this hour. It's Dwayne."

"What's wrong?"

Caitlin sat up. "Who is it?"

Matt put his hand over the receiver. "It's Dwayne. It's okay."

She collapsed back onto the pillow and rolled over.

"Matt, you still there? Matt?"

"Yeah, sorry, what's going on?"

"I got a call late this evening. I'm at the West Hollywood substation. A deputy found Rashid dead in Plummer Park with a single gunshot wound to the head."

"Rashid? You mean Omar's brother?"

"Yeah."

"Murder?" Matt asked.

"It looks like murder. I don't think it's suicide. Might be a robbery gone bad. They notified me after they checked L.A. Clear."

L.A. Clear was a law enforcement clearinghouse in which the various agencies in and around Los Angeles County "registered" the subjects of their investigations. It began with drug investigations in the late '80s when a subject brokered a cocaine deal between an informant for one agency and an undercover officer with another department. The ensuing arrest of all the interested parties resulted in a near "friendly fire" shootout, "blue on blue" as it was known in law enforcement circles. No one was hurt, but the clearinghouse was borne out of that incident.

"It took awhile to identify the body," said Dwayne. "He wasn't carrying any ID. I'm going with deputies to the motel to notify Omar."

"So what happened?"

"I'm not sure. They found the Explorer parked on the street. Rashid was wearing the sweatshirt with the green paint on the right sleeve."

"The bank robbery suspect? You think Rashid could have been behind that string of robberies?" asked Matt.

"He fits the general description in terms of size and weight. Several witnesses thought the robber might be Middle Eastern. One described the get-away car as a green SUV. I think he may have been our suspect."

Matt was awake now. Caitlin slept through the entire discussion. "So who did it, his own people or a tweeker looking to grab some easy cash?"

"No clues yet. We're going to hit Omar pretty hard. If we don't arrest him, keep a close eye on him at the clinic the next few days, assuming he even shows up."

"I can't believe Omar's involved in the robberies," Matt said. "He's at the clinic every afternoon and late into the evenings. Most banks are closed before we finish up. When were the robberies?"

"They were all during the day. He may not have participated, but he just might know about them and where the money went. More than $90,000 has been taken. We need to trace the funds."

"I've seen the motel," said Matt. "It's no penthouse suite at the Ritz."

"I'm guessing the money went back to the Middle East or to support cell activity here."

"I need to see you. I picked up something at the clinic today that may be important. Looks like a recruiting brochure for terrorists. I need you to get it to a translator."

"Did you get it from Omar?"

"Yeah, sorta, I found it on his desk." Matt wasn't about to tell Dwayne how he really found it.

"Sounds good. Get it to me, and I'll have one of our people take a look at it. I'll call you after our meeting with Omar."

Dwayne followed the two deputies in a marked black-and-white unit from the substation to the Venice motel. It was 3:30 a.m., and the streets were nearly deserted. There was little reason to be out at this hour. However, when the patrol car turned on to Lincoln Boulevard, a prostitute was standing near the corner negotiating with two potential customers. Once they spotted the deputies, they scattered like roaches exposed to light.

A travel brochure might describe the motel as within walking distance of the Pacific. It probably wouldn't say you have to walk through a gang-infested neighborhood to reach the ocean.

The Shoreline Crips controlled much of this area. Their graffiti was everywhere, marking their territory, recording their history, telling the world, "Enter at your own risk."

This neighborhood was in LAPD's Pacific Division. As a courtesy Dwayne called the Watch Commander at Pacific and advised him of the situation. The Watch Commander offered to send one of his own units over, but Dwayne said that wouldn't be necessary. There was little sense tying up more units than needed, especially since this was only a notification. The Watch Commander appreciated the heads-up and said he would increase patrols in the area for the next hour or so.

The motel was a horseshoe-shaped, one-story building with fifteen units. There was one parking space for each unit. No pool. No amenities. No turn-down service with a mint on the pillow. Although at one time it may have catered to vacationers, the motel now serviced residential transients who stayed a week or a month at a time. In all actuality a few of the rooms were subrented at hourly rates by women practicing the world's oldest profession.

Dwayne and the deputies pulled into the parking area. The headlights illuminated the motel trimmed in a distinctive green. Even with the naked eye, Dwayne knew it matched the color on the sleeve of Rashid's sweatshirt.

There were few cars in the parking lot so Dwayne assumed there were rooms available. The surveillance team had previously identified Omar and Rashid's room. Dwayne and the deputies walked directly to it. There was little sense in disturbing the manager at 3:30 in the morning. If he needed to be interviewed, that could be done at a more reasonable hour.

The motel complex wasn't well lit. Three light poles were supposed to illuminate the parking lot, but only one was operational. Broken glass under two of the poles confirmed the lights had been shot out. All the residents must have been asleep. The chairs in front of each unit were empty, and there were no lights on in any of the rooms.

The deputies stood back away from and off to the side of the door in a defensive posture and unfastened their holster snaps. Experience and training taught them not to stand directly in front of the door where an unexpected shotgun blast could end their careers if not their lives.

Dwayne also stood to the side and reached over to knock on the door to Omar's room. There was no response. He knocked louder. Again no response. One of the deputies stepped forward and with the business end of his nightstick banged a couple of times on the door.

From inside Omar's room came a faint response. "Who is it?"

Neither Dwayne nor the deputies responded. Dwayne continued to knock. When Omar came to the window and pulled back the curtain, he saw the two uniformed officers.

Dwayne held up his credentials and pressed it to the glass. Omar nodded his head, acknowledging their presence. Dwayne could hear the chain latch being unhooked and saw the door handle turn. Instinctively the deputies placed their hands on their weapons. Dwayne cleared his jacket but no one drew his weapon.

Omar opened the door, standing there in his boxers, obviously unarmed.

"Omar Azia Khan?" said Dwayne.

"Yes," responded Omar, "what is this all about?"

"Sir, may we come in? We'd like to talk to you."

Omar complied. All three officials entered the tiny motel room, a dark, damp residence whose stale air discouraged hospitality. The younger deputy headed straight to the bathroom and cautiously opened the door. "It's clear."

"There is no one else here," said Omar.

The furnishings were sparse, as would be expected. Two twin beds, a TV, a single nightstand, a small table with two chairs, a refrigerator, a hot plate, and a microwave were included in the monthly charge. The room was cluttered with several boxes of clothes and a stack of newspapers, magazines, and books.

Omar cleared Rashid's bed and brought out the two chairs, offering the three men places to sit. One of the deputies took a chair and sat close to the door blocking the only avenue for entry or egress. The second deputy placed the chair at the opposite end of the room. Both deputies remained silent during the interview; their uniformed presence at 3:30 was sufficient.

Omar sat on his bed, and Dwayne sat across from him on Rashid's bed.

Looking in Dwayne's direction but failing to make eye contact, Omar said, "This is most troubling you would come to me at this hour. What is wrong?"

"Do you have a brother named Rashid?"

"Yes, of course. If you know my name, then you must know I have a brother."

"Where is he?" asked Dwayne.

"I do not know. My brother sometimes works late."

"You mean he works until 3:30 in the morning?"

Omar was confused and still not quite awake. He was visibly shaken by the presence of the three. "I am sorry. What is all this about? My brother is not here. I do not know where he is. He has been in this country several years. He has many friends. He may be with his friends. He does not tell me where he goes."

Dwayne pulled out a small notebook and continued the questioning, taking notes as Omar answered. He still had not told him Rashid was dead.

Omar explained he had been in the United States for only a few weeks and worked for World Angel Ministries. He described his work at the clinic and the classes at UCLA. From everything Dwayne knew, Omar was telling him the truth.

"Does your brother have a sweatshirt with green paint on the sleeve?"

Omar ran his fingers through his hair as he answered, "Yes. He told me he leaned up against the pillar in front of our door just after it was painted a few months ago."

Dwayne continued the questioning. He never took his eyes off Omar, who refused to make eye contact. "Omar, an individual matching a description of your brother and wearing a sweatshirt with green paint on the right sleeve, is suspected in a half-dozen bank robberies over the past two months?"

"Are you saying my brother robbed these banks?"

"That's exactly what I am saying."

Omar put his head down and shook it. He paused before answering.

"Omar, do you know anything about this?"

Still no response.

Dwayne repeated his question and added, "We know he did this. He's committed a crime. He's done something that is wrong in any country and by the rules of any religion. We have photos of him in the bank, taking the money, using a gun, walking out of the bank with the money in his hands. By doing this so openly, with so much evidence, your brother has brought shame to himself, to you, and to your family."

With that Omar raised his head. "You are right. If my brother did this, he has brought shame upon our family."

There was a long moment of silence. Dwayne had opened the door with "shame," and Omar responded.

Omar continued, "I do not know exactly what he has been doing. Sometimes he comes here with much money. But he does not keep it. He calls someone I do not know. They meet. He gives that person the money. I did not know he was robbing your banks. My brother does not like this country, and he wants to support my people back home who do not like the Western ways."

"Do you like this country?" asked Dwayne.

Omar responded with a series of questions. "What does it matter what I like? Why did you come at this hour to ask about bank robberies? What do you want?" Omar glanced at the bedside clock. "Why would you decide to question me and my brother at 3:30 in the morning?"

Dwayne did not directly respond to Omar's questions but continued to press for answers about Rashid's associates. Omar could provide few answers. Dwayne was cautious but wanted to believe in Omar's sincerity.

Again Dwayne looked him in the eye. "Omar, I came here to tell you something. I have some bad news. Tonight we found your brother dead. He had been shot. We're not sure if he committed suicide or was murdered."

Shock overcame Omar. He lowered his head and placed his face in his hands. He and his brother survived the Soviet invasion. They survived the civil war by which the Taliban assumed control. They survived the United States efforts to destroy the Taliban. Now his brother was dead.

Dwayne attempted to ask a few more questions, but Omar said nothing.

Finally Omar raised his head and looked Dwayne in the eye. With anger he asked, "Why did you wait to tell me about his death until after you asked many questions?"

Tension hung in the air. The deputies readied themselves for action, if need be.

Dwayne leaned forward and in a calm voice said, "When I came here tonight, I thought you and your brother were involved together in the bank robberies, and I wasn't sure whether you knew about his death. I don't believe that now. I am sorry for your loss, and I am sorry for the deception. I now know I was wrong."

As soon as he completed the last sentence, Dwayne questioned its wisdom. An apology might be perceived as weakness. Dwayne still maintained the upper hand in this interview and didn't want to lose the momentum. Had he been interviewing someone from the West, the apology would have been good strategy. Now it was questionable.

Dwayne continued the questioning. The responses were somewhat more hostile, but nonetheless Omar responded.

As Dwayne was about to complete the interview, he had a final request. "I would like your permission to take your brother's personal belongings, papers, notebooks, phone directories, checkbooks, any documents that might identify the killer, if, in fact, it was murder."

"In my country you would not even ask. I guess I have no choice. You may take what you wish."

"In this country you do have a choice, but if you deny us, I'll ask a judge for permission to search the entire room and take those items."

Omar nodded his head, acquiescing to Dwayne's request.

Dwayne and the deputies quickly gathered the items. Dwayne left a detailed inventory and promised to return them in a few days. He also provided information about how to claim the body and offered help in notifying relatives overseas. He left his business card and told Omar to call him if he had any questions. Dwayne hoped he had appeased Omar and neutralized the anger, but an air of distrust remained when he and the deputies left.

Chapter Thirty-Seven

Matt awoke at 5:30 a.m., threw on a pair of gym shorts, and went for a run. He was meeting Dwayne for coffee and had already told David he would have to miss the morning training session because of a prior commitment. He promised to be at the clinic by noon.

It had been three days since Rashid's body had been found, and Matt had yet to sit down with Dwayne and learn the details of the death or the specifics of the interview with Omar.

At Monday's staff meeting David announced Omar's brother's death. He said Omar was taking the next several days off to get his brother's affairs in order and then would return to his duties at the clinic.

Although Matt stopped by the motel and left a note, he had yet to speak with Omar. Ordinarily he hated taking advantage of someone during such a time, but the mission was far more important than Omar's grieving. Besides, Matt wasn't too concerned with the

Afghan's feelings. There were so many questions about the murder needing to be resolved, and if it related to terrorist activity, this might be the best time for the FBI to gain an advantage.

The morning skies were dark. The previous two days had been overcast, and the only light available was projected by a streetlamp or the headlights of an occasional car. Matt liked this quiet time. He thought more clearly during a run than while fighting traffic on the L.A. freeway system.

For Matt one of the most difficult things about working undercover was blocking the case from his mind. He awoke with thoughts of the case and went to bed with similar thoughts. His mind was constantly working as he attempted to design a scenario by which he could learn the truth of Omar's involvement. Was he a terrorist? If so, what were his plans? Rashid's death certainly added fuel to the fire of speculation. How and why would Omar ever confide in a stranger? Matt was at a loss. He was certain cultural differences would prevent Omar from quickly confiding his darkest secrets. Maybe by befriending him and spending hours in his company, Matt could discern some fact that might fit in the larger puzzle. It was a long shot. Matt needed to take advantage of Omar's loss. At this point there seemed to be no other course of action.

Matt continued his run through the city streets of Thousand Oaks. It was mostly flat, but a few rolling hills made the run challenging. When he reached the high school, he ran over to the track. Several joggers were there, running around the all-weather surface. Matt hit the track with a gallop and turned it into high gear. He ran a lap at a near full sprint, completing the quarter-mile in impressive time, at least impressive for a thirty-five-year-old ex-jock. He slowed his pace and headed home, completing five miles in a respectable time.

He slipped in the back door and walked into the kitchen, soaked in sweat from the run. Caitlin was sitting at the tiny dining room table reading her Bible while she ate breakfast. With outstretched arms he said, "Good morning, the love of my life. How about a hug for your hero?"

"Not before a shower, Cowboy," she said with a slight grin as she rose from her chair and headed for the kitchen counter.

"Well, then how about a kiss?"

"A kiss you can have. Just don't drip sweat on me."

Matt leaned over and kissed her.

"Here, I squeezed you a glass of orange juice," said Caitlin, handing him a large glass.

"I like my orange juice and women the same way . . . fresh." He swatted her on her behind and went back to the bedroom to get ready for his meeting with Dwayne.

Dr. Ubadiah al-Banna's huge smile confirmed his pleasure with Wadi's success in obtaining the Israeli consulate blueprints.

The two sat in a vinyl-covered booth inside a rundown West Hollywood coffee shop. Magazine photos of movie queens from the fifties covered the walls, and dust covered the photos. The restaurant was convenient but hardly comfortable or clean.

As al-Banna reviewed the blueprints, he said, "It is too bad about Rashid."

"I do not weep for him. He was sloppy. He had been warned yet continued his clumsy ways. It was only a matter of time before his incompetence exposed the cause."

Al-Banna returned the photos of the blueprints to the manila envelope. "I will see these are delivered to the appropriate people. This was an amazing victory. When the time is right, these will be most important. I must leave. I have many patients to see this morning. Thank you again for all you do for the cause."

"Our cause is just. It is an honor to serve."

THE JOINT TERRORISM TASK Force consisted of four squads of FBI agents supplemented with the finest agents and officers from various federal, state, and local agencies. The concept worked well. Institutional egos were set aside, and a great deal of unheralded success could be attributed to the work of the task force. By working together, dots that might not have been connected were. Convictions were obtained, but more importantly, terrorist acts had been prevented. Sometimes those acts received little or no attention because of the sensitive way in which the intelligence was developed. People with a "need to know" knew the valuable and sometimes thankless work of the JTTF.

For the past three years Pete Garcia, a veteran LAPD detective, had been assigned to the task force. Pete took his job seriously and was checking computerized crime reports filed by the various divisions throughout the city. One report was of particular interest this morning. He printed it and sought out Dwayne, who was sitting in his office.

"Got a minute?"

"Sure, Pete, what you got?"

Pete handed the report to Dwayne. "Ran across this report filed by Wilshire patrol. Possible break-in at the building that houses the Israeli Consulate. Thought you might find the description of one of the suspects interesting."

Dwayne reviewed the report, his eyes stopping at the clothing and suspect description provided by the retired patrolman. "Green paint stain on right sleeve of sweatshirt."

Pete continued, "Look at the time and date. It happened shortly before the sheriff's deputy found the body in Plummer Park."

Dwayne grinned. "Detective Garcia, on any given night how many sweatshirts in the greater Los Angeles area have a green paint stain on the right sleeve?"

Pete returned the grin. "Supervisory Special Agent Washington, my expert professional opinion is one."

"I will second that opinion. Let's take a closer look. Great work, Pete."

Matt was a few minutes early for his meeting with Dwayne. He sat inside the Brentwood café. The heavy morning fog lingered, preventing the sun and its radiant heat from breaking through. It was too chilly to sit on the patio, but the noise of the cappuccino machine was annoying. Matt debated moving the meeting to another location once Dwayne arrived, but he knew Dwayne had another meeting at eleven. Matt figured he would just tolerate the consistent racket of what the gentry thought was the quaint sound of their favorite latte being prepared. Matt picked a table near the window. As he was perusing the paper, his cell phone rang. It was Dwayne.

"So, are you standing me up again? My ego can't take this constant inattention."

"Something's come up. Can you meet Pete and me at the Israeli Consulate parking lot?"

"Sure, what's up?"

"I think we had an attempted break-in at the building that houses the consulate. Rashid may have been part of it."

"You're kidding. That's big time if Rashid's involved."

"I'm not kidding. I'll explain when you get here. I checked with immigration. It will come as no shock that Rashid overstayed his visa."

Matt let out a mock gasp. "How dare he fail to comply with our laws and penetrate our borders!"

"Did Omar ever discuss Rashid's status?"

"I never asked. Not sure I could bring it up without arousing suspicion," said Matt. "That night at the motel, did you ask about it?"

"No, didn't even think about it at the time. We didn't exactly leave on the best of terms, but I should go back to clear up a few questions. Meet us as soon as you can outside the consulate."

"I'm on my way."

Chapter Thirty-Eight

Matt drove into the parking lot of the Wilshire Boulevard office building and pulled alongside Dwayne. Pete Garcia was in the passenger seat.

"Thanks for the call," said Matt.

"You're the undercover. Your stake in this is greater than ours. Wasn't sure it was wise for you to show up, but you're a big boy. Thought I'd leave it up to you."

"I don't think I'll run into too many Islamic terrorists at the Israeli consulate, at least at this hour. I'll be okay."

The three exited their cars and headed toward the alley entrance of the building.

"By the way," said Dwayne, "I had one of the translators look at that brochure you found on Omar's desk. It's almost like a religious tract justifying a call to arms against Israel and the West. It seems rather careless he would leave it on top of his desk or even have it for that matter. A confirmed terrorist shouldn't need daily reminders of why he's fighting the Great Satan. It's an interesting piece of intel."

"Maybe our boy's strictly minor leagues and needs more practice before he gets called up to the bigs," said Matt.

"Could be; we still have a lot to learn about terrorists. It's probably naïve to expect them all to fit into the same neat little box."

As they continued walking, Pete handed Matt a copy of the crime report. He gave it a quick read.

"This doesn't tell us much; pretty generic," said Matt.

"I know. I called the guard this morning and spoke with him in more detail. Don't be too hard on the patrol unit. The Schoolyard Crips did a drive-by over in Eighteenth Street hood, and all available units were called. This just looked like a botched burglary. A drive-by 187 beats that any day."

"I understand. At least they filed the report. Some guys wouldn't have bothered with the paper. I don't suppose the crime lab responded?" asked Matt.

"No," said Pete. "There was really no need. The patrol unit spent less than fifteen minutes on this thing. The security guard had no reason to believe anything was stolen or they got farther than the basement. The only alarm activated was a door to one of the utility rooms, and that door was never opened. No one made entry otherwise; the motion detector inside the room would have been activated. The guard thinks he spooked 'em before they got down to business."

"But there's an exterior alarm?" asked Matt.

Pete nodded.

"So how'd they get in the building if it was alarmed?" asked Matt.

"According to the guard, the exterior alarm was set when he checked it earlier in the evening. The only plausible explanation is they bypassed the exterior system."

Matt ran his fingers through his hair and looked at Dwayne. "If they bypassed one alarm, they could have easily bypassed others. They may have been in there much longer than the guard calculated and just accidentally brushed up against the door. They may have already gotten down to business and were on their way out."

The three approached the exterior alley door. The metal door was worn, dented, and scratched from a variety of boxes and items moved in and out of the entrance over the years. Many of the scratches were rusted so they could easily be dismissed as being too old. Matt carefully examined the area around the perimeter sensor alarm. The sunlight reflected off the exposed metal of several tiny scratches. Matt pointed out the tiny marks to Dwayne and Pete.

"This is fresh. No discoloration. No rust. No sign of aging. My guess is they bypassed the alarm."

Dwayne turned the doorknob. Since it was a regular workday, the building was accessible from the alley, and the door was unlocked. All three entered. They walked down the well-lit hallway. Pete counted down the doors until they came to the one identified by the security guard.

"This is it."

Stenciled on the door were the words "Restricted Access." Pete opened the door to the room housing a massive electrical panel.

"This could have been their target. You could do a lot of damage from this panel under the right circumstances," said Pete.

Matt looked over the panel. "I'm not so sure. It seems to me they could inconvenience or embarrass the consulate during a political function, but turning the lights off in the middle of a heavy workday seems more like a college prank than terrorism."

Dwayne's attention was drawn elsewhere.

"Check this out," said Dwayne. "The building administrator's office is directly across the hall. Maybe one of our friends leaned up against the door as his buddies were going in or coming out of this office."

Matt carefully examined the door frame to the administrator's office. The interior door sensor had several fresh scratch marks. "Dwayne, I think you're right. It looks like they got a little sloppy. Whoever their alarm man is, was rushing to get everybody inside before they were detected. I bet he bypassed this, and they were in the office."

As Matt was examining the wiring at the base of the door frame, the door opened. Lisa Hughes, one of the building managers, walked out with a box of papers and almost tripped over Matt. Dwayne caught her before she fell.

"I'm so sorry. Are you okay?" asked Dwayne.

"Yeah, I'm fine," said Lisa, a little annoyed and embarrassed. "Can I help you?"

Dwayne pulled out his credentials and introduced Matt and Peter. "We're investigating the break-in."

"Not sure there's much to investigate. I certainly didn't think it warranted the FBI showing up," said Lisa.

"Do you mind if we ask you a few questions?"

"Not at all, but let me deliver these boxes to one of the tenants upstairs. Make yourself at home in my office. You can actually walk in, no need to crawl." Lisa was referring to Matt, who was still on his hands and knees, sheepishly looking up at the building manager.

Before she returned, Matt and Pete gave the office a "quick toss." They were both wearing surgical gloves. They spotted the file cabinets and carefully opened the drawers.

Matt pointed out the file containing the information on the consulate. It was difficult to tell if anything had been disturbed. Pete suggested they should call his crime lab and dust the place for prints. Matt agreed. Just as Pete was picking up the phone to make the call, Lisa returned.

"Now, how can I help you? I've been here about a year. You're my first FBI agents, but we get Secret Service and Israeli Intelligence fairly often, especially when governmental big shots are planning to visit the consulate."

Lisa was aware of the break-in but found nothing disturbed in her office and accepted the belief of the guard that he interrupted the intruders before they were able to accomplish their goal, "whatever that might be." No one in the building reported any problems, and it was highly unlikely the intruders made it above the lobby because the guard had been on duty for more than three hours before the alarm was activated. She cooperated fully with the investigation and allowed the men to remain in the office until the technician from the LAPD crime lab arrived.

Pete could hear the technician as she lugged her case down the hallway toward the office. Pete turned to Matt and Dwayne. "She's not going to be happy. She's going to lift a lot of latents. Make her feel important. Oh well, nobody said police work was easy."

Allison Block had been an evidence technician with the police department for three years. She had a bachelor's degree with a dual major in criminology and chemistry and was working part-time on her master's in chemistry. She enjoyed the forensic side of the house and hoped to move into the lab full-time in a year or two. She was gaining valuable experience as an evidence technician, but dusting for prints did not rank at the pinnacle of law enforcement excitement.

She extended her hand. "Pete, good to see you again. It's been awhile."

"Yeah, several months. Let me introduce you to a couple of FBI agents I work with on the task force. Allison Block, this is Supervisory Special Agent Dwayne Washington and Special Agent Matt Hogan."

They exchanged pleasantries and Dwayne explained the situation. Despite Pete's warning, Allison was enthusiastic about an opportunity to work a terrorism case and immediately began dusting the exterior door frame and the two interior doors in question. Once she completed that task, she began examining the administrative office area, a Herculean effort.

Matt pulled Dwayne aside.

"Let's narrow this down. If Rashid and his buddies made it into this room, the only thing of importance would be documents pertaining to the consulate. Do we really care if they ransacked the drawers or checked out the water cooler?" Matt pointed to the file cabinet on the left. "Lisa said that's the only place containing any information about the consulate. Let's concentrate our efforts on the second drawer where the file is located."

Dwayne thought for a second before he answered. "I understand what you're saying, but I doubt all four of the intruders spent their whole time surrounding the file cabinet. If they weren't wearing gloves, they may have touched the water cooler or the drawers and left a latent. If you need to get going, go. Pete and I can stay. I'd rather be thorough than expedient. It only takes one good latent to get a conviction."

Matt thanked Allison for her assistance and headed back to the clinic. The others remained behind, completing a game of evidence hide-and-seek.

Chapter Thirty-Nine

Matt returned to the clinic and spent most of the afternoon doing the menial chores he learned to hate—restocking supplies, rolling bandages, and his all-time favorite, painting. The outdoor storage shed, located in the far corner behind the large Jacaranda tree, needed several coats of an all-weather paint to withstand the salt air. Matt took his time completing the painting, knowing Omar was at a seminar at UCLA and Ibrahim was having dinner with friends. Matt wanted to use the early evening hours, when minimal staff walked the floors, to search Ibrahim's office. Although Matt tried several times, someone always managed to interrupt his plans before he was able to execute his surreptitious, if not illegal, examination of the contents of Ibrahim's personal belongings. Tonight he hoped to bend the Constitution again . . . just a little.

Matt finished the painting as the sun was setting. He took his time in cleaning the rollers and brushes. He then showered and put on clean clothes. His belabored actions provided enough time for the day staff and volunteers to head home for the evening. Only two nurses would be on duty for the night shift, and both would spend most of their time at the nurses' station located near the front of the clinic.

Matt kept the noise to a minimum. He didn't want to appear to be hiding if caught, but, in fact, that's exactly what he was doing.

After almost forty-five minutes, he completed the clean-up efforts. He needed to return the cleaning supplies to the large walk-in closet. Just as he was about to exit the supply closet, he heard David at the end of the hallway talking to a man with a strong Middle Eastern accent. Matt quickly ducked back into the storage room, leaving the door cracked enough to hear the conversation.

"I am very nervous about taking this much cash," said David.

"But it is for a good cause," said the man, irritated he had to force the money upon David. "I want to help you, help her, and the others."

"I understand that and I appreciate your gifts, but it is a problem to take cash."

"It is more of a problem for me to pay in any other way. Please take my cash," said the man.

Matt sensed David relented when he heard, "This is very kind. I can assure you, just as before, the money will be used for a good cause."

"Thank you for your help with the children and being receptive to our gifts. I must go now. My car is parked out back. I will leave by the side door." The man turned and headed down the hallway. As he passed the cracked door of the supply closet, Matt saw Yasir Mehsud, Humpty Dumpty as Caitlin called him, waddling toward the door leading to the alley.

David continued walking toward the front of the building and failed to see what Matt saw: Yasir slipping into the restroom.

Matt waited quietly, peering through the small opening. Yasir remained in the restroom for almost five minutes before finally exiting. But even then, his actions were deliberate and suspicious. He popped his head around the corner of the door frame, almost the sneak-and-peek technique Matt employed on numerous arrests. When it was obvious Yasir determined he was alone, he walked back toward the individual hospital rooms, rather than toward the alley exit. Matt watched Yasir enter Shahla's darkened room.

Hoping to prevent the storage room door from squeaking, Matt slowly opened it, grabbing a pillow, sheets, and a blanket as he exited the closet. Matt then padded toward Shahla's room, hoping the linens would provide sufficient cover and a reason for entering the room.

Matt knew weapons drawn and guns blazing would endanger Shahla and spell the end of the undercover operation. At the same time Yasir's suspicious actions required Shahla be protected.

Matt walked into the room, carrying the pillow and blanket on his weak side, readying his right hand to draw his weapon, concealed under his shirt on his strong side.

Yasir jumped when Matt entered the room.

"Can I help you?" whispered Matt.

Yasir turned and headed toward the door without uttering a word. Matt didn't want to confront him in Shahla's room and so let him leave. Matt's immediate concern was the girl. He raced to Shahla to determine whether she had been hurt. He heard the door leading to the alley close. Shahla stirred and looked up at Matt. When she smiled, Matt knew she was okay. He returned the smile, patted her head, and mouthed, "Go back to sleep," even though she didn't understand the words. She rolled over and fell back asleep. Matt rushed out of the room and headed toward the door.

Once outside Matt looked in both directions of the darkened alley. He saw nothing, but then the headlights of a car coming eastbound illuminated Yasir as he stood flat against the wall in an unsuccessful attempt to conceal himself. His corpulent stomach protruded beyond the shadows. The car passed, turning left at the street. Matt walked deliberately toward Yasir's position. As Matt closed, Yasir stepped from the wall and wheeled toward Matt. Even in the faint light, Matt saw the reflection of a gun in the man's right hand.

The loud noises of the traffic on Wilshire Boulevard drowned out the sound of the single gunshot fired from Yasir's weapon, but the muzzle flash momentarily lit up the alley. The bullet missed. Matt's training proved more valuable. He reacted with lightning speed—double-tap—two shots center mass. The rounds entered midchest, striking the heart. The first round was probably the fatal blow, but the second insured Yasir's expeditious trip to whatever afterlife terrorists enjoyed. Yasir dropped immediately.

FBI agents believed in General Patton's creed; battles fought decisively with brute force save lives, maybe this time Matt's.

Matt rushed to the site where the rotund corpse lay in a puddle of his own blood. Matt grabbed the 9mm mini-Glock that fell from Yasir's grip. Holstering his own weapon, Matt cleared the Glock and stuck it inside his belt before placing his middle and index fingers over Yasir's carotid artery. There was no pulse. He was dead, and no amount of medical attention would bring back the life of this obese terrorist.

Matt looked around. The dark alley was empty. The incident brought no curious onlookers. Matt squatted next to the body trying to gather his senses, now upset he reacted the way he was trained. Yasir's actions and Matt's reactions not only cost Yasir his life but placed the entire undercover operation in jeopardy. Matt thought for a few seconds before grabbing his cell phone and punching in Dwayne's number.

As expected Dwayne was livid when he heard the news. Matt had to hold his cell phone away from his ear as Dwayne spewed his anger.

"What'd you want me to do, let him keep firing? He wheeled on me, Dwayne. He had a gun," said Matt, remaining calm.

"Where are you now?"

"I got out of Dodge. I cleared out of the alley before anyone came. I'm down the street."

"Where's the body?"

"Still in the alley, I guess. He's not going anywhere under his own power."

"Did you call 911?"

"I called you. This just happened."

"The Queen Mother's gonna shut us down. This thing is over," said Dwayne.

"Don't panic just yet. Let's call the Boss. Tell him what happened. Figure out who this guy is. I'm telling you, Dwayne, he's a player. He's tied to terrorism in some way. He was at the market. Zerak knows him. He sells counterfeit cigarettes. He has some type of relationship with Shahla, and he's paying this charity in cash for some unknown reason. He's no good, and before we close up shop, we need to make sure we have him fully identified. As of right now my cover is still intact. Let's play this thing out."

"Maybe you make sense."

"Dwayne, please trust my instincts. Call Pete Garcia. Have him work with the Santa Monica PD. It was a righteous shoot. We'll cooperate fully. We just don't need all the facts to come out now. This will give you a reason to interview David and find out what the relationship is with Humpty Dumpty and the clinic."

"Okay, I'll make the calls. Then I might just go get drunk. Maybe the Queen Mother was right to fear your cowboy antics. You do make a supervisor question why he ever went the administrative route."

For the first time in several hours, Matt smiled.

Chapter Forty

The church bells from the chapel rang out at 8:00 a.m., just as they did every morning. The tiny Catholic chapel, located off Santa Monica Boulevard about three miles from the ocean, was open to the public from 6:00 a.m. until 10:00 p.m.

Although the parish priest welcomed everyone, he occasionally had to police the sanctuary to prevent the homeless from taking adverse possession of the pews. It was not unusual to see an empty grocery cart parked on the walkway just outside the door with its homeless owner inside the chapel stretched out asleep on one of the wooden pews, trash bags of empty cans, bottles, and newspapers at his feet.

This morning the chapel was empty. The sunlight reflected through the stained-glass windows, depicting the Stations of the Cross surrounding the chapel. A large wooden crucifix hung from the ceiling just above the altar. Somehow, no matter where you sat in the chapel, Christ appeared to be looking directly at you. At twilight it was both awesome and eerie.

Wadi walked in, crossed himself, and took a seat in a pew toward the back. The cover was perfect. Muslim terrorists are not known to frequent Catholic churches. Wadi made one mistake, the same mistake he made every day he entered the chapel.

Today, as was usual, he went in unobserved. Wadi learned the technique of crossing himself watching American TV. He watched Karl Malden one too many times in *On the Waterfront*. Wadi practiced crossing himself in the mirror, and now every time he entered the chapel, he crossed himself backward. It certainly was a habit no Muslim would notice but would quickly catch the attention of anyone familiar with the religious practice.

Wadi sat there quietly for a few minutes and enjoyed the serenity. He liked the little chapel for its beauty and its peace. He was familiar with Jesus, as were all Muslims. Jesus is one of more than twenty prophets discussed in the Koran and is believed to be one of the most significant along with Adam, Noah, Abraham, Moses, and, of course, Mohammed, the last prophet.

Wadi studied each window, and every time he looked at the cross, he felt the eyes of Jesus peering at him.

Ismad walked into the chapel and shook his head in disgust. He saw Wadi and walked toward him. Before Ismad could say anything, Wadi instructed him in a whisper to sit down and look straight ahead toward the cross. This time Wadi was determined to take control.

"I must leave soon for a meeting," said Ismad.

"This will not take long."

"I understand the cause lost another soldier last night," said Ismad.

"It does not affect your assignment."

"Everything has the potential to impact my mission."

"Yasir is my problem. I will handle it."

"Let us hope you handle it better than I have seen you manage the other incidents since my arrival in this country."

Wadi ignored the criticism. "Do you have the date and the place?"

"Yes."

"Have you worked with this material before?" asked Wadi.

"Of course, I trained at Khalden and Mes Aynak. Where did you take your training? The Sudan with the al-amal?"

Wadi laughed out loud. It was a cold, deadly laugh. Then he said brusquely, "When it is time, contact the name on this business card."

Ismad looked at the card. It read, "Ubadiah Adel al-Banna, MD."

Wadi continued to look straight ahead as he said, "Use a pay phone when you call. Set up an appointment under this name."

Wadi handed Ismad a driver's license and insurance card. Ismad took the items, read the name, and placed the identification papers in his pocket.

Wadi continued, "No one in his office knows he is with the cause. He is a dedicated longtime member of the movement. I objected to his direct involvement in this action, but he insisted. He is proud to serve the cause and looks forward to meeting you. At the meeting he will give you further instructions and will assist you in completing your assignment. We can bring America to its knees."

Wadi leaned closer to Ismad and whispered, "Allah will be pleased."

Ismad prepared to leave and rose from his seat. With contempt he said, "Do you worship here?" He walked away, not waiting for a response.

David opened the staff meeting with prayer.

"Dear Heavenly Father, we thank you for another day, a day to worship you and to serve you. Soften the hearts of those we touch. Allow us to be your light in a world so filled with darkness. Amen."

Matt loved David's prayers; they were always short, and they seemed sincere, but how sincere was a man who played host to terrorists and took their money? Before Matt's undercover assignment could even answer the most elementary questions, more questions arose. Was David, a Christian, imbedded with radical Muslim terrorists? Was World Angel, in fact, a front for Islamic fascism?

Last night's shooting was not Matt's first, and it was not the first time he killed a man. That did not make this incident any easier, but he learned to deal with the psychological trauma of discharging a weapon in the heat of combat. The Bureau had a well-planned protocol for dealing with such matters, but the nature of the undercover operation required him to remain in character. He had little time for the counseling typically required. He and Caitlin spent the early morning hours discussing the situation, easing much of the anxiety. She was his rock and his tether, a role he cherished and appreciated even more each time he faced the turmoil the world threw at him.

Matt looked around the conference room table and marveled at the dedication of those at the session. All were educated and skilled. They could be successful in the world, at least from a financial standpoint, but chose instead to serve God, often for less than minimum wage. He was thankful he had a great job that paid reasonably well and could still bring the personal satisfaction of knowing he was making the world a better and safer place in which to live. He was not, however, ready to make the financial sacrifice those around the table were making.

Matt sat across from Omar, who was drinking his usual early morning Coke. If he had a vice, and Matt saw none, it was Coca Cola. Omar went through at least a six-pack every day. After weeks of working with him on a daily basis, at least for an hour or so each day, Matt saw nothing identifying him as a terrorist or anything clearing him of being one either. They shared lunches and Cokes. They talked at length about life in Afghanistan. Matt engaged him in some political discussions, but Omar never said anything sounding a warning bell. Sure he was opinionated, but so was Ibrahim. So was Caitlin for that matter. "Opinionated" doesn't make you the target of an FBI investigation.

Matt's mind wandered, and he realized he missed the announcements for the day. David said something about a fund-raising banquet. Matt made a mental note to check on the particulars. Matt also realized Ibrahim was absent. *Good, at least he can't close us with prayer.* But just as he began to question why Ibrahim was missing, the door to the conference room opened, and Ibrahim quietly slipped in the back of the room. *Nuts, please don't ask him to pray.* Kim, the receptionist, followed closely behind with a fresh pot of coffee and a smile on her face. Matt and Ibrahim acknowledged each other with a nod.

The morning sun reflected off the walls of the conference room, creating an almost halo-like effect over David's head as he stood at the front of the room. If angels did walk the earth, David might be one, unless he was aiding and abetting terrorism, a question still begging an answer.

David devoted the morning session to discussing witnessing opportunities to Muslims. Matt started to tune out, hearing something about "the painful memories of the Crusades." Matt looked engaged, but he really wasn't interested in a history lesson. Then he heard, "We must not ignore history and if we are to succeed in bringing the gospel, we must be sensitive."

Matt smiled at the thought of being sensitive. He remembered the "camel jockey" comment to Karim that night at the restaurant, and he recently shot Humpty Dumpty. Sensitivity, as Caitlin would attest, was not his strongest quality.

Matt glanced around the room. Everyone seemed to be listening except Omar, who was staring out the window with apparent indifference to what was being said.

"Although our understanding may be vastly different on the various issues, Christianity and Islam have a great deal of common themes. The recognition of prophets, the belief that the Torah and the Gospels are holy books, a belief in angels and demons, a judgment day—all of these provide topics of discussion. Muslims genuinely want to please Allah. Their five pillars of faith are all done to seek favor with God. This dedication should be acknowledged and praised. We, as Christians, would do well to adopt the same dedication many of the Muslim faith demonstrate.

"Islam is a religion of rules. Christianity is a religion of relationship, a relationship with Jesus Christ who overcame death. In simple terms your mission is clear. You must help your Muslim friend understand the need for a savior, for *the* Savior."

Chapter Forty-One

As Dwayne stood at the window in the FBI conference room, he saw the news vans pulling into the parking lot of the Federal Building on Wilshire Boulevard. Each of the major networks and the local independent stations in Los Angeles were represented. Cameramen trudged into the building lugging their equipment to the elevator and up to the eleventh floor where the press conference was being held.

Standing along the back wall, Dwayne watched reporters jockeying for a position near the front. Dwayne spent almost an hour on the phone the night before talking with Jason Barnes, who was out of town, attending a conference at headquarters. Barnes was supportive of Matt's plan, and the trade-off was Pamela Clinton would have an opportunity to grab her fifteen minutes of fame in front of the cameras. She agreed to participate in the journalistic charade as long as she could conduct the press conference.

She was punctual, entering the room at the precise time the media office scheduled the conference. Her long, slender figure was accented by the striped, charcoal pantsuit she wore. Her brunette, shoulder-length hair was perfectly styled, not a hair out of place. The media moguls at headquarters would be pleased at her professional appearance. She marched directly to the podium, where she stood, flanked on either side by the flag, and centered in front of the large FBI seal hanging on the wall. *A real Kodak moment,* thought Dwayne. She looked comfortable in front of the cameras, scanning the audience, and taking a breath before beginning.

"Ladies and gentlemen, I am Pamela Clinton, the Acting Special Agent in Charge of the Terrorism Section of the Los Angeles Field Office of the FBI. We are announcing today that last evening the body of Yasir Ali Mehsud was discovered shot in an alley off Wilshire Boulevard in Santa Monica. We have confirmed with the CIA that Yasir was the brother of former al-Qaeda leader Haji Mohammed Mehsud. The latter, along with members of his family, was killed in August of this year in Afghanistan. Members of the Joint Terrorism Task Force are working closely with the Santa Monica Police Department investigating the homicide."

To Dwayne's surprise she handled the press with aplomb. Clinton opened the press conference to questions and managed to say a lot without saying anything, carefully crafting her answers to reveal absolutely nothing. Even though she had few skills to investigate cases or handle the rigors of the street, she manipulated the press masterfully.

Dwayne slipped out the back door.

Boris Gregorian labored at the workbench, tinkering with the soda-can-sized canister as Dr. U watched.

Boris laughed at the question. "The suitcase nuclear bombs of my country that are still supposed to exist are more of what the Americans might call an urban legend. They each consisted of three canisters filled with uranium or plutonium, depending on availability.

But they had a life span of maybe three years. Any that would still exist are nothing more than radioactive scrap metal. They were just too difficult to maintain. I wish I could get my hands on one. I read once where the Chechen Mafia sold bin Laden twenty such devices for $30 million. What is the old saying, 'A fool and his money are soon parted'? Who would ever trust the Chechens?"

"So you don't think he has them?" asked Dr. U.

"If bin Laden has them, why hasn't he detonated one, and why are you seeking my assistance?"

Dr. U frowned, disappointed Boris couldn't deliver a real nuclear bomb sending an unforgettable message to the Americans.

Boris took a sip of beer. "It takes more than a suitcase of explosives to do the job you are asking."

"How large?"

"I could fill a fifty-five-gallon drum with ammonium nitrate and fuel oil, and that would serve your purpose." Boris laughed.

"That would not be practical."

"My device will serve your purpose."

"When can you deliver?" asked Dr. U.

"As soon as the caesium-137 is delivered, I will be ready. Give it a few more days. My people are reliable, but it is still a matter of getting the material to me," said Boris. "You realize the initial blast will cause the most damage. The airborne radioactive contaminants spread by the explosion will only cover a few blocks but will eventually inflict sickness and possibly death."

Dr. U smiled and nodded, acknowledging he understood this attack would not have the impact of a true nuclear device. "Our goal is to create chaos as the infidels deal with our newest attack vehicle. I want to watch the panic in the streets as they scramble to determine who and where our next target will be. The clean-up costs alone will seriously impact their economy, and what new bureaucracies will they create to deal with the new round of potential attacks? We shall devastate the morale and the will of a weak people. America is not safe. Her leaders are not safe. We can destroy this country just as we will destroy the Zionist movement."

Boris loved a zealot. They were so gullible.

"Will it be safe for my man to handle?" asked Dr. U.

"Of course. This container prevents any contamination until the actual explosion. Then it will be dispersed."

Boris held up what appeared to be a small cell phone. "This device will activate the timer."

"How far will that be operable?"

"This will work within a few hundred feet."

"Is that far enough? We are not asking him to martyr himself," said Dr. U.

"As long as he doesn't stand around and count the radioactive snowflakes falling around him, America will not be his final battle. But when he pushes this button, he should run like there's no tomorrow, or there will be no tomorrow for him. History will be written either way." Boris let out a huge belly laugh. "Not to worry. I will set the timer so he will have lots of time to escape. I, too, want you to succeed."

Dwayne was at the outdoor café awaiting Matt. Several elderly couples were seated at the tables, but there was plenty of room for Matt and Dwayne to discuss their business without curious observers overhearing. There was a slight fall chill in the air, but the bright sunshine made for a perfect autumn afternoon. Dwayne had a stack of Bureau mail for Matt and needed him to initial several reports. Matt pulled up a few minutes late and quickly ordered coffee as he sat down.

"Sorry. I was helping Omar with one of the kids and just couldn't get away."

"That's okay. How are you doing?"

"I'm fine."

"You sure? Take a few days off if you need it. The trauma of a shooting isn't the easiest thing to shake."

"Really, I'm fine. I've been through this before. It's never easy. But I know I had no other choice. I did what I was trained to do. If I need some time, I'll take it, but I'm handling it."

"Is Caitlin okay?"

"Yeah, she has her faith."

"You're lucky to have her. Just let me know if you need some time off. We can arrange something."

"Thanks, I really appreciate it. How'd the press conference go?"

"I left early to be on time here, but I didn't miss much. I have to admit, though, she handled herself like a pro."

"You mean like a Quantico-trained management marionette."

"You really do have issues. Maybe we need to up your medication. On your next psychiatric evaluation I'll recommend that to the shrink. At least when she's in front of the press, she's not calling me every ten minutes asking for an update on the investigation. Every time one of the eight people at headquarters who has a piece of this case calls, she immediately calls me for the latest. I want to say, 'Give it a rest, lady. Nothing's changed since your last call, ten minutes ago. Don't call us; we'll call you.' I want to say that, but then I think I'd like to go somewhere in this organization, so I bite my tongue and take a breath."

Matt grinned. "Sure hope I can join the management team someday. The thrill of filling out surveys, answering inane questions from the Bureau, and being tethered to a desk all day just gives me goose bumps."

"There are some advantages."

"I'll stick to the streets. Besides, I wouldn't want to have to supervise someone like me."

"We confirmed that Yasir was the brother of Haji, and apparently Shahla is the daughter that survived the blast."

"That is amazing. The bold move is often the right move. I guess my shoot-first-ask-questions-later investigative technique paid off."

Dwayne shook his head. "Don't even joke about that. I'm serious. I know it was a good shoot, but if the wrong people hear a comment like that, it could cause tremendous problems."

"So how is the clinic involved? Is this all linked to the terrorist plot NSA and the CIA keep reporting?"

"I'm not sure we have an answer. I'm taking a run at David this afternoon. I'll let you know how that goes."

"Any overhears on the shooting?"

"I haven't heard from NSA or the Agency. We're bound to pick up something. Analysts at the NCTC—"

"The what?" interrupted Matt.

"The National Counterterrorism Center at Tyson's Corner. Their analysts are privy to every piece of intelligence being gathered on this matter and are briefing the White House on the alleged attack."

"Alleged? You don't think something's brewing?"

"In the words of management, I can neither confirm nor deny. We're still no closer than we were when we started in terms of a specific incident. But if Rashid and Omar are involved, their visits to Disneyland and the Staples Center make sense. HQ—and of course, now that headquarters rendered an opinion, the Queen Mother is onboard—are convinced those would be the high value targets the terrorists would seek."

"A packed house at a Lakers or Clippers game or a holiday weekend at Disneyland would exceed the World Trade Center numbers. I wish I knew how to get us the information we need. What'd you get at the Israeli Consulate building?" asked Matt.

"We lifted over thirty-five good latents from the office building. Obviously, there were lots of partials and smudges, but thirty-five is a sizable number. The real task was in the comparisons. We printed the office staff and quickly eliminated them. The coroner gave us a set of Rashid's prints. We found his prints all over the consulate file and the building maintenance file containing the electrical, plumbing, heating, and air-conditioning blueprints."

"So we can assume the other side has the floor plans."

"It sure looks that way," said Dwayne.

"Would you consider that a high-value target?"

"Not really. An embassy yes, but a consulate? I really don't think so."

"So why steal the plans?"

"I'm guessing to build an intelligence base in case they ever need it. But that's just speculation on my part."

"Did you identify any other latents?" asked Matt.

"No, that's just it. Rashid was the only unknown we identified. We could account for every other print."

"That seems odd. We know from the guard there were four intruders, yet Rashid is the only one who left prints."

Dwayne took another sip of his coffee. "I'm wondering if Rashid was sloppy and didn't wear gloves, but the rest did. The evidence tech did a great job. She pointed out several spots where a talcum-like powder residue was left on the carpet. Could have been from surgical gloves worn by the others."

Dwayne handed Matt his mail and then pulled from his briefcase the initial crime reports and surveillance photos of the bank robberies in which Rashid was a suspect.

"Thought you might want to look at these. We obviously aren't going to prosecute a dead man, but we've linked Rashid to eight bank robberies based upon the M.O., description of the robber, location of the banks, and the time frame of the robberies."

Matt set the mail aside and began to review the reports and photos. Each report described the robber as of dark or olive complexion, wearing a hooded gray sweatshirt. At least five of the reports identified the green paint on the right sleeve. Some witnesses described the suspect as Hispanic or Middle Eastern and listed his height as five-six to five-eight with a slight to medium build. Matt reviewed the complete set of reports and then perused them a second time.

"How carefully did you read these?" asked Matt as he took a drink of his coffee.

"I just skimmed them. We have our subject, and he won't be robbing anyone else. I'm tethered to a desk and have surveys to complete, remember?"

"Did you notice the victim tellers?"

"Not particularly."

"Of the eight reports, six of the victim tellers have Middle Eastern names. I've never worked banks and realize L.A. is the ethnic diversity capital of the world, but six out of eight victim tellers, all from the Middle East, seem like more than a coincidence."

Dwayne took the reports and reviewed the victim teller information. "You're right. I'm surprised the bank robbery coordinator didn't pick up on that. When I get back to the office, I'll pull the files and review the statements from each of the tellers. It could be a coincidence, but I seriously doubt it. Good job."

"And check this out. Look at these photos."

Dwayne looked at each of the photos. "Doesn't show much. The hood is always pulled up. You can't see his face."

"No you can't, but in every photo his left hand is in the sweatshirt pocket. The right hand is holding the money."

"So."

"As I recall in the crime scene photos at the park, Rashid was holding the automatic in his right hand. I'm betting the reason he has his left hand in the pocket in the bank robbery surveillance photos is because he's holding the gun with his left hand. He's left-handed, not right."

"Maybe we don't want to hide you behind a desk. That makes sense. Now how do we find out if Rashid was left-handed?" said Dwayne.

"Hey, I came up with the theory. You come up with the facts to match it."

Dwayne rose from the table, leaving the bill for Matt. "I have to get back to a meeting with the Queen Mother."

Matt held up the check and waved it at Dwayne as he was walking away. "Thanks."

Chapter Forty-Two

Matt's cell phone rang as he was driving back to the clinic.

"This is Matt."

"Matt, it's Steve Barnett. Just picked up an overhear that may be of interest."

"Shoot."

"That may be a poor choice of words coming from you. You doing okay?"

"Yeah, thanks for asking. So what you got?"

"Zerak just got off the phone with his wife. He saw the press conference the Queen Mother held. He said he had no idea Yasir was Haji's brother and had he known this had any link to al-Qaeda he would have never gone into business with him."

"Thanks, Steve."

"That should ease some of the concerns you and your wife have with the father."

"Yeah, that helps a lot. Thanks."

Once the sun set, the temperature dropped significantly. Tonight it was in the upper forties. At noon it was seventy-eight degrees. Dwayne and Matt pulled in front of a twelve-unit apartment complex in Culver City.

"You sure you haven't seen him?" said Dwayne as Matt was reviewing a driver's license photo.

"Dwayne, I'm sure. I've met three guys from the Middle East: Omar, Ibrahim, and Dr. U. I'd remember this guy if he showed up at the clinic."

"I just don't want to take any chances."

"We aren't. Look, you're short of man power; and for all we know, my charade at the clinic may be one big exercise in futility. If this guy's a player, I'll deal with it when the situation arises. I'll do a Humpty Dumpty on him. It worked the last time."

"Don't go there, Matt."

The two exited the car.

They were preparing to interview Abu Sayyid al-Doori, the victim teller of a recent bank robbery.

Dwayne pulled all eight victim teller interviews and had an analyst complete background checks on each. Six of the eight tellers were Middle Eastern immigrants, two males and four females. A seventh was female and married to an Australian. She was using her married name but was born in Syria. The eighth victim teller, a female, was a graduate student at UCLA and had no known Middle Eastern connections.

Al-Doori was born in Egypt and came to the United States as a student in 1999. He was a permanent resident and had applied for citizenship, which could happen as early as next spring.

This was one of eight reinterviews that teams of JTTF agents would conduct this evening.

Dwayne exercised supervisory privilege and picked one of the two male tellers: al-Doori. Dwayne spoke to the agent who interviewed the Egyptian. The agent recalled al-Doori was shaken, as were many tellers by such a traumatic experience; being face-to-face with a bank robber is pleasant for no one. But the agent remembered one witness thought the robber lingered in the line until al-Doori's teller window was available.

The apartment complex had a security gate; and just as Matt and Dwayne approached, one of the tenants, a female who looked to be in her early thirties, exited. Dwayne smiled and held the door as the tenant was leaving. Both casually walked in.

"That was easy. Some security," said Matt. "We both have guns, and you look like you belong on a wanted poster."

"Thanks. Act like you know what you're doing, and you can get away with almost anything."

"That's how I've managed to fool the Bureau for these many years," said Matt.

"Yeah, but in your case, we have to continue to employ you. If we loosed you on society, it might upset the delicate balance of good versus evil."

They continued walking until they came to unit nine. The lights were on, and Matt could hear the television. Dwayne knocked on the door. Someone came to the window and peeked out. Dwayne held up his badge and credentials to the window. Within a few seconds, the door opened, but the security chain was still attached.

"Yes, can I help you?"

"Mr. Abu al-Doori?" said Dwayne.

"Who are you?"

"Sir, we're with the FBI. If you are Abu al-Doori, we'd like to talk with you."

"I am Abu. What is this about?"

"About the bank robbery."

Al-Doori hesitated. "It is late. Could we do this at the bank tomorrow?"

"Sir, it shouldn't take long. We just have a few follow-up questions we need you to answer. We'd like to do it tonight if at all possible."

When al-Doori cracked open the door, Matt realized he was watching Al-Jazeera television. The door closed. It took a little longer than Matt thought was necessary to unlatch the chain and open the door. Just as Matt began to knock again, the door opened.

Matt and Dwayne entered the room and displayed their credentials identifying them as FBI agents. They took a seat on the couch. Abu offered them something to drink, but both declined. Al-Doori's roommate was taking a night class so they were alone in the two-bedroom apartment.

Dwayne began by asking detailed background questions about al-Doori, including his family history, marital status, and the circumstances behind his coming to the United States.

The TV was still on, and al-Doori watched that rather than look the agents in the eye.

Al-Doori said his family remained in Egypt, as did his fiancée. Once he obtained his citizenship, he planned on returning to Egypt, marrying his fiancé, and returning with her to the U.S.

Dwayne then carefully reviewed al-Doori's previous statement and confirmed its accuracy. When Dwayne asked if al-Doori had anything to add, al-Doori responded by saying, "What is this all about? I thought the robber was killed? It was in the papers."

"You're correct. The robber was killed, but we are doing some follow-up investigation," said Dwayne.

Matt began to get impatient with the speed at which the interview was proceeding. He grabbed the remote and turned off the TV. "You can watch *CSI: Baghdad* some other time. We're with the Joint Terrorism Task Force. We aren't with the bank robbery squad."

With a sweeping motion of his arm, Matt cleared the coffee table of several magazines, knocking them to the floor. He spread before al-Doori surveillance photos of Rashid, several crime scene photos from Plummer Park, and an autopsy photo.

"Look at these photos. Is this the man who robbed you?"

"Yes."

"Prior to that day, had you ever seen this man?"

Al-Doori shook his head, looking at all the photos a second time, stopping at the crime scene photos. "Never."

"Are you sure?"

"Yes, I'm sure. The only time I ever saw this man was when he came into my bank that day."

"We have evidence to the contrary."

Dwayne maintained his eye contact with al-Doori but was unaware of any contrary evidence.

"I don't know what you mean?" said al-Doori.

Matt picked up the most gruesome crime scene photo, a color photo of Rashid's head, turned to the side, lying in a pool of blood. "This man worked for a terrorist organization. We have evidence you are associated with that organization."

"That is not true."

Matt raised his voice, ever so slightly, "But it is, Abu, and unless you decide to cooperate tonight, not tomorrow at the bank, not next week in jail, not from Egypt where I will see you're returned after you complete your prison sentence, you better tell us all you know about Rashid. No half stepping, my friend. It's a felony to lie to an FBI agent, and you're lying when you say you don't know him."

"I am not lying. I do not know him."

Matt never wavered and leaned in closer. "You know of him. You know of the organization. You knew about the bank robbery in advance."

Al-Doori said nothing.

Matt continued, "My next phone call is to the United States Attorney's office and then Immigration. I'll see to it they begin processing you immediately. This country does not harbor terrorists or those who support terrorism. You supported terrorism. We know it and you know it."

Matt paused, waiting for a response. He was beginning to think the strategy was failing.

Al-Doori said nothing.

Matt leaned in closer and raised his voice slightly. "After you complete the jail sentence and the deportation procedures, you can spend the rest of your life in Egypt. You will not be welcome here, and neither will your wife or your children. Do you understand what I'm saying?"

Al-Doori looked down at the photos again. "You don't understand. I had to."

"Had to what?" asked Matt.

"I had to cooperate with them."

"We know that. Tell us about it." Matt was bluffing but the bluff worked. He had no idea what al-Doori was about to say.

"I want to be a citizen. I want to live in the United States. I want my fiancée to join me, and I want my children to be born here. I am grateful for the opportunities this country has to offer."

Matt interrupted, "You have a strange way of expressing your gratitude."

Al-Doori hung his head but continued, "Several weeks ago a man came to my apartment. He knew about my family and about my fiancée. He knew where they lived and showed me photos of the house where my fiancée's family lives. I had never seen this man before, and I have not seen him since. He knew I worked at the bank. He told me he needed my help for the cause and, if I cooperated, nothing would happen to my family in Egypt."

Al-Doori choked back tears, but the emotional response didn't move Matt, who glared at the Egyptian.

Al-Doori continued, "He said I would receive a phone call one night and, the next day when a man came into the bank to rob it, I was to give him all the money I had. He said he would only ask once. If I refused, someone would die. If I agreed, no one would ever contact me again. If I went to the police, he would know, and everyone in my family would die. He told me the bank was insured by the government, and it was that same government, the government of the United States, that had been responsible for all the problems in the Middle East. He said the West must pay for defiling the land of Allah."

Al-Doori picked up a photo of Rashid. "I knew when I saw this man in my bank he was sent for the cause. I did not want to give him all the money in my drawer, but I had no other choice. I was afraid. I was afraid for my family. I have not heard from anyone since that day. When I saw on the news this man had been killed, I was even more frightened. I have told no one about this. Not my roommate, no one in my family, not my fiancé."

Both Matt and Dwayne believed al-Doori. His explanation made sense and he seemed sincere. Although al-Doori was guilty of conspiracy, his defense of duress would probably prevail. There was no sense seeking an arrest warrant that evening. They had the information they wanted.

Matt concluded with a few final questions and al-Doori's assurance he would tell no one of the visit until he heard again from the FBI. Al-Doori was all too happy to cooperate.

The bank robberies were part of a scheme to support terrorism. To prevent future robberies would require a strategy not ready to be employed that evening. The tentacles of terrorism were spreading beyond the rumored attack on an unknown date.

Chapter Forty-Three

Matt was uncertain how he was going to handle the Thanksgiving holiday. Caitlin's mom loved to entertain, and the holidays were her chance to shine. Matt called her "a regular Martha Stewart without the felony conviction." She usually prepared a feast for Thanksgiving with enough food to feed a platoon of Marines. She would be disappointed if he were a no-show. Matt would be expected to join Caitlin's family for the celebration, but he felt an obligation to the children at the clinic. He couldn't tell Caitlin's parents about the undercover assignment, but when he said he had to work a four-to-midnight shift, Caitlin's mom accommodated his work schedule by moving the meal to noon.

Omar said he was driving to San Diego for Thursday and Friday and would be returning Saturday afternoon. When David invited the out-of-town staffers to his house for Thanksgiving and Ibrahim accepted, Matt invited Caitlin to help him host a Thanksgiving dinner at the clinic for the children.

Matt alerted the surveillance team, who were less than thrilled they would be spending Thanksgiving on the road. San Diego has a sizable Middle Eastern community and was a temporary home to some of the 9/11 hijackers. The FBI could not take any chances a significant meeting might occur on a holiday. In fact, it made perfect sense. Matt often joked, "Crime takes no holiday," so why should terrorism be any different. The 24-7 surveillance of Omar would continue.

Since Matt had an undercover budget, he decided to spend part of it treating the children to a traditional Thanksgiving, turkey with all the fixings. He wasn't sure how he could justify the expenditure to the Bureau accountants, but a little creative writing would do the trick. He could justify the costs because it helped "maintain his cover" and "enhanced his credibility with the target." The bean counters bought that argument before so he would attempt it again.

Every room at the clinic was occupied. Sixteen children had been brought to the United States for medical treatment. Most were severely burned, but several like Shahla were amputees. David arranged to get the necessary plastic surgery for the burn victims, not only for cosmetic reasons to treat the horrible scars but also to provide new skin allowing the body to function as normally as possible. Matt's heart ached each time he saw these young people who suffered so terribly through no fault of their own.

Matt hired a local caterer to prepare the meal—turkey, mashed potatoes, stuffing, green beans, and a strawberry fruit salad. Caitlin baked pumpkin pies for the event.

It was Caitlin's first visit to the clinic. He proudly showed off the facility but conspicuously avoided pointing out any rooms he painted. To do otherwise might remind her of the painting she had been nagging him to do for the past six months.

A minimal staff was on hand for the evening.

Caitlin and Matt brought the children into the cafeteria and filled each of their plates. Caitlin led the group in prayer. Since only two of the children spoke English, few may have appreciated her heartfelt thanks not only for the food but also for each of the children.

Like Matt, Caitlin's heart broke as she saw the pain and suffering reflected in the faces of each child. Most managed a weak smile, but more often than not the children had vacant, faraway looks in their eyes. Caitlin hovered over the children like a mother hen, giving hugs and extra helpings of any food they desired. She was particularly pleased the pumpkin pie was so well received. It was a treat few ever experienced, and each giggled as she topped off the dessert with Reddi-wip. Of course, Matt, being the child who refused to grow up, delighted each child by directly squirting whipped cream into opened mouths. Even a language barrier couldn't prevent the satisfaction of the sweet delicacy.

Matt's joy, however, abruptly halted when he received a call on his cell phone from the SOG team leader. Omar had not gone to San Diego. He was exiting his car and walking up the entrance to the clinic. It was too late to hustle Caitlin out of the clinic, but he warned her of the unexpected visitor just as Omar entered the room.

"Omar, I thought you were going to San Diego for a couple of days?"

"Yes, I planned to go, but I slept late this morning; and by the time I got up, it seemed as though I wasted the day, so I decided to stay here. I had no one in particular to see there and thought I would just come here and spend time with the children."

Matt stumbled with a response. "That's too bad. San Diego is a beautiful city. I'm sure you would have enjoyed seeing it."

"Maybe some other day I will go," said Omar, who was looking at Caitlin. "Is this your wife?"

"Yes."

Matt introduced them, and Omar immediately asked about Jaana, remembering the telephone conversation he overheard when Jaana was originally hospitalized.

Caitlin was struck by his apparent sincere concern for Jaana's well-being and his offer to help in any way he could. He proudly told Caitlin he was in the bone marrow donor program and was looking forward to the day when he could help someone who needed a transplant.

Following dessert, the three returned the children to their rooms and cleaned up the cafeteria. Caitlin and Omar spoke for quite some time, often outside of Matt's hearing. Caitlin carefully watched her responses but generally seemed to enjoy the conversation. Omar was more talkative than usual, which aroused Matt's suspicion.

The evening ended and they said their good-byes.

As Matt and Caitlin were walking to their car, Caitlin said, "I don't know what to make of him. He seems sincere, but then I don't know how a terrorist is supposed to act. I'm still trying to figure out Jaana's father."

"My point exactly."

"At first I was nervous, but he put me at ease rather quickly. I guess my first UC assignment, smuggling a kitten into the hospital, better prepared me for tonight's adventure."

"I'm really sorry to have put you through this. I certainly didn't expect him to show up. I didn't even think to call the surveillance team to confirm whether he went out of town. They wouldn't have called except they saw my car parked in the driveway in front of the clinic when Omar pulled up."

"I survived. It was actually exciting. I don't want to do it full time, but I am beginning to understand the rush."

"What did he say when I was in the kitchen cleaning up?"

"He talked mostly about his work here and in Afghanistan, but he also asked about you in a roundabout manner."

"How so?"

Caitlin had trouble expressing her thoughts. "It's hard to explain. I don't know if he was probing or just trying to make conversation. He mentioned the trust fund and how nice it is you don't have to work for a living. I had no trouble agreeing with him there. I still can't get over the fact you get paid to play cops and robbers, something you did for free as a child."

"Get to the point."

"He talked about you being a paramedic and investing in stocks. It was almost like he was trying to get me to confirm your cover. Maybe I'm just a little paranoid. I know I didn't say anything I shouldn't have. Does it bother you he met me?"

"Yeah."

"Are you going to say anything to Dwayne?"

"No. He probably wouldn't care, but this was a big no-no tonight, and I don't want to put him on the spot by forcing him to report I disclosed a sensitive undercover operation to a non-Bureau employee. No sense getting OPR involved until after I save the world from the vise grip of terrorism."

Caitlin shook her head and kissed him on the cheek. "I didn't think this was exactly kosher, but thanks for letting me come. Those kids are precious."

Chapter Forty-Four

Caitlin took a personal day at school and picked the perfect morning to take Jaana to the clinic. It had been almost four weeks since the surgery, and Jaana was recovering nicely. She immediately began weekly chemotherapy treatments to kill any lingering cancer cells. The side effects were predictable. Her hair fell out, and the nausea from the chemo usually lasted a day following each treatment. It was difficult to explain to a seven-year-old why something that made her sick was actually good for her, but at least for today her gray pallor was gone. Most importantly, the joy in her countenance was back.

Caitlin gave her a beautiful multicolored scarf to cover her head, and Jaana wore the gift proudly.

The sun was shining, and Jaana sang most of the way to the clinic. Nahid went with them, while Zerak, hoping to make up for all the business lost during the hospitalization, remained at the store.

Timing was of critical importance this morning. Ibrahim and Omar were at the morning training session and would return to the clinic in a couple of hours. Caitlin told Jaana about the clinic and that she met several children who lost limbs because of the wars going on all over the world. Caitlin described Shahla and said she was also from Afghanistan. Jaana made Caitlin promise to introduce her once she was allowed to go out. Today Caitlin was fulfilling that promise.

They arrived at the clinic around ten. Caitlin hoped to leave late enough from Jaana's apartment to allow the morning commute to subside, but an overturned pickup truck on the Sunset off-ramp of the 405 backed up traffic to the Valley. It was a slow crawl, and Caitlin was already on the freeway before she learned of the accident. In any event, Jaana's excitement at being able to meet someone from Afghanistan made up for the near-jog pace of the traffic.

When they finally arrived, Matt greeted them in the parking lot. He took the wheelchair from the trunk, opened it, and locked the brakes. Matt carefully lifted Jaana from the car and placed her in the chair. Her mom put a light pink blanket over her legs, covering the stump. This would be Jaana's first time in public since the surgery, and Nahid was uncertain as to whether she would be self-conscious about her leg and her hair.

Matt wheeled her up the walk through the front doors. Several of the nurses Matt had been assisting were walking out as they were entering. Both Gina and Sherri greeted Jaana and made her feel welcome at the clinic. They chatted briefly, and Jaana was not the least bit shy in telling them about her cancer and the operation. The nurses immediately fell in love with Jaana, as did everyone who met her.

Matt took them on the nickel tour of the clinic before heading for Shahla's room. When they arrived, Shahla was in her bed, staring out the window at a bird perched on her windowsill. Matt lightly tapped on the open door, and Shahla turned.

"Hi, Shahla. I hope you don't mind, but I brought a friend. I thought you might like to meet another little girl from Afghanistan. This is Jaana."

Shahla's English was still very limited, and she had no idea what Matt was saying. Matt rolled Jaana closer to the bed. Jaana looked at Shahla's amputated leg and threw off her blanket.

With a huge smile, Jaana said in Pashto, "Hey, I've only got one too, just like you. We could be twins."

For the first time Matt saw Shahla smile. Jaana began to chatter as if they had been friends for years. Matt, Caitlin, and Nahid walked out into the hallway and let the two young victims of evil, seen and unseen, be little girls.

Nahid and Caitlin stayed outside the room while Matt left, promising to return in fifteen minutes. When he did, he was carrying hamburgers, fries, and milk shakes for five. He entered the room and announced he had a special surprise for lunch. Both little girls squealed for joy. They may have been Afghan by birth, but they quickly assumed the makings of all-American girls.

Far too quickly the morning was up, and Caitlin announced it was time to go, causing both girls to groan. Caitlin told Shahla and Jaana they could visit again. Jaana made Nahid promise to bring her back on the weekend, and Nahid acceded. It was difficult, if not impossible, to deny such a small wish to two who had faced so much recently. Each said good-bye with promises to see each other soon.

As Matt was wheeling Jaana down the hallway, Caitlin asked her if she had a good time.

"It was wonderful," she replied. "I told her about Jesus."

Caitlin smiled and Matt could only marvel at the courage this little immigrant child showed. She truly was special.

It was a parklike setting behind the clinic. The grounds were well maintained. California oaks surrounded the eight-foot high stucco walls blocking out the noises of the world. Three orange trees in the northwest corner provided a quick snack for anyone willing to pick the ripened fruit. Pink and white oleander sporadically lined the edge of the yard, and the two men sat in a large wooden gazebo.

Matt handed Omar a Coke.

Omar looked at the Coke, then looked at Matt. "In 1987, to bring attention to the Palestinian cause, bin Laden called for the boycott of American goods. He repeated the call after the United States imposed sanctions on my country. It was difficult to get your Coke."

There was pain in his voice. Omar's Coke comment was merely meant to momentarily take his mind off death. They both popped the tops of the cans at the same time. Matt leaned back in his chair and said nothing. He waited for Omar to continue the conversation.

As if talking to no one in particular, Omar finally began, "He didn't do it."

Matt waited to respond then said, "Do what?"

"I have told no one. I do not know why I am telling you. There is something different about you. I think I can trust you. I trust very few. That is how I survived in my country. Please tell no one."

Matt started to promise he would maintain a confidence, but Omar went on without waiting for assurances.

"I was questioned by your FBI. They think my brother robbed banks and used the money to support the terrorists. They are not sure if he was murdered or committed suicide. . . . He didn't commit suicide."

"Why do you think that?"

"My brother was part of a cause and was willing to die for that cause because he believed it to be just. The Koran says he who leaves his dwelling to fight for God and his apostle and is then overtaken by death shall be rewarded by God. Rashid believed that. The cause has assigned martyrdom the highest priority. We call it *shuhada*, martyrs in the name of Allah. Rashid would make that sacrifice."

Omar took a long drink from the can and waited several seconds before continuing. "But the Koran teaches suicide is wrong, just as in your religion. Jannah, what you call Paradise, does not await one who takes his own life. Israel calls the terrorist attacks 'suicide missions' as a way to discredit those willing to make the ultimate sacrifice. The Jews hoped the word *suicide* would discourage the actions of those dedicated to jihad. But it is wrong to describe as suicide the act of one who willingly gives his life out of dedication for the victory of Islam. That is what we call a martyr."

"Would your brother martyr himself?"

"Of course, that is what I am saying."

"So you believe he was murdered?"

"I know he was murdered." Omar put his head down and lowered his voice. "I loved my brother, but we did not believe the same. We both saw decades of horror in our country, but it brought us to different views. I saw death, and it made me want to save lives. He saw death and wanted to eradicate those responsible for the destruction he witnessed."

"Who did he blame?" asked Matt.

"My brother was a warrior in what many Muslims believe is a true jihad. Even as a child he fought the Soviets who invaded our country. Your government supported that fight. I read that your President Carter would not support the Olympics in Moscow, and then my country got help, your help. Even though Osama bin Laden took your money, he hated you because of your presence in our world. The Prophet Mohammed said, 'Let there be no two religions in Arabia.' My brother believed now you, rather than the Russians, are the infidels and will remain our enemy as long as you stay on the Arabian Peninsula . . . and as long as you support the Israeli occupation of Palestine."

"Do you believe that?"

"It is not important what I believe. My brother believed it. He used to give me booklets explaining why the cause was just. Why the sixth pillar, jihad, meant armed conflict. I now know from the FBI that jihad for him also included robbing banks. I knew he was doing something wrong, but I did not know what. He would come home at night with money, sometimes stacks of money, but he never would spend it.

"Once at the motel I received a strange call telling me about a bank and the name of a teller. I said nothing to my brother. It meant nothing to me. It did not seem important. But Rashid got very angry with me for not telling him. He said he was supposed to meet the teller and didn't because I didn't give him the message. The next day I saw on the news the bank was robbed. I said something to Rashid. He got upset and said never to discuss it again."

"What happened on the night he died?"

Omar looked off into the distance before answering. "I knew that night he was doing something for the cause. I don't know what. He complained once that everything he earned he gave to others. He kept nothing for himself. But others used the money he earned for themselves. I believe they killed him. My brother was very brave. He fought for many years. Whoever he answered to here was young. My brother feared him but did not respect him. His superior did not experience life as my brother knew it."

Matt watched Omar carefully, trying to discern insincerity. He saw none. Because Omar was opening up, Matt was comfortable probing deeper. It was a fine line between interested comrade and inquisitor. Matt wanted to be cautious.

"Did you know your brother's associates?"

"No, my brother was protective of me. It may sound strange to you, but even though we did not agree on the cause, my brother was proud of me. He knew I worked for a Christian organization, but he knew I was helping children maimed by the war. He supported me in that work. He did not want me involved in his world. I never met others."

"Did he train at a terrorist camp?"

Omar looked at Matt. There was no anger in Omar's eyes, but the look suggested Matt was about to get a lecture. "Americans use the word *terrorist* very freely. If you want to invade our land, kill our people, or tell us how to govern ourselves, it is in the name of freedom. If you support the occupation of Palestine or support Israeli troops that kill women and children, that is justice. If someone of the

Islamic faith engages in such activities, it is terrorism. The Palestinian child who throws rocks is a terrorist. The American soldier who comes to our country and kills our citizens, is what, a patriot? Were not your revolutionaries who fought against British rule terrorists? Some might say, it is the United States who is the terrorist. But to answer your question, my brother was trained at a camp in Khost, a camp your tax dollars indirectly supported. Does that make it a terrorist training camp?"

Matt thought it best to back away. Omar opened up far more than he would have ever suspected. The door was left open for further discussion.

Omar stood up. Matt also rose.

"Was your brother left-handed?"

Omar answered without hesitation. "Yes, it caused him many problems. In the Muslim faith the left hand is for bodily functions and is considered unclean. During the Russian invasion of my country, Rashid was shot in the finger on his right hand, and it did not heal properly." Omar held up his index finger, the trigger finger, bent at a slight angle. "He was unable to bend it any further than that. So for many things like writing, he learned to use his left hand." Omar looked at Matt with obvious confusion. "Why is that important?"

Matt never answered the question but with all sincerity said, "Omar, I am sorry about your brother. I understand your hurt. Let's go honor him by treating the children."

Although it was uncharacteristic of Matt, he gave Omar a hug.

Matt stood out front of the clinic and punched the speed dial to Dwayne's cold phone.

"Dwayne, it's Matt."

"I'm a trained investigator. I recognize the voice. Besides, you're the only one with this number," said Dwayne. "What's going on?"

"He was left-handed."

"Who?"

"Rashid. This wasn't a suicide. Has the coroner's office issued a ruling?"

"I haven't seen a thing. I can call over to homicide, if you want, and see where they stand."

"Would you please? Check out the right index finger. See if the report mentions any deformity or malfunction. According to Omar the finger couldn't pull a trigger. It couldn't bend. Also check for fingerprints on the magazine and the individual rounds."

"Yeah, I can check on that," said Dwayne.

"This was an inside job; it wasn't suicide. Omar says Rashid didn't always play well with others and had problems with management."

"Sounds familiar. No wonder you're taking an interest. I'll check on it and get back to you."

Chapter Forty-Five

Matt sat on the patio and waited for Dwayne, who was late. To date, the investigation had yielded more questions than answers. Matt's frustration grew.

Dwayne arrived and apologized for being late.

"Don't worry about it. Even if you were early, I'm not sure we'd be any closer to solving this thing. If there's a thing to solve," said Matt. "I can't find anything tangible that links Omar, Ibrahim, or anyone for that matter to a specific terrorist plot."

"I understand your frustration. In some respects this is a fishing expedition."

"Well, the fish aren't biting."

"Are you familiar with Echelon?" asked Dwayne.

"Never heard of it."

"It's one of those chatter-gathering tools we use. It's a global electronic communications surveillance system that can intercept millions of communications every day. Phone calls, e-mails, Internet downloads, satellite transmissions—"

"Does the ACLU know about this?" interrupted Matt.

Dwayne smirked. "Yeah, they know. NSA now believes this may be a dirty bomb and is convinced something is going down in L.A. within the next two weeks."

"A dirty bomb? How'd they come up with that?"

"I don't know, but we have some true believers at headquarters."

"But what and who are we looking for?"

"We just don't know. No one believes this is some sort of campaign of disinformation. Al-Qaeda certainly isn't above that tactic. After all, how many times have we heightened security only to see another day pass without incident? But analysts from several different intelligence organizations believe this to be real. The fuse is lit. We just aren't sure how fast it's burning. Stick with Omar. He's our best lead so far."

Matt shrugged his shoulders with resignation. "He's not our only lead. Did you ever go back to David and interview him about Yasir?"

"Yeah, but he stonewalled me. Denied meeting Yasir or even knowing him. When I said a witness in the alley thought he saw Yasir coming out the back of the clinic, David was very convincing the witness must have been mistaken."

"We know that's a lie."

"But what can I do? I can't say we've got someone on the inside who knows differently."

Matt ran his fingers through his hair, pausing long enough to think. "Let me see what I can do. I have an idea that might work. Did you interview anyone else at the clinic?"

"I spoke with the two nurses on duty that night, but they didn't see anything."

"Good, that's my cover."

"Do I want to know?"

"No, plausible deniability. If it doesn't work, you can't be blamed; and if it does, headquarters will take credit anyway. Give me your business card."

"What, now you plan on impersonating a supervisor?"

"I'm a great liar, but I don't think I could pose as Bureau management and keep a straight face."

Dwayne handed Matt a business card.

"Oh, by the way, that fingerprint lead panned out. The sheriff's crime lab checked the magazine. They lifted several prints off the individual rounds in the magazine. None matched Rashid."

"He didn't load the weapon?"

"Nope," said Dwayne.

"Well, I guess that's something. Could they match the latents?"

"Yeah, but it's no one on our radar. They came back to a Nabil al-Sherif."

"Look, I have to get going," said Matt.

"Hang in there. You're doing a great job."

"Glad you think so. It sure doesn't feel so great, and now you're telling me this needle in the haystack just became a radioactive needle. Thanks for ratcheting it up another notch."

It was almost 6:00 when Matt pulled in front of the World Angel headquarters. The lights were still on in David's office so Matt decided on plan B.

His initial plan was to break into the offices and rifle through David's desk to determine what the connection was with Yasir, the dead terrorist in the alley. Now rather than committing another felony, he would try an indirect confrontation.

Just as he walked into the reception area, David, Ibrahim, and Kim were exiting David's office. Ibrahim and Kim towered over David. All were formally dressed, David in a tuxedo with a bright cummerbund.

"Wow! You guys must have big plans for this evening. Birthday? Anniversary? Celebrate winning the lottery?"

"Hi, Matt. No, we're going to a premiere in Westwood," said David. "My wife is picking us up in a few minutes."

Kim was all smiles. She and Ibrahim continued walking as David stopped briefly to talk.

"A premiere? You guys run in some elite circles."

"James Goldstone."

"The producer?"

"That's the one. He has a new movie coming out called *Red Glare*."

"Oh, yeah, I saw the trailers on that. It's about an embassy bombing in Africa, isn't it?" said Matt.

Matt could hear Kim and Ibrahim descend the wooden stairs.

"That's it. It's based on a true story. He takes on the controversial topics but has been commercially successful so the industry sticks with him. I'm anxious to see his latest. He's a strong supporter of ours, and I want to support him. Besides, the premieres are always exciting."

"Sounds like fun, rubbing elbows with the Hollywood elite."

"You can meet him next week," said David.

"Next week?"

David nodded, "He's being honored at the Children First banquet next Friday."

"Children First banquet?"

"You're going, aren't you?"

"What is it?"

"I've announced it at several of the staff meetings."

This caught Matt completely off guard.

"Don't tell me you don't listen to my meditations either?" asked David with an impish grin. "Children First is a multiagency fundraising event in which we participate each year. This year James Goldstone is our featured speaker, and I expect you to be there."

"Absolutely. I don't know how I missed the announcement. I'll definitely be there. I can't afford to be fired."

"Did you need something? We need to run. My wife could be waiting."

Matt's tone changed abruptly. "Something came up today, and I need to speak with you briefly."

"Certainly, as long as it is brief."

"Alone."

David hollered down the stairs. "This will just take a second. Please wait for me outside. If my wife arrives, tell her I will be there shortly."

David looked toward Matt.

"The FBI stopped by my house this morning." Matt pulled Dwayne's wrinkled up card from his pants pocket and handed it to David. "Some agent left a card in my door. May not be anything, but I'm assuming it has to do with the shooting in the alley."

The concern on David's face could not be masked. "Did you call the agent back?"

"No, not yet. I heard someone mention the guy came to the clinic and met with you. I don't want to lie to the FBI, but before I said anything, I thought maybe I should check with you."

"Thanks for coming to me."

David was visibly shaken. "Please, sit down."

Matt and David sat on the brown leather couch in the waiting room. David paused as he gathered his thoughts. "This is very difficult for me to say. I saw that man the day he was killed. I met with him once before. His name was Yasir Mehsud, and he was Shahla's uncle. He made two very large donations to the clinic, all in cash. I know I was wrong to accept the money in that way, but we needed it to help get the clinic ready. He wanted to ensure Shahla would be brought to the United States for the best possible treatment. I believed then, as I do now, she was deserving of the finest care we could provide. The night Yasir died, he asked me to bring in other children. He was willing to pay. But I was unwilling to commit until I knew the extent of the injuries the children suffered. He was upset when he left and must have taken out his anger on someone in the alley. I did not know he was a terrorist until the FBI announced it following his death. The FBI did question me and I lied. I know it was wrong, but I was so afraid if people knew I accepted money from terrorists, we would lose all our funding or, worse yet, be shut down by the government."

"So you had no idea he was a terrorist when you were meeting with him?" asked Matt.

"Of course not. Many people donate in cash because they are paid in cash, but never in the amounts Yasir provided. It was probably a violation of the law since I didn't report his contribution, but I answer to God, not the United States government."

"I'm not sure the IRS is going to look at it that way."

"Please, Matt, I beg of you, don't say anything to the FBI."

Matt paused, more for dramatic effect, as if thinking through his response. He looked David in the eye and then with a reluctant smile nodded, agreeing to David's request.

David rose from the couch and Matt followed. David offered his hand and shook Matt's with conviction. They headed down the stairs.

"So what's up with Kim and the doctor?"

"They are just friends. He is much too old for her. I had two extra tickets to tonight's event. Not too many men pay attention to her. When I suggested she join us, she mentioned Ibrahim might like the excitement of the premiere. I asked the doctor, and he agreed to accompany us."

At the bottom of the staircase, David set the alarm, turned off the lights, and locked the door. As they walked outside, Matt whispered, "I didn't see the man at the clinic, and that's what I'll tell the FBI."

"Thanks, Matt, for understanding."

Chapter Forty-Six

Matt knocked on the partially opened door and walked into Ibrahim's small office. Kim was sitting on the edge of the desk and quickly stood up, blushing at the intrusion. She stumbled through an awkward cover-up and, marching past Matt, said, "Doctor, I'll get those travel vouchers to you by the end of the day."

"How was the premiere?"

"It was pretty exciting," said Kim as she left the office.

Ibrahim turned in his chair and began stuffing a few papers in a briefcase.

"You have time for lunch?" asked Matt.

"Not today. I have a one o'clock appointment and need to get on the road. I still am not used to the traffic in Southern California. I never seem to leave myself enough time."

Matt grinned. "I'm not sure anyone gets used to it."

Ismad arrived early for his appointment. The small gray stucco medical building near Farmer's Market was easier to find than he anticipated. As instructed, he turned right into the driveway and drove around to the rear where he parked.

The warmth from the sun directly overhead felt good. He grew up in the desert so he enjoyed the dry climate. Since being in the United States, he had not been exposed to the kind of heat he craved. The main heat he experienced was the uncomfortable feeling that maybe the FBI detected his presence.

Ismad was careful wherever he went. He regularly checked his mirrors, changed lanes frequently when driving the freeways, and would occasionally make a U-turn on the surface streets just to determine if he was being followed. To his knowledge he was successful at eluding any surveillance team.

But caution was the key. He practiced it every day. Important calls were made from pay phones, never the same phone twice. Phone cards supplied by Wadi were used for every long-distance call. He paid cash whenever possible. He used different names when making reservations at any place not requiring identification and avoided socializing except when necessary. His task would be complete in a few days. His success was guaranteed if Allah so willed.

He walked up the steps to the second floor, looking for room 238. It was just past the water fountain. On the door were the names of four doctors, all part of a family practice. One name was familiar: Ubadiah Adel al-Banna, MD.

Ismad opened the door and walked into a waiting room crowded with several mothers and their children. A man who appeared to be by himself was also seated and reading a magazine. Ismad signed in at the desk, filled out the necessary paperwork, and waited. One by one the patients were called. It seemed as though as one patient was called another entered by the front door. The practice was thriving.

After ten minutes the nurse opened the door and called for Ismad under the name he was told to use, Arif Rahman. He put the magazine back on the coffee table and followed the nurse to an examination room. As instructed he told the nurse he was experiencing dizziness. She took his temperature and blood pressure and said the doctor would be in shortly. He waited a few more minutes.

Al-Banna entered with his chart and, while closing the door, said, "Mr. Rahman, I am Dr. al-Banna."

Ismad smiled and the two embraced.

"*Allahu Akbar*," they said simultaneously.

Al-Banna began, "It is an honor to meet you. You are truly a holy warrior to take on the assignment you have been given."

The two exchanged pleasantries and chatted briefly. They were both aware this meeting was to be brief and singular in purpose. This was no time to establish a friendship, but trust had already been built.

Al-Banna was in place. He had been in the United States for years. He blended in to both the medical community and society in general. He had wealth and therefore could plausibly attend extravagant affairs. With his medical practice he could meet with anyone from any walk of life. His door was open to all in need.

He was part of the support team helping with fund-raising and procurement. He used his medical background to obtain medical supplies for overseas operations. He convinced medical manufacturers in the United States of the genuine needs of his people overseas. Those same manufacturers, who supported the war on terrorism with their tax dollars, unwittingly healed the terrorists who were inflicting damage to the cause of freedom.

Through his good credit he also financed the purchase of safe houses. Al-Banna owned several apartment complexes in the greater Los Angeles area. Each was corporately owned under a different name. In each of these multiunit complexes, one unit was devoted to the cause. Occupants came and went without the need for credit checks or identification. As with many apartment buildings, the turnover in renters was frequent. No one questioned residents who only stayed a month or two at a time. The units were always on the ground floor to allow easy escape in case of detection. Each unit provided a secure area where contraband of any type could be concealed. Behind hidden walls were lockers for weapons, explosives, false identification, and cash. Al-Banna owned these properties, but those availing themselves of his largess did not know his name or his connection to the cause. Intermediaries set up the services he provided.

On this day he had exposed himself to Ismad. Other than Wadi, no one else in the United States knew of his importance. Al-Banna trusted Wadi with his life. Now he trusted Ismad.

Al-Banna handed Ismad a key. "This is to a locker at the Hollywood bus terminal. The number is on the key. Inside the locker you will find directions to a storage facility that will have all you will need for that day. And what a glorious day it will be when the infidels learn no one is safe if Allah so wills."

"Thank you for your service to the cause," said Ismad.

"Until we serve together again," said al-Banna.

"If not in our homeland, then in Paradise."

"*Allah Issalmak.*"

Chapter Forty-Seven

Omar practically floated into the room.

Matt laughed, "What are you grinnin' at?"

"I've been selected to be a bone marrow donor."

"That's terrific. When do you go in for the procedure?"

"I am to report on Monday. It will only take a short time, but I may miss a few days of work. Do you think Dr. David will allow me?"

"Absolutely, you're gonna save a life. No one can be upset with that. I'll cover as best I can for you. Just let me know if there is anything I can do to help. Will you need a ride to the hospital? Anything, just ask."

"Thanks, Matt. I will. I better go tell Dr. David now."

Omar left the room, and Matt immediately called Dwayne.

"I can't talk long. Omar just told me he was selected to be a bone marrow donor. What kind of terrorist donates bone marrow? He's going to have the procedure on Monday."

"SOG followed him to a doctor's office. That may explain the visit. They were unable to determine which doctor he visited. Maybe it's true. Or maybe it's part of the ruse to keep us guessing."

"It just doesn't make sense. I better go. Here come a couple of nurses." Matt ended the call more confused than ever.

THE SUN SET, AND Ismad sat by himself at a quiet restaurant along the ocean. The waves crashed along the rocks below, and the white foam glistened from the illumination given off by the restaurant's outdoor lights. The sounds of the surf could be heard even through the heavy plateglass windows. The scene was intoxicating.

Ismad knew the time for his mission was near. After he completed dinner, he would drive to the storage facility and pick up the explosive device. In less than forty-eight hours, the mission would be complete. Success would come with Allah's help.

More than thirty years ago a missile reduced his home to rubble, killing both his parents. Ismad returned home from school that afternoon to find the death of all he knew and loved.

Both his parents could be defined as moderate Shiite Muslims. The family worshipped Allah, prayed five times a day, and gave 2.5 percent of everything they earned. Every few years they even traveled to Mecca. But his parents were not political. They did not hate. In fact, his father had many business dealings with "people of the book," as Muslims refer to Christians and Jews. His parents entertained them in their home when the infidels, his father's business associates, traveled to his country.

Unlike Ismad's neighbors, his father taught tolerance and wanted his son and daughter to understand both sides of the Palestinian issue. Although Ismad's father opposed the creation of the state of Israel, he knew history. He knew the Israelites once occupied the land of Canaan, and the Jews, without a homeland, suffered atrocities at the hands of Hitler. Yet the United Nations created an independent state of Israel in an area occupied by Arabs for more than a thousand years.

The day of his parents' death marked the beginning of Ismad's personal jihad. Like others in the cause, he believed the destruction of Israel, the little Satan, was a religious obligation, an obligation he gladly assumed.

He contemplated all he witnessed during this most recent trip to the United States and was disturbed by Wadi's leadership. Money raised for the cause supported Wadi's Western lifestyle—an expensive car, designer clothes, lavish gifts for American women. Wadi excused his actions by saying he was blending in with the culture, but Ismad knew better. Wadi compromised his beliefs in the name of expediency. The passion was gone. He ran the cell like a business, seeking to profit from the success. Allah could not be pleased.

As Ismad looked out into the ocean, his cell phone rang.

"Yes," said Ismad.

"*Allahu Akbar*," was Wadi's response.

"*Allahu*."

"You need to be at my apartment tomorrow morning to discuss any last-minute details. I also have another set of identification in case you need it to make your escape."

With contempt Ismad responded, "I do not believe that is necessary. I know my instructions."

"Report tomorrow," said Wadi as he hung up the phone, not waiting for a response.

Matt's cell phone rang just as he and Caitlin began dinner. Matt was about to let the call go to voice mail when he looked at the caller ID. Dwayne was on the other end so he took the call.

"Hey, Dwayne."

"Hi, Matt. Got a minute?"

"Yeah, I guess. Caitlin and I just sat down for dinner."

"Oh, I'm sorry. I thought you guys ate like rich people around eight o'clock."

"No, I only play a rich person on TV. In my real life I work for a government agency where some of its employees qualify for food stamps and federal subsidies. What's up?"

"I'm looking over transcripts of Zerak's calls," said Dwayne, referring to Jaana's father. "I've married up a few of the solicitations to a number in West Hollywood. I'll call the phone company tomorrow and get subscriber information. According to the transcripts, one call was from a Palestinian relief organization, and a second call from the same number was for an Afghan orphan fund. Both callers were male. So these guys may be posing as separate organizations, soliciting funds for the cause de jour."

"That's interesting. Maybe it's a legitimate fund-raising organization contracted out to raise funds for various charities."

"Yeah, and you got a shot at being the next Director. I'll let you get back to your dinner. I'll call you with the subscriber information in the morning."

Chapter Forty-Eight

Ismad knocked on the door. He could hear loud music coming from inside the apartment. The sounds disgusted him.

Wadi answered the door and greeted Ismad as if all were well. Wadi was not oblivious to Ismad's contempt; he just chose to ignore it. He returned to the dining room table and continued eating breakfast.

Before Ismad sat down, he walked past the stereo and turned off the music.

"This music is wrong," said Ismad. "Don't you understand the significance?"

"I know what it is and what it means. I don't need another lecture from you. You still don't understand my role. I am in America. I must be an American. I must think like an American. I must blend into this society so no one suspects my loyalties are elsewhere. I'm sorry you can't understand that. We all must do what is necessary to bring about the liberation of Jerusalem and the destruction of the West. You criticize me, but do you pray? Do you give?"

"I do when I can. When I am alone with my God, I can pray. When I must be among the infidels, I cannot. At least I am making the effort. You are not even trying to please Allah." Ismad threw a newspaper at the fifty-inch flat-screen TV. "You used money for the cause to buy this. And that sound system, playing music that defiles Allah. Was that bought with his funds also, like your car and your clothes?"

Wadi raised his voice. "You don't know what I do to please Allah. I am doing all that is asked of me. Those I report to overseas have no problems with the way in which I am managing my work. Who are you to tell me what I should and should not do? What I watch? What I listen to? If I want to eat while the sun is up during Ramadan, that is my business. Soldiers are not required to fast during this time. I am a soldier. I have been in this war for many years, and I am on the front lines. Thanks to my efforts, hundreds of thousands of dollars have been raised for the cause. I am supporting cells throughout the world. Since you reported to me, I have seen your scorn. Is it because of my age? Or my success? Or are you just jealous I can serve the cause here and you must return to your country when this is over?"

Ismad started to speak, but Wadi waved his hand, cutting him off, and continued, "I am offended by your pettiness. I provide you with all you need to succeed. You have but one mission. Every day is a new mission for me. I am proud of my efforts, and I know Allah is pleased."

Ismad yelled, "Allah cannot be pleased. It is about the cause, not about you and your wants, needs, and desires!"

"That is where you are wrong. It is about me and the cause. For the cause to succeed, I must succeed. Go back to the desert and serve the cause. I will continue to serve here!"

Wadi reached over to a manila envelope lying on the table. He flung it at Ismad. A Frisbee-like spin on the envelope caused it to flip and land at Ismad's feet. Ismad glared at Wadi.

Wadi looked him directly in the eye. "Pick it up."

Ismad sat there without moving.

"Pick it up! It contains a passport and new identification in case you need it following your mission. There is also $5,000 in emergency funds. If all goes well, return the envelope and money to me. It will be used by others. If you need it, use it."

Ismad reached down and examined the contents.

Wadi rose from the table and walked toward the bedroom. "I must make a phone call. You know the way out." Wadi turned on the sound system as he walked past. The music resumed.

Ismad sat there in silence. After hearing Wadi complete his call, Ismad padded into the bedroom undetected.

Wadi would sin no more.

When Ismad returned from the bedroom, he walked to the kitchen sink and washed his hands. It is defilement to pray to Allah with blood on one's hands.

As he left the apartment, he turned off the music and set the TV to Al-Jazeera.

Matt was driving down the Pacific Coast Highway on his way to the clinic. It was almost 10:30, and the morning fog was all but cleared. Although he missed a staff meeting, he planned on spending the entire afternoon at the clinic working with Omar. The waves were crashing against the shoreline, thanks to a fierce storm hundreds of miles out to sea. It was so beautiful he debated stopping and enjoying the beach for what he believed would be some well-deserved R&R.

The early morning commuters reached their destination, and it was Teflon traffic all the way—no sticking, slick, smooth, and easy. *Do you walk the beach or take advantage of a perfect commute?* Perfect commutes were less frequent than crashing waves along the shoreline. He would continue to drive.

Matt had the windows down and a Charlie Daniels CD blasting. It was so loud he didn't hear the cell phone until the fifth ring. He answered without looking at the caller ID, then reached over to turn down the volume.

"Hang on a sec. Let me turn this down. . . . There, hello."

"You really are a white-trash hillbilly. When this case is over, let me introduce you to some smooth jazz," said Dwayne.

"Excuse me, sir, could you connect me to my EEO counselor. I believe I've been dis'd by my superior."

"Where are you?"

"Cruisin' down PCH. You got something for me, or you just don't trust me?"

"No, yes. Well, I don't trust you, but that's not the issue this morning. That subscriber information came back to an apartment on Havenhurst in West Hollywood. I sent two of the guys down to the U.S. Attorney's office to get a search warrant. They're waiting for the judge to come off the bench and sign it. We plan on hitting it early this afternoon. Wanna come?"

"Absolutely. When and where are you gonna brief?"

"Let's shoot for one at Plummer Park."

"I'll be there. I'll stop by the clinic for a few minutes, then head on out."

Chapter Forty-Nine

Five casually dressed task force members were waiting in the parking lot when Matt arrived at Plummer Park. Individually they did not look like agents. But collectively, standing around, with soft drinks and coffee cups in their hands and leaning next to American-made cars, it was pretty obvious to anyone with street smarts these "cops" were about to roll.

Dwayne was waiting for the two agents to return from the courthouse with the search warrant, and then the team would hit the Havenhurst apartment. The CIA had picked up overseas chatter that some type of incident was to take place in Los Angeles within forty-eight hours. Normally search warrants were served in the early morning hours to ensure the sleeping occupants were at home, but the clock was ticking. Agents did not have the luxury of waiting until sunrise tomorrow.

The affidavit and search warrant flew through the rather cumbersome process without any problems. That in and of itself was a minor miracle. The probable cause was weak; and the duty judge this week, David Borenstein, did not have a history of being law enforcement friendly. The former criminal defense attorney actually prided himself on making agents change almost every affidavit submitted, at least once. Usually the requested modifications were more a judicial power trip than a desire to ensure compliance with the Constitution. With lifetime appointments to the bench, absolutely nothing could be done other than stroke the judge's fragile ego and make the necessary changes. Today he signed the affidavit without comment. Apparently terrorists bent on destroying Israel impacted his decision to give the legal document a quick signature.

Brian Fletcher was already set up as the point. He had been watching the apartment since the subscriber information was obtained earlier in the morning. No one had come in or out of the apartment in the three hours he was there. When he first arrived, he walked past the unit and could hear Al-Jazeera on the TV. He assumed someone was in the apartment watching television. Dwayne kept checking periodically with Brian, but the report remained the same—no activity.

Once the warrant arrived, Dwayne briefed the team.

Tim Warren, a Naval Academy graduate who had been a Navy SEAL for eight years prior to joining the Bureau, was on the task force. He had set off more explosions than a topless dancer in church and would be in charge of making the entry. Dwayne assigned two agents to cover the back of the ground-floor apartment. The others would assist on the entry. Matt would remain in the van until the apartment was cleared just in case there was a connection to the clinic.

Dwayne concluded with, "This is no white-collar boiler room. We all know what happened at the warehouse. If in doubt, back away and we'll regroup. Terrorists with plans to wreak havoc on L.A. are believed to be behind doors number one, two, and three. Extreme caution is the order of the day."

The agents piled into a Chevy Suburban and drove the few blocks to the Havenhurst address.

Upon arrival the agents dispatched quickly to their respective positions. The front door to the apartment was concealed by heavy brush along the walkway paralleling the building. It provided perfect cover from the street so no one could see the agents closing.

Tim approached the door with caution and carefully examined the door frame, looking for wires, sensors, or contact points. Nothing appeared to be out of the ordinary. The TV could be heard through the closed door.

Dwayne standing behind Tim gave a signal to Matt, who was back at the van, parked at the curb. Matt phoned the apartment. Dwayne could hear the ringing through the door, but no one answered. Matt let the phone ring twenty times, hung up, and dialed again. It rang ten more times before Dwayne knocked on the door. No response.

Rather than kick the door in, which would have been John Wayne's style, Tim picked the lock and carefully cracked open the door. Dwayne and the other agents had their weapons drawn. Tim carefully examined the inside of the door frame and with a small fiber-optic camera scanned the back of the door and as much of the apartment as he could see. The door and room appeared clear.

Tim pushed open the door, and the agents entered, crisscrossing through the opened door and covering the room as they entered. The living room was clear. The bedroom door was open. The agents dispatched quickly to the bedroom door. Again standing on both sides of the door, they prepared to enter when Tim shouted for everyone to stop. The agents froze. Inside the bedroom a surprise awaited.

Chapter Fifty

A crimsonlike halo surrounded the head of a limp body lying on the floor. The victim was fully clothed. His neck had a thin cut from ear to ear, the raw skin laid open.

Tim carefully approached while the other agents provided cover. He checked for a pulse, but it was futile. The victim, a Middle Eastern male, was dead. The condition of the body and the blood demonstrated the death was several hours old. Tim radioed all units the apartment was cleared.

"That's him!" said Matt who had now entered the room.

"Who?" asked Dwayne.

"That's the guy from the warehouse. That's *GQ*, the guy in the Porsche."

"Are you sure?"

"I'll never forget that face. I was less than thirty feet from him and have played that night over in my mind every day since."

Wadi al-Habishi had been garroted, a favorite tool of assassins, because of the silent, violent, and message-sending nature in which a person died. Matt had seen it once before, a mob hit in Encino about five years ago. Piano wire connected to two wooden handgrips, quickly looped from behind around the neck of an unsuspecting victim, crossed hands, and pulled tightly. In the hands of someone trained, death would be almost instantaneous.

"Whoever did this was either dedicated to the cause or lacked a conscience," said Dwayne.

"Maybe both," said Matt.

Based on the blood-splatter pattern on the bed sheets and on an opened telephone directory, as well as shoe marks on the wall where the victim kicked as he struggled, it appeared as though the victim had been sitting on the side of the bed, searching through the directory, preparing to make a call. The killer must have walked up from behind, leaned over the twin bed, and completed the task.

Matt and Dwayne presumed it was a hit. Burglars aren't known to garrote residents, and West Hollywood apartments weren't high priority for the professional thief. Robbery wasn't an apparent motive. The flat-screen TV and expensive sound system were still intact. With the exception of the dead body, little seemed disturbed.

Dwayne called the Evidence Recovery Team, FBI agents who maintained a regular caseload but were specially trained to search significant crime scenes. Normally the search would be discontinued until the ERT agents arrived to avoid disturbing any evidence of the homicide. Once the ERT supervisor cleared the location, the search would resume. But the issues were different this afternoon. It would take the ERT agents several hours to arrive from throughout the division.

With the discovery of the body, time was a commodity not to be wasted. The death raised even more questions. Waiting another hour could be costly. The agents had discovered the working office of a terrorist cell, and the knowledge gained from the continued search could save lives.

Dwayne ordered the agents to resume the search, carefully preserving as much of the crime scene as possible.

The kitchen and living room area provided few pieces of evidence. The only interesting item was a calendar with the next day's date circled. The bedroom where the deceased was lying appeared more significant.

Inside the closet was a reinforced crawl space. Secreted in the space was a Kalashinikov automatic weapon and four mini-Glocks, the same model Yasir Mehsud, Caitlin's Humpty Dumpty, used in the alley behind the clinic. A shoebox held several cell phones and GPS devices, all terrorist tools of the trade.

When one of the agents moved a dresser in the bedroom, he discovered a large wall safe hidden behind a false vent.

It took only a few minutes for Tim to open the safe, but its contents were the types of evidence the agents hoped to find—passports and identification from various countries, many blank but some under various names containing the deceased's photo; eighty-five thousand in cash; three dozen prepaid SIM cards; twenty credit cards under various names.

"Hey Dwayne, you might want to take a look at this," said Pete Garcia. Pete held the Egyptian passport of Nabil al-Sherif. The picture on the passport was of Wadi. "Remember those prints on the magazine of Rashid's .32 caliber?"

"Yeah," said Dwayne.

"He's our boy. Our vic loaded the magazine."

Another agent searching the dresser drawer found a California driver's license, a social security card, and a UCLA student identification card, all in the name of Wadi Ali al-Habishi aka Nabil al-Sherif.

Answers were beginning to come, and parts of the puzzle were starting to make sense.

Chapter Fifty-One

"Why wasn't I told about this?" screamed Dwayne over the cell phone. "I have my whole team out here trying to connect the pieces to a puzzle we must solve, and I am just learning about this now. When were you going to tell me?"

The ASAC, Pamela Clinton, was on the other end of Dwayne's tirade. She nervously apologized for not notifying him, saying she didn't think he needed to know.

"I have kept you fully informed of our investigation, and you don't think something like this is significant?" He took a breath, captured his anger, and said, "Well, thanks for telling me now."

He ended the call and held his emotions in check, though tempted to hurl the cell phone across the room.

To no one in particular, Dwayne said aloud, "That was the Queen Mother. There is a secret reception tomorrow night at the Israeli consulate for the vice president and several Israeli weapons dealers in town for an arms convention in Long Beach. The new administration is trying to smooth ruffled Israeli feathers. Tomorrow night . . . the date circled on the calendar. The plans for that building were copied in the burglary of the maintenance office, and we have chatter of a terrorist incident planned for L.A. this week. She just happens to pick this moment to mention the reception to me. Since HQ was convinced it was Disneyland or the Staples Center, she didn't think to share the intel with us. How could anyone be so naïve? She doesn't see a connection, or is she trying to grab the glory?"

He slammed his fist on the table. "I think we have our connection. Matt, get out of here! Get back over to the clinic. I want you on Omar like flies on the stuff she has for brains. I can't believe this. What is she thinking? Tim, you take over until ERT arrives. Dust everything for prints. I'm more concerned with terrorism than I am a murder. I want everyone who was ever in this room identified. I want every resident interviewed, especially the manager, and I want it yesterday. Time is not on our side. Pete, you come with me. I want LAPD present when I sit down with our people. Besides, I need someone to hold me back. I may fly across that conference table if Clinton pulls another stupid stunt like this one."

It was three o'clock by the time Dwayne and Pete arrived at the FBI offices. They went straight to the eleventh floor SCIF. The Sensitive Compartmented Information Facility was a secure, restricted access room designed to prevent electronic intrusion during discussions of the nation's most sensitive secrets. As required, Dwayne and Pete placed their cell phones in lockers outside the facility. Inside the entire upper management of the Los Angeles FBI awaited their arrival. Decisions had to be made about how best to handle the information the task force obtained earlier in the afternoon.

Dwayne laid out his reasons for believing the consulate was the target tomorrow night. His argument was compelling. He was articulate and convincing; more important, he made sense.

Jason Barnes, the ADIC, asked numerous probing questions about the investigation to date. He had an excellent grasp of the situation and agreed with Dwayne's analysis of the facts. Once Barnes expressed his opinion, the rest of management acceded; the consulate was the perfect target. There were only two symbols of the Israeli government in Los Angeles—El-Al Airlines, the Israeli government-run airlines that flew out of LAX, and the Israeli consulate. LAX was targeted twice before—Karim Mohamed Ali Hedayat's attack on July 4, 2002, killing an El-Al employee and passenger; and Omar Ressam, who was caught at the Canadian border and later admitted to planning the millennium bombing of LAX. What better way to attack the Big Satan and the Little Satan than by killing the vice president of the United States while on a sensitive diplomatic mission at the consulate?

Decisions had to be made regarding the secret meeting that might no longer be a secret. Should it be canceled? Should it be moved? The Israelis have always taken the position their actions would not be dictated by terrorists. Everyone in the room concurred the Israelis would want to hold the meeting as scheduled but increase security to ensure safety.

Barnes said he would notify the consulate and Secret Service. The Service would certainly want to cancel the meeting, but canceling had political ramifications. The vice president was seeking to assure the Israelis the U.S. administration supported Israel. Bowing to terrorist threats would not instill confidence.

Barnes specifically tasked Dwayne and Pete to go straight to the consulate to discuss security measures for tomorrow's event. They left immediately without ever acknowledging the ASAC.

As instructed by Dwayne, Matt returned to the clinic. He finished the afternoon, working closely with Omar and several of the patients, including Shahla. She was progressing well and would soon be fitted with a prosthetic device. She found a friend in Jaana, who visited often.

Matt grew to love his job when it involved the children. He still wasn't thrilled with the janitorial duties or the heavy lifting, but he tolerated those tasks for the sake of the assignment.

Evening was approaching. He and Omar were putting away the exercise equipment. Omar stopped and stared, captivated by the view. Through the westerly facing window, the setting sun seemed to explode in orange and crimson. Even Matt was awestruck.

"Let me take you to dinner," said Matt.

"That is not necessary."

"I know it's not, but I want to. You'll be returning to your country soon, and there's still so much I would like to learn about your culture."

Omar finally agreed. "Have you ever eaten Middle Eastern food?"

"Yeah."

"There is a restaurant in Beverly Hills called the Mediterranean Enchantment. Maybe we could try it. I have never eaten there, but I understand the food is good."

Matt hesitated. "I heard they're under new management and the food isn't nearly as good as it used to be. I would hate for you to be disappointed. I know a great little steak place in Santa Monica. Let me take you for an All-American meal."

Dwayne and Pete met with the Israeli officials and shared the overseas intelligence regarding an attack in Los Angeles and the results of the afternoon search at Wadi's apartment. Dwayne did not tell them about the undercover operation or of their suspicions about World Angel. Jeopardizing the safety of an undercover agent or the compromise of an undercover operation was not part of any cooperation package with a foreign government. The Israelis knew all they needed to know.

In reality, the information the FBI provided did little to change the security plans. The consulate planned all its affairs as if they were going to be compromised by terrorists. Security was always tight, and virtually every event received at least one threatening call, letter, or piece of overseas intelligence suggesting a terrorist act might take place. The consulate officials were grateful for the information, promised to work closely with U.S. law enforcement regarding security issues, but had no intention of canceling, moving, or postponing the event. The Israeli businessmen were already in town anticipating the meeting with the vice president.

As one official said, "We live our daily lives under the threat of a terrorist attack. We will not yield to their intimidation. Even if no representative from the U.S. government chooses to attend our reception tomorrow, we will not cancel."

Chapter Fifty-Two

Matt and Omar finished their work at the clinic and headed west on Wilshire Boulevard with Matt driving. Omar was staring out the window, observing the bright lights and Christmas decorations.

"I am anxious to get back to my country and work with my friends at the clinic, but I will also miss many things about your country—the beautiful lights, large grocery stores with the abundance of fresh foods, movie theaters with so many choices. There is so much to do here, almost too much. Sometimes I feel overwhelmed. Even with the war, I love my country and the work I do there."

A terrorist who likes our country because of fresh fruit—it just doesn't make sense.

Matt pulled into the canopy-covered entrance to the Steak Brigade, known for its prime rib. The bright lights of the parking lot made it seem like midday; anymore candle power and you would need sunglasses.

The valet parking attendants opened the door for Omar and took the car keys from Matt. Omar continued to be overwhelmed by the opulence of the United States.

"People open the doors for you and park your car. For that you must pay."

Matt laughed. "Don't go to the restroom here. Some guy hangs out there, and after you wash your hands, he gives you several paper towels and expects a tip."

"I should have gone when we were back at the clinic," said Omar with a smile.

Because of the bright lights of the parking lot, it took a minute or so for their eyes to adjust to the contrasting darkness inside the dining room. A college-age hostess led them to a quiet table in the back. Servers, bringing sizzling steaks to the tables, marched past the two as they were being seated.

Matt had eaten here several times but only once with Caitlin. The other times the government picked up the tab as part of an undercover operation. Linen tablecloths spelled more extravagance than an agent could afford except for truly special occasions. It actually was ideal for romance or an undercover meet. It was a relaxed, quiet atmosphere, perfect for conversation, recorded or not.

Omar looked over the menu and was intimidated by the prices. In his country entire families could eat for weeks on the cost of an entree. He mentioned the cheapest item when Matt asked what he wanted.

"Nonsense," said Matt, who ordered for both. Prime rib, medium rare, baked potato, butter, sour cream on the side, mixed vegetables and a salad with the house dressing. Matt winked at Omar, who returned a smile.

The restaurant's reputation was well deserved. The food was delicious, the atmosphere superb. The five-star rating and continued accolades from restaurant critics were most appropriate. Both enjoyed the meal and the pleasant conversation that went with it.

A busboy cleared the plates, and their server asked if they wanted dessert. They both passed on dessert but ordered coffee as the conversation continued.

As a second cup of coffee was being poured, Omar's question startled Matt. It was as much a statement as a question.

"You lost someone close to you."

"Why would you say that?"

Omar looked Matt in the eye. "I have watched you work with the children, and I sensed your sincere understanding when I lost my brother. You are different. It is difficult for me to explain. At first, I believed it was because you are an American, but it is more. There is a hard edge beneath your compassionate exterior. It is almost like you are two different people."

"Don't ruin dinner by playing amateur psychologist," said Matt.

"I am not playing. Who was it?"

Matt paused, then, took another sip of coffee, maintaining eye contact the entire time. "I lost my younger brother several years ago."

"You were close to him."

"He was my hero and my best friend."

"Was it to disease or by accident?"

"It was no accident. He died in your country on Christmas Day 2005."

"He was in the military?" asked Omar.

"He was a Marine."

"That makes your compassion even more remarkable. Thank you for accepting me. It must be difficult to work so closely with people you maybe blame for your brother's death. But maybe also it explains why you understand my hurt."

"It hasn't always been easy."

"Nor has it been easy for me. We have much in common," said Omar.

Matt dropped Omar off at the motel and headed home. Memories of Scott flooded his thoughts. In January 2001 Matt left the Marines for the FBI. He wasn't interested in another West Pac deployment giving Caitlin seven months to rethink their engagement. They were married in June just after Matt graduated from the FBI Academy in Quantico, Virginia. When 9/11 happened, Matt almost quit the Bureau to return to the Corps. Marines were warriors, and Matt wanted to take the fight to the enemy. The SAC talked him out of his decision to quit, promising him all the opportunities he could ever want to be a warrior at home. But the thoughts of being separated from Caitlin provided more than enough incentive to remain with the FBI.

Matt's younger brother Scott spurned a football scholarship, dropped out of college after two games in his sophomore year, and enlisted the day after the attack. Scott loved the Corps and its mission. He lived the ideals: honor, courage, and commitment. He relished every opportunity to tease Matt, calling him a "former Marine" and a "pogue"—a "person other than a grunt." Matt took it all in stride until Christmas Day 2005 when his family received the notification. Scott was killed trying to rescue a fallen Marine near the northwest frontier dividing Afghanistan and Pakistan.

On January 10, 2006, the family stood in freezing rain as Scott's body was laid to rest in Arlington. It was the only time Matt ever saw his father cry. Scott died a hero, fighting for a cause in which he truly believed. Consumed by guilt, Matt knew he let his brother down as well as every Marine who chose to put a nation and a cause before self-interest. It wasn't Caitlin's fault, but sometimes he blamed her. He should have been there for Scott, with Scott.

Representatives from the various law enforcement agencies met at dawn at the consulate. The discussions centered on the information the task force accumulated and the potential attack believed to be scheduled that evening. There still was no confirmation of the attack.

Security was tightened. Dogs, trained in detecting explosives, paraded throughout the building. Each office was searched, and every visitor was required to provide identification to plainclothes Secret Service agents monitoring the entrance. The measures were inconvenient to say the least, and several building tenants were getting annoyed at the continual need for increased security. No one wanted to see another terrorist attack, but with so many terror alerts and warnings over the past decade, it seemed like a great deal of caution for something that might never happen.

Of course, the general public never knew how many attacks were thwarted because of the protections in place. "Terrorist Acts Prevented" was not a statistic headlining the evening news. Too much knowledge might frighten an already nervous public, but the revelation of such potential acts might also compromise highly sophisticated tools if the terrorists learned the intelligence community knew about their plans. Every precaution was being taken for this evening's affair. The secret meeting was still a go. Maybe as disturbing as a potential attack was the possibility that somehow the meeting leaked, if in fact the consulate was the target.

Again the agencies reviewed the facts. The date seemed certain. The target made sense. The 9/11 attacks focused on commerce, the World Trade Center; the military, the Pentagon; and potentially the government, the White House, the destination most experts believed the plane that crashed in Pennsylvania was headed. Since that date, officials in L.A. have speculated entertainment such as Disneyland or one of the movie studios might be next, or perhaps a major transportation hub like LAX. But any attack would be significant: a school, a hotel, the convention center, or a sports arena. No one and no institution seemed immune. Targeting the Israeli Consulate inside the United States while the vice president was in attendance would bring more than just embarrassment to both countries. A clear message would be sent.

Tonight Israeli officials had no intention of cowering to the terrorist threat, but an uneasy calm prevailed as the evening's activities were being prepared. The Israelis insisted they would be in attendance, and if the vice president of the United States chose not to come, the administration could suffer the diplomatic consequences.

Chapter Fifty-Three

Matt looked at his watch. It was past eleven; Omar was uncharacteristically late. Matt walked toward the front of the clinic, debating whether to call Dwayne. A surveillance team was supposed to be on Omar, but trained foreign operatives had a knack for losing even professional surveillance agents. If everyone's guess was correct, today was D-Day, and Omar's change in pattern was cause for concern. Matt was cautious. He didn't want to appear to be watching for Omar, so he slipped into Shahla's room. Their two-way communication skills were still minimal, but Matt grabbed her wheelchair and made a welcoming motion directed at the chair. She acknowledged the offer with a smile, and Matt helped her into the chair. Shahla provided a great cover as the two wheeled toward the front entrance.

Matt spotted Ibrahim in the hallway. "I'm going to order out for sandwiches from the deli across the street. Can I get you one?"

Ibrahim was preoccupied and continued walking, then said over his shoulder, "No, I have to go to the hotel and set up our booth for the banquet. I promised David and Kim I would help."

"Okay, I'll see you tonight at the banquet."

The noon sun warmed the air as Ismad arrived at the towering Wilshire structure housing the consulate. Allah provided a perfect day to bring America to its knees again. Ismad was dressed in a maintenance uniform and was looking for a parking place on the street. He quickly noticed the heightened activity around the building and realized the attack was anticipated. Could he get all that was needed to succeed this day past the increased security? He wanted to blame Wadi's incompetence, but maybe his actions alerted the infidels.

He appreciated the challenge this presented. What a message he would send if law enforcement officials, even with advance suspicions of his plans, failed to protect their vice president and Israeli capitalists. He would gladly martyr himself if directed, but before proceeding, he made a phone call.

As Matt and Shahla were returning from the deli, Omar arrived. Matt kidded him about partying too late on rich American food. Omar was embarrassed by the inquiry and claimed he overslept for the first time since coming to America.

As quickly as Matt was able to return Shahla to her room, he called Dwayne. Dwayne confirmed Omar had apparently overslept. The van riding point saw no activity in the motel room until a few minutes ago, and the agent swore Omar hadn't been out since Matt deposited him at the motel late last night. Dwayne repeated his orders and instructed Matt to monitor Omar closely the rest of the day.

Matt and Omar worked with the children throughout the afternoon. Omar was never out of Matt's sight for more than a few minutes. Nothing appeared unusual. It was a typical workday with the anticipation of the Children First fund-raising banquet that evening. They still had a great deal of work to do in preparation for next week's scheduled arrival of new patients, replacing two children who returned home the day before. Matt and Omar kept busy.

Omar had never been to a formal affair and was looking forward to the pomp surrounding such an event. If he were the terrorist, he said or did nothing identifying the consulate as his target.

The foundation fund-raising event was billed as a "formal affair." Even the word *formal* made Matt uncomfortable. Tonight was beyond his discount clothing wardrobe. Matt joked if Costco didn't sell it, he didn't wear it. Caitlin helped him pick out a nice suit and tie for the occasion. Matt balked at buying the silk tie because it cost more than his entire outfit for a typical workday. Caitlin convinced him "just once to spring for class." He vowed not to spill anything on the tie, and maybe he could take it back for a full refund.

He changed at the clinic and drove Omar back to the motel so he could get ready. Dwayne's instructions were clear—"Keep a close eye on him during the scheduled hours of the Israeli consulate affair"—so Matt volunteered to play chauffeur for the evening.

At the motel Matt excused himself to go to the bathroom. The screen to the bathroom window was missing, and the opening was large enough for Omar to have escaped earlier in the morning. Matt climbed up on to the toilet and peered out the window. A wooden pallet was leaning against the wall beneath the window, a handy makeshift ladder to climb back into the room.

"Are you okay?" said Omar.

The inquiry startled Matt, who braced himself before he slipped off the toilet bowl. Matt flushed the john and ran the water. He quickly called Dwayne and in a hushed voice reported his findings, suggesting Omar might have eluded SOG.

Matt turned off the faucet and walked out of the bathroom.

"You ready?" asked Matt.

"I am ready. I thought maybe you decided to set up residence in the bathroom."

"The sauerkraut on my Reuben at lunch decided it was time to move on."

They arrived at the Century City Renaissance Hotel as many of the other guests were arriving. Matt approached the circular driveway and headed toward the valet parking. He could have chosen the "self-park," but the Bureau was reimbursing all his expenses this evening so why not play this to the hilt. He pulled up to the front door and was quickly greeted by the parking attendant. The young Hispanic, dressed in black pants and a spotless white shirt, took Matt's keys and handed him one of those receipts a lawyer wrote absolving the hotel of everything from theft to nuclear holocaust. Just as Matt and Omar were exiting the car, Ibrahim arrived, walking up the driveway.

"Good evening, doctor," said Omar greeting Ibrahim.

Ibrahim grunted "hello" but joined the two as they entered the hotel.

"You didn't walk, did you?" inquired Matt.

"No," said Ibrahim. "I found a spot on the street and thought I'd save a few American dollars."

"Just hope you don't get a ticket. Then it will cost you many American dollars," replied Matt.

"I checked the sign. I am okay."

Matt said, "You get the booth set up this afternoon?"

"Everything went fine."

The three entered the hotel through the automatic doors. A large "Welcome Children First Foundation" banner greeted them. The lobby was breathtaking. It rivaled a modern museum in its design and was large enough to house a par-three golf course. A thirty-eight-foot cascading waterfall with a dancing water-laser light show welcomed the visitors.

Omar was overwhelmed. He stood in awe, gaping at the fountain. Even Matt was impressed. This was the first time he had been inside the lobby. This sight alone almost made the evening worthwhile.

"This is incredible!" remarked Omar.

"I've never seen anything like it," said Matt.

"The money spent to make such a device could have gone to a better cause," said Ibrahim.

"I don't believe money spent on beauty can ever be misspent. Too much of the world I have known has been destroyed. I am glad to see beauty being encouraged," replied Omar.

They followed the sounds of a jazz quartet emanating from the banquet hall; every third or fourth song was a popular Christmas number. Large tables were set up along the walls of the ballroom with more than three hundred items available for the auction, a Christmas boutique for the wealthy. Each table was divided into specific categories—family vacations, sporting events, art, personal gifts such as massages, beauty treatments, makeovers. There was even a liposuction gift certificate. Each registered guest had a number. In order to bid at the auction, you merely signed your name and number and wrote the amount of your bid. If someone came after you with a higher bid, that person took the prize. Ibrahim seemed distracted, but Matt and Omar looked over each table and studied the items available.

Matt bid on four Dodger tickets, two Laker floor-level seats, and a weeklong vacation in Hawaii. He was into the rhythm of the auction and was disappointed when someone quickly outbid him for the vacation and the Dodger tickets. He smiled when he came upon some items he donated through Caitlin—an FBI baseball cap, sweatshirt, and barbecue apron. Omar was enthralled by the prize and bid on it. *Confess to being a terrorist and you get an orange jumpsuit to go with that FBI logo ball cap.*

Matt looked for Ibrahim, who was at the dais talking with several of the guests.

Along one wall were booths with representatives from various charities and medical facilities that treat the victims of land mines. World Angel set up an emotionally provocative display showing photos of the children being treated at the various clinics.

Kim was behind the booth, answering questions and providing brochures on the ministry. David was standing in front, trying to enlist financial support for the children. What he lacked in height, he made up for in tenacity and dedication. His charismatic personality made it difficult for anyone to say no.

Matt and Omar walked over. David introduced them to a potential supporter. As Omar was explaining the work he was doing at the clinic, Matt turned to Kim.

"The display looks great, very professional."

"It's supposed to be portable, but setting it up this afternoon was a bear. I could have used some help."

"I'm sorry. You should've called. I thought Ibrahim came over to help."

She hesitated briefly, "Yeah, he did, but he got tied up with other business. It's okay. Now I know how to do it."

Chapter Fifty-Four

Omar completed his discussion with the donor, and everyone decided to take a seat at the assigned table. If the consulate was the target and Omar was not the terrorist, tonight might be the last night for this assignment. So far Omar was doing absolutely nothing pointing to terrorism. The longer he spent with Omar, the more confused he became with Omar's role in anything untoward.

Ibrahim joined them at the table. Their nameplates written in calligraphy identified their individual seats.

With a hint of sarcasm in his voice, Matt leaned into Ibrahim and whispered, "Hey, nice job on the display. You must have worked hard."

Ibrahim looked at him, smiled, but failed to respond.

More than fifty tables, each catering to ten guests, were set up in the banquet hall. There was little doubt this evening would be a financial success. Although the audience did not contain the usual Hollywood celebrities, among the five hundred in attendance were some of L.A.'s top entrepreneurs and businessmen, including many representing the "industry," mainly producers, network executives, and studio big shots. Many came in support of the guest of honor.

A strong supporter of World Angel, James Goldstone was an Academy Award-winning producer, influential in raising not only awareness but also hundreds of thousands of dollars. Because World Angel was a Christian organization, it was not always welcomed or accepted by the world relief community. Even though Goldstone was a devout Jew, he was vocal in his support of David.

Goldstone was a somewhat controversial choice for tonight's guest of honor. People from all faiths would be attending, and Goldstone was criticized by segments of the Islamic community for a documentary he had done several years before on the Palestinian issue. In fact, some called for his assassination. The Ayatollah Khomeini of Iran sentenced author Salman Rushdie of India to death for his publication of *The Satanic Verses*. Rushdie went underground once the pronouncement went public and to this day is flanked by bodyguards who screen all visitors.

Goldstone was bewildered and confused by the controversy. He denied any hidden agenda in his documentary, and most critics believed it to be as critical of Israel as it was of Palestine. Goldstone refused to run from any stated or implied terrorist threat and remained open and accessible. Few people even believed the issue was still viable; no action had been taken in the years since the airing of the documentary.

All the guests were seated, and the servers were about to begin bringing out the salads. Unapologetically, David asked everyone at his table to bow their heads, and he blessed the meal and the evening.

David introduced everyone at the table to ensure they knew one another. The guests included David, his wife and daughter, Ibrahim, Omar, Matt, and two businessmen and their wives.

Matt put his cell phone on silent mode, and before the salad arrived the phone vibrated. He glanced at the caller ID and found it was Dwayne.

He looked at the guests. "Please excuse me; this is important."

"This is Matt," he answered.

"Matt, thank God you got my call. Keep this conversation one way, you understand?"

"Sure, I'm in the middle of dinner. How can I help you?"

"Walk away from the table and call me back immediately. You understand, immediately."

Matt maintained his composure but could obviously sense the near panic in Dwayne's call. He calmly replied to Dwayne. "Sure. Just let me excuse myself, and I'll call you right back."

Matt looked at David across the table. "I'm terribly sorry; something has come up with one of my rentals, and I need to settle it immediately with the property manager. I have to take this call. I'll be right back."

Matt rose from the table and walked with purpose toward the back of the room. Ibrahim looked at David. "Please excuse me also. I need to wash my hands before we eat."

When Matt got to the back of the room, he quickly turned and looked for Omar, who was still at the table. After dialing Dwayne, Matt focused on Omar. "Dwayne, what is it?"

"It's not here. It's not the consulate. It's the banquet!"

"What are you talking about?"

"Matt, NSA picked up an intercept and confirmed the conversation. It's a dirty bomb. The attack was scheduled for the consulate but changed at the last minute to the banquet this evening. It is not the consulate. I repeat. It is the banquet, not the consulate. The attacker is named Ismad. We are deploying now. We've got hazmat teams en route."

"Ismad? Not Omar?"

"No, I asked and confirmed, the name is Ismad. Does that mean anything?"

"No, I don't know of anyone at the clinic or with World Angel named Ismad."

"Who is there?"

"Just a bunch of fat cats. No high profile politicians or celebrities. The guest speaker is James Goldstone, a controversial producer but not really a household name. He's been pretty public for a long time. Doesn't make sense to hit him now. They could have done it at any time. What do you want me to do? If I clear this place now, we lose everything, and there will be chaos."

"We're deploying now. We should be there shortly. Do not evacuate until we arrive. We will handle that when we get there. See if you can ID Ismad. I'll call you when we arrive."

Chapter Fifty-Five

Matt rushed back to the table. He leaned over to David. In a voice louder than a whisper, he said to him, "I need to see you in the hallway now. It's important. Please hurry."

As he was speaking to David, he saw that Ibrahim was gone. He looked at the nameplate. "Ibrahim Saleh Mohammad al-Dirani" was written in calligraphy. The letter of each name prominently displayed, I-S-M-A-D.

"Ismad," he said out loud.

"What?" said Omar.

Matt looked directly at Omar, "Where is he? Where did he go?"

"Who?" asked Omar.

"Ibrahim," said Matt.

David said, "He said he was going to wash his hands."

Matt ran toward the restrooms. Omar followed. They ran past the tables. Matt bumped a server who dropped a salad bowl just as he was putting it in front of a guest. Matt and Omar reached the hallway together.

"What is it?" asked Omar.

"I'm looking for Ismad."

"Who?"

"Ibrahim. His code name is Ismad."

"His code name?"

Matt spotted one of the hotel employees in the hallway. Matt yelled, "Where are the restrooms?" The employee smiled and pointed back down the hallway.

Matt reached into the back of his waistband and pulled out a Glock 22. The .40 caliber automatic startled Omar.

"Who are you? Why do you carry that weapon?" asked Omar.

Matt pointed the weapon toward Omar. "I don't have time to explain. Just back off. Return to the dining hall."

Omar hesitated.

"Do it now!"

Matt ran into the restroom. He kicked open each stall door. They were empty. Matt stopped to collect his thoughts.

As Matt exited the restroom, Omar was still standing near the entrance.

"I told you to back off."

Omar asked, "What is wrong?"

"I need to find Ibrahim, and I need to find him now."

Matt thought the kitchen would be too crowded for any terrorist activity and began looking for the room housing the power plant. As he was running, he grabbed his cell phone and pushed redial. He was quickly connected to Dwayne.

"Ibrahim's initials spell Ismad. He has to be our man. He excused himself from the table right after your call, and now I can't find him. I'm guessing he's in the . . ."

"We're less than five away."

The cell phone beeped, signaling low battery. "Dwayne, Dwayne. Can you hear me?"

No response. It was useless. The battery was dead. Matt continued running down the hallway.

Omar followed but from a safe distance.

Matt spotted a door. "Power Plant. Authorized Personnel Only." It was slightly ajar. He opened it and did a quick sneak and peek around the door frame. He saw the stairwell, determined the entrance was clear, and ran in. He took the stairs three at a time and was confronted by a dungeon-like dark maze of pipes and ducts. Matt could hear faint whispers and a scraping type sound.

Matt knew he was beneath the banquet room and guessed he was close to where the podium was located. As he made his way through the maze, he came upon Ibrahim.

Ibrahim was dragging a large container, about half the size of a fifty-five-gallon metal drum, across the concrete floor. He settled the drum near the base of a support beam. A translucent plastic device the size of a cable modem was attached to the lid with multicolored wires peaking out one end leading inside the drum. Ibrahim knew the box consisted of enough brick-orange Semtex to level the banquet hall above. But more important was the soda can-sized container within the drum; its contents, the radioactive material, caesium-137. Ibrahim sensed a presence. With his back partially turned to Matt, Ibrahim discreetly drew his 9mm automatic from inside his waistband, concealing the Mini-Glock from Matt.

Matt had his weapon trained on Ibrahim, his finger on the trigger, ready to fire but also wanting answers.

Ibrahim turned slowly.

"Step back, Matt, I must do this."

Watch his eyes!

"Do what?"

"You Americans are so stupid. I serve only Allah, not your God at some clinic." His voice was cold with death.

"How is this serving him?" asked Matt.

"Tonight I will strike at the belly of your economic system. The costs of 9/11 will be multiplied greatly. Your vice president would have made a tasty target, but with this I will eliminate not only the business leaders of your city but also the man who made a movie critical of Islam."

"And is it worth destroying the young lives represented up in that room and the medical personnel treating those children regardless what god they worship?"

"There are no innocents in a land that defiles Allah."

Ibrahim held the remote detonator in one hand. *Watch the eyes!* Ibrahim's eyes betrayed nothing.

Matt spotted the weapon at Ibrahim's side.

"Drop the gun, Ibrahim."

"Make war on the infidels who dwell around you!" shouted Ibrahim.

"Drop the gun and step away . . ."

Before Matt could complete his sentence, an iron pipe came from out of the shadows, crashing down on his right arm, crushing the bone and dislodging the Glock which skidded several feet on the concrete floor. With lightning speed, the pipe came back toward Matt a second time catching him just below the neck, striking him in the chest, causing him to loose his balance. He fell and grasped his arm; excruciating pain radiating toward his shoulder.

Kim stepped out from the shadows. "Kill him!" She shouted to Ibrahim.

"In due time. Let the infidel suffer."

Kim struck another brutal blow with the pipe, tears of anger flowing as she screamed incoherently, protecting the only man who had ever paid attention to her.

Omar rushed in from behind and grabbed the pipe as Kim attempted yet another strike. Omar twisted the pipe from her hands and in a sweeping motion pulled her body against his. The pipe pressed up against her throat, choking her as he pulled the pipe tighter.

Pointing the gun at Omar, who was using Kim as a shield, Ibrahim said, "Why do you side with the infidel? Don't you understand this must be done for our cause? Only through blood and martyrdom can we succeed!"

Omar showed no fear. "It may be your cause, but it is not mine. This country, these people, their God . . . they care about you, and me, and the children. You twist the word of Allah. The murder of innocents will not get you into Paradise."

Matt started to his feet, still dazed from the blow, pain pulsating through his body.

"Don't talk to me about the word! You have aligned yourself with the infidel. The Koran says, 'Believers, take neither Jews nor Christians for your friends. Whoever of you seeks their friendship will become one of their number.' Allah does not guide the wrong-doers!" shouted Ibrahim.

Omar screamed his response pulling the pipe tighter. "I serve the children! I have seen enough killing in the name of God and Allah. I say no more death. It must be stopped! You must be stopped!"

Kim lost consciousness. When Omar released the pipe, her limp body fell to the floor.

Matt inched toward his weapon lying on the ground a few feet from Ibrahim. Ibrahim turned to his right. He pulled the hammer back on the automatic. "One more step and you will die."

Matt continued forward slowly, his arm swelling from the blow. "I'm a dead man. If I stay, the bomb will kill me. If I try to leave, you will kill me."

"One more step and I will kill you!" shouted Ibrahim.

"Pull the trigger. Show me how right your cause is."

"*Allahu Akbar!*" screamed Ibrahim.

Omar lunged toward the gun. Ibrahim turned and fired one shot hitting Omar in the left thigh severing the femoral artery. Omar collapsed, writhing in pain.

Matt rushed toward Ibrahim and knocked the gun and remote from his hands. Matt threw a hard left jab to the face and followed with a quick left uppercut to the solar plexus.

Ibrahim's nose shattered. Blood gushed, splattering both men. Ibrahim folded, and Matt continued to pummel his body with a combination of blows, using only his left hand and his right knee. Ibrahim collapsed to the ground.

Omar was conscious, but blood poured from the gunshot wound. Matt rushed over to apply pressure to the wound.

"The bomb!" Omar cried out with anguish. "Stop the bomb now!"

Matt ripped off his shirt and wrapped it tightly around the wound hoping to suppress the bleeding.

Matt shouted to Omar, who was lapsing in and out of consciousness, "Omar, stay with me! Place your hand on your thigh. Hold it as tight as you can."

Omar tried, but his hand slipped off the leg as he weakened.

"Omar, stay with me!"

Matt dragged Omar over to the support beam. To his left was Omar, to his right the bomb. He placed his hand on Omar's thigh and applied pressure. Matt's left hand was preventing life's blood from freely flowing onto the concrete floor. The injured right arm was touching the device set for another act of senseless terrorism on the shores of America.

From the banquet hall above, Matt could hear applause as producer James Goldstone was being introduced.

Matt looked at the bomb. Three wires, electrical leads, connected the timing device to the detonator. Matt had no idea how much time remained. He wasn't even sure Ibrahim activated the timer. This wasn't Hollywood with a digital clock on the device counting backward. He had no idea whether he could save the lives of hundreds of guests upstairs. Not only that, he needed to save the life of Omar if the young patient awaiting his bone marrow on Monday were to live. Omar lacked the strength to supply sufficient pressure to stop the bleeding.

"Omar, stay with me. Dead men don't make good bone marrow donors."

Omar managed a half smile.

Ibrahim started to stir and attempted to rise on his elbow, reaching toward Matt's weapon still on the floor. Matt jumped over Omar and, with the most powerful left he ever landed, hit Ibrahim in the face. Ibrahim's head snapped with a loud crunch, and he collapsed to the floor.

Out of nowhere Kim jumped toward the remote device and grabbed it. "I am a seeker! *Allahu Akbar!*" she screamed, limping toward the stairs, carrying the remote in her right hand.

Matt reached for his weapon a few feet away on the concrete. He grabbed it with his left hand. His right hand was useless. "Stop! Kim, stop!"

She continued to run. She left Matt little choice.

He fired once. The shot struck her in the back. She fell to the floor, her body convulsing. Matt saw the red light on the remote device flash.

Matt turned toward the drum. A green LED light on the timing device atop the container was now flashing. At any moment an electric current would curse down the wire to the detonator secreted within the container.

In a weakened voice Omar said, "Save yourself. Leave me. Go warn the others."

"I think we're joined at the hip on this one, partner. We're out of options. Only God's grace is pulling our fannies out of this fire."

Matt looked at the wires. He had one chance. He had to cut the wire connecting the timing device to the detonator. He had no clue which wire. He had taken a four-hour class several years before on bombs and bomb making when members of an L.A. street gang decided to get ambitious. The case ended when the two shot-callers blew themselves up in a gang member's garage.

Matt's knowledge was so rudimentary it was of little use. He remembered from the course one wire was a ground wire, one connected the detonator, and one would by-pass the detonator, so if the other wire were cut, the device would automatically explode.

He hollered at the top of his lungs, hoping by now Dwayne had arrived. No response.

Omar agonized in pain but was conscious.

Matt looked at him. "You got a favorite color."

Omar gave a weak laugh.

Matt looked toward heaven. "God, I guess I'm ready. Give me the courage to trust. I've made a lot of mistakes. Thanks for a wife who tried to make you real in my life. But right now we could use a miracle." He looked at Omar. "Let's go with red."

He closed his eyes and pulled the wire. Nothing. No explosion. He opened his eyes and gave Omar an ear-to-ear smile. "We did it!"

Matt looked at the bomb. His ears were ringing from the gunshots, but when he placed his hands on the timing device, he could feel the vibration; the green light still flashing. Matt had no choice and no time to debate. He pulled the blue wire.

The vibration stopped. The bomb was deactivated.

From outside the door Matt could hear Dwayne's screams.

Matt hollered, "Dwayne, down here!"

Epilogue

It was Christmas Eve at Grace Community Church. The sanctuary was bathed in the fragrance of evergreen boughs and the warm glow of candlelight. It was a time of worship, praise, and reflection. The choir completed a number of traditional Christmas carols, and the spirit of the season permeated the church. The curtain closed as the lights to the sanctuary dimmed. You could hear the bustling of small children and a few giggles as the actors took their places on stage.

When the curtain opened, the scene was set. A five-year-old Joseph, dressed in a long burlap robe, stood next to Mary, kneeling at the manger. Mary, dressed in a blue shawl and a tattered dress, was also a member of the kindergarten class. The wise men flanked Joseph on the left and the shepherds stood on the right toward the back. Angels surrounded the manger.

The two most beautiful angels were wheelchair bound. Jaana and Shahla were both dressed in white and had wings springing from the back of their chairs.

Matt choked back tears as he watched his two newest heroes on stage. He was glad the lights were lowered. *FBI agents don't cry.*

This was one Christmas season he would never forget. He looked down the row of seats. Omar was sitting on the other side of Caitlin, David Mulumbo next to him. Rock Gallo, Matt's boxing guru, was seated next to Jaana's parents, who were sitting at the far end of the row next to Dwayne. Everyone important in Matt's life the past several months joined him tonight.

Caitlin gingerly grabbed Matt's left arm and squeezed it as the stage lights brightened. Matt's right arm, both bones shattered from Kim's blow, was in a cast. He also broke his left index finger with the powerful left hook to Ibrahim's jaw. Would he ever learn to stay away from the face? He had surgery the day following the arrest, and doctors put in two pins just above the right wrist. Most of the pain subsided, but it was difficult even then to complain, knowing the pain and agony his two little angels recently encountered. He watched their cherub faces on stage, hope beaming, with smiles larger than life.

Jaana was going to get her wish, a big sister. Always the optimist, Jaana, in arguing for the addition of Shahla to the family, said they would only have to buy one pair of shoes for the both of them. Jaana said she would wear the right shoe and Shahla could wear the left. The Anwaris were in the process of obtaining custody of Shahla. Matt was working through a contact at ICE to expedite the immigration process, allowing Shahla to stay in the United States beyond the period of her visa and obtain permanent resident status. Jaana told everyone about seeing Jesus that day in the operating room, and a seven-year-old child led her parents and her "new big sister" to a relationship with Christ.

David forgave Matt the deception, just as Matt successfully argued charges of impeding an investigation not be brought against David. Matt reasoned since David told him the truth regarding Yasir Mehsud, David had in fact corrected the lie to Dwayne. Maybe it was the Christmas spirit, but the U.S. Attorney's office declined prosecution of David Mulumbo. Yasir's donations to the clinic never were made public. The publicity from the arrest actually provided an opportunity to publicize all the positive work of World Angel, and contributions increased since the incident went public. The national spotlight gave David a forum to reflect his love for the innocent children ravaged by war and brutality.

Following the arrest, the attorney general personally called Dwayne and congratulated him on a job well done. Matt learned from Bureau sources a headquarters administrator who oversaw the case from Washington was miffed when the Director invited Dwayne to testify behind closed doors before a select congressional intelligence committee on the investigation. Matt would have traded any incentive award for the opportunity to hear the headquarters higher-up complain about his lack of recognition.

Kim recovered from her gunshot wound and was awaiting trial. The federal magistrate refused to set bond. Her attorney was attempting to work a deal. Kim realized she had been used. With cooperation she might see daylight in a decade or two.

Ibrahim was in the hospital ward of Terminal Island Federal Correctional Facility. His mission was a failure. A federal grand jury returned a twenty-one-page indictment. The evidence was solid. After the feds finished with their trial, the district attorney's office also wanted to exact revenge. The DA filed a one-count murder charge for Wadi's death and attempted murder charges naming each one in attendance at the banquet as a separate count. Ibrahim would never see freedom again. He even failed at being a martyr. Neither the feds nor the locals were seeking the death penalty. Ibrahim would spend the rest of his life in jail and in shame. The dirty bomb proved to be little more than a weak solution of caesium-137. The impact beyond the initial explosion would have been minimal. If the terrorists paid good money for the nuclear waste, they were cheated, but Judge Judy probably wouldn't find for the plaintiffs. Ibrahim's immediate future was also less than rosy. During the arrest Matt broke Ibrahim's jaw and fractured the C2 vertebrae in his neck. He was wearing a medical halo and drinking prison fare through a straw. Matt doubted Ibrahim would ever qualify for a heavenly halo.

Rashid's murder was solved. Wadi's prints matched those on the magazine and expended shell casing. Omar had that satisfaction.

What for the longest time appeared to be an unsuccessful assignment turned into the most exciting investigation of Matt's career.

There was still work to do. Covert cells would continue to operate within U.S. borders. Ibrahim refused to cooperate or speak with the agents. Although the FBI prevented a tragedy, they were still seeking cell members who assisted Ibrahim. Follow-up investigation of Ibrahim's phone records and bank records yielded little solid evidence linking any of his contacts to terrorism. The Havenhurst apartment provided no links to other terrorists. But as Pamela Clinton told the press, "The investigation is ongoing."

However, tonight was not the time to dwell on death. As a result of this investigation, lives were spared and souls were saved. Tonight was a night to celebrate hope, the hope that exists because of the birth of a child more than two thousand years ago.

Maybe this Christmas Matt could find peace. Two weeks before in the basement beneath a banquet hall, he had been willing to trust Jesus with his death. Would he now be willing to trust him with his life?

Acknowledgments

Thanks to Brad Waggoner, president and publisher of B&H Publishing Group, Oliver North, my "Commanding Editor," and Gary Terashita, my executive editor, for taking a chance on a first-time novelist. Thanks to Kim Stanford, Julie Gwinn, Jean Eckenrode, Jeff Godby, and all the great people at Fidelis Books for making this project a reality. I am truly honored to be part of the team.

To Bucky Rosenbaum, my agent and friend.

To Cara Highsmith, Lori Vanden Bosch, Becky Towle, Monika Baker, Kim Nunez, and Abeer O. Mansur for your input, feedback, encouragement, and support.

To Lawana Jones at the FBI Prepublication Unit for ushering the manuscript through the process.

But most of all, thanks to a gracious God, who blessed me with parents who served as role models and a wife who stood by me these past three-plus decades. Thanks, God, for the two greatest children a father could ever want, who married wisely and provided grandchildren who have this former macho FBI agent wrapped around their collective fingers.